OUT
of the
BLUE

The McCallister Series

Book One

MARK THOMPSON

ISBN: 978-1-4834-5930-1 (sc)
ISBN: 978-1-4834-5929-5 (e)

Because of the dynamic nature of the Internet, any web addresses or links contained in this book may have changed since publication and may no longer be valid. The views expressed in this work are solely those of the author and do not necessarily reflect the views of the publisher, and the publisher hereby disclaims any responsibility for them.

Any people depicted in stock imagery provided by Thinkstock are models, and such images are being used for illustrative purposes only.
Certain stock imagery © Thinkstock.

Lulu Publishing Services rev. date: 10/25/2016

Contents

PRELUDE

Present day Saltburn is a Victorian town built on the back of Middlesbrough becoming an industrial centre after the discovery of Iron Stone in the local hills. The brain child of Henry Pease a local entrepreneur, it is said that after walking the coastal path to visit his brother Joseph in Marske, he had a vision of a town crowning the clifftop and pleasant gardens in the glen below. The town was built around the existing railway which arrived in 1861.

Prior to this there was only a small seaside village hugging the coast which it is believed was named after the stream or burn that flows through the now Valley Gardens and was so called because of the amount of saltwater that flows back in from the sea on a high tide. The position that the village holds would have been difficult to access from inland it being steep valley walls and dense woodland the only real means of access would have been across the top of Hunt Cliff from the South, along the beach from Marske and Redcar from the North or from the sea by boat. This is why it was an ideal spot for smuggling because any approaching excise men could be seen from miles away, and any contraband quickly hidden from view.

John Andrew was a real character who lived in Saltburn from 1780 and was known as the King of the smugglers. His talents for this however I may have over exaggerated somewhat for this novel, but then again maybe not. Scottish by birth and a master stone mason by trade, in partnership with a local brewer he co-ordinated the areas smuggling trade from the Ship Inn. He was a well-respected member of the community and in 1817 he was elected Master of the Cleveland hounds. His many descendants still live in the local area as do descendants of the Verrel family and the Bashams.

I have strived to keep the details of this book as factual as possible, however history doesn't always walk the same path as you would like it to. As such the details of Napoleon's calamitous attack on Russia are true, Robert Bank Jenkinson, was the British Prime Minister at the time and Sir Harry Calvert had just been given the honour of Knight Grand Cross.

Napoleon Bonaparte was the same age as John Andrew but while John was attacking the English Taxation system on his own doorstep, Napoleon was attacking Tsar Alexander 1st for breaking the continental agreement and trading with the English, Frances arch enemy.

John Andrew would have presumably known all about the French/ Russian war through the media of the day, however I think I can safely say that Napoleon Bonaparte knew nothing of John Andrew.

FIG.1

FIG 2.

FIG 3.

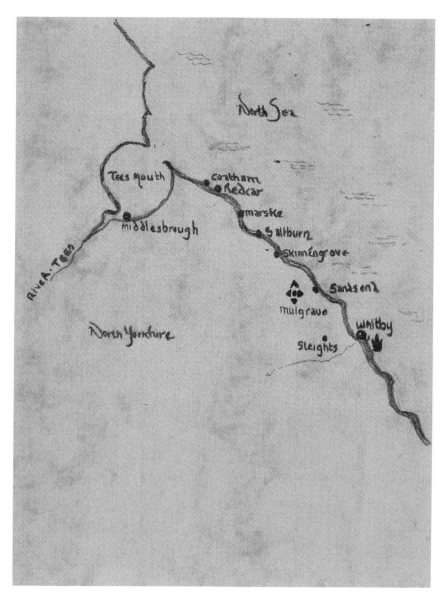

FIG 4.

1812 SALTBURN MID-MARCH,

John Andrew handed the muted lamp to his partner in crime and hauled at the first of the barrels, these will fetch a fine price over at Whitby he thought, not wanting to speak aloud albeit a fine landing spot, quiet and dark in the lee of Hunt cliff that was towering above them. The night fraught with people ever keen to hand him over to the excise men, for the price of a half decent meal and a flagon or two. When he had all four barrels safely above the high tide line he turned and helped the fisherman push the small craft till it was afloat once again, the two men shook hands, the sail filled and soon the boat was headed back out to sea.

John knew he had to get the barrels into hiding long before daylight and so started to roll them along the beach in front of the few small cottages that lined the shore front of Saltburn. Thankfully no one stirred at this ungodly hour. He laboured long and hard to conceal his prize in the deathly quiet surroundings of the newly acquired morgue at the far end of the village. Finished only six months ago, the morgue was built to house the many seamen that lost their lives in the treacherous waters of the great North Sea. Prior to this, bodies were dragged along the sand and left at the high tide mark, until they could be transported by mule inland the couple of miles to Brotton, a treacherous journey at the best of times. The poor souls that had spent a few hours or even weeks in the water were never in a very good condition, and being left on the sands for up to a week, the kind folk of Brotton received the dead with disgust rather than pity and so the parish council decided to give funds to build a morgue to contain the corpses unmolested by crab and gull. Funds were also given for a cart to transport the unfortunate the six miles along the beach to Redcar to be received by Father O'Toole and his Sacred Heart, so when the decision was made by the council it was deemed by all concerned to be money well spent including John because when labour was sought to build the morgue he was keen to help out for the extra income which was just what he needed for his future plans. He worked long and hard often popping back after dark to do a few modifications of his own and even now that the structure was complete he still spent more time in the building than most of the residents, always keen to cover his tracks before the sun rose over Hunt Cliff.

PRESENT DAY SALTBURN EARLY AUGUST.

Ryan strolled casually along the sea front, he had taken in the pier and turned at the end to take a few landward snap shots. It seems unbelievable that Saltburn had lay hidden from him for all these years strange when this charming place existed only an hour away. Finding Saltburn on his lap top whilst surfing the internet on his lunch break he decided to take a visit at the weekend. At first he was going to drive but decided to take the train on the off chance that any of the local watering holes tempted his thirst on such a beautiful day. Sauntering along the sea front he crossed the road bridge and headed onward to what he later found out that was the original hamlet of Saltburn, just a row of small cottages and a tavern aptly named the Ship Inn. He walked inside and in the cool dark interior ordered a pint of pear cider over ice just what he needed it being so warm. Taking his drink

outside he sat on the low sea wall and glanced around taking in all that the place had to offer (FIG 1.) Ryan was a tall barrel chested young man with a shock of ginger hair and tidy beard as the fashion of the day, well dressed in casual attire he thought suitable for the beach, his short sleeved white cotton shirt showing his tattooed thick set arms, the sleeves he had often thought cost more than a designer shirt ever could and much more personal. A good artistic talent he had designed every piece himself and was hugely proud of the final result, showing them off at every opportunity. Glancing over towards the beach he noticed a couple of young boys carrying surfboards under their arms and heading over to the cliff, mesmerized he watched them for some time wondering what they were up to after all as everyone knew, surfers lived in California and Hawaii not the North East of England. His glass now being empty he ordered a sandwich and another cider from a pretty barmaid that was collecting empty glasses she gave him a shy smile and hurried back inside. Sitting back on the wall he squinted over to the beach and could just make out the youngsters playing amongst the waves at the base of the cliff not the safest of pursuits he thought.

1812 SALTBURN

The next evening as John sat in front of the roaring fire with a couple of old fishermen in the Ship Inn his thoughts wandered to his bounty

hidden away in Cat-Nab or blue mountain(FIG 2.), as the hillock had always been known, it backed upto the rear of the morgue and over the months he had been secretly tunnelling into it. It was a slow venture but he had persevered to the point whereby it was a good thirty foot long and two levels high and his four barrels looked lost in there. Thinking of the barrels he needed to get in touch with an acquaintance he knew over in Whitby to try and move the contraband on and make a tidy little profit, so he promised himself that the very next morning he would walk south across the cliff tops and meet with him (FIG 4.)

The morning broke bright and clear, unusual for the time of year and John set off in good spirits determined to get there before lunch and back before sun down which would only give him a short time to find his contact and make the deal. The journey was always a firm favourite of his, walking past the ruins of the old Roman watch tower, and down to Skiningrove where as a child he used to come to scrap with the local kids alas no more as most of the community had long moved on to Middlesbrough, Sunderland or Newcastle to sail with the herring fleets, in the quiet moments he wondered if he should up and leave himself and join his old adversaries but hopefully this new venture of his would mean he wouldn't have to move from his family home even if he was the

3

only family left. At length he reached Port Mulgrave and in the distance he noticed two riders heading in his direction. It wasn't long before he could make them out and who should they be but his new adversaries the excise men easily recognised in their bright uniforms, although he was just a man on the road, he still blushed red as if guilty as hell and lent his face to the floor as they passed, by the nature of their business they studied him closely and as he passed them the second man shouted him to stop and explain his passage, struggling to think of any excuse he stuttered to try and explain. 'Are you a simpleton' the first man yelled as he climbed down from his horse and handed the reigns to his colleague, reaching for his whip he lashed out at John and caught him just above his left eye, furious for this unprovoked attack, on the second strike he grabbed the whip and pulled the man towards him at the same time bringing his knee up to land hard in the man's groin, with a grunt he fell but not quick enough and before he hit the ground John hit him with a vicious right to the side of the head snapping his neck sideways and he lay there motionless. This all happened so fast that it took the other man a second to realise what had just happened and as he reached for his pistol John bellowed and waved at his horse which made the nervous creature rear toppling its rider just as he pulled the trigger, the lead shot went high and left but not enough and it grazed John's shoulder before hammering safely into the ground fifteen feet away. John knew he was in deep trouble and had to act fast, dropping on top of his assailant he made for the pistol and wrestled it from his grip however his adversary knowing that it was now useless having being fired the once let it go without a fight reaching instead for a hidden knife he was carrying inside his tunic, seeing this John reversed the gun and using the heavy grip pommel took a huge swipe at the man's head the impact shattering his skull sending fragments of bone deep into his brain, the man was dead within seconds. John took a deep breath and examined his shoulder, it wasn't a deep wound but it hurt like hell and was bleeding down his arm, he reached down and took hold of the man's tunic, tore a strip and wrapped it around the wound to stem the blood, once done he took a step or two back to take stock of the situation. It wasn't good.

SALTBURN PRESENT DAY

The cider had added to Ryan's sense of wellbeing, and although it had been a long time coming he had decided that he would definitely visit this part of the world again, just then the barmaid came back and asked him if he would be requiring another drink because she would be clocking off at three, glancing at his watch and noting that it was five too he said *'ok but only if you will join me'*, The sly smile was back, and she accepted the offer, *'I'll just ditch the apron and be right out'*. Moments later she was back carrying another cider and a glass of wine for herself. Sitting down she introduced herself as *Victoria Dunn* and taking her offered hand he said *'Ryan...Ryan Thompson very pleased to meet you Victoria Dunn'*. He informed Vicky that he was visiting for the first time having travelled over from Darlington, Oh a townie she thought but didn't express it as she didn't want to offended him, *'where are you from he said in reply, I'm from here! what Saltburn? yes you could say that, I'm one of the few that can boast that I am from old Saltburn your sitting in it right now, what? You mean right here, she smiled, yes that's correct I live in the pub my dad owns it, in fact it was he who bought the drinks although he doesn't know it yet, won't you get into trouble doing that? no I'll tell him you're a holiday maker, first time at the beach, He's done the same plenty of times, yes but look at the tattoos I've got on show, I bet I'm not his first choice of customer, maybe, but you are mine'*, and the smile was back.

Having finished their drinks and Ryan not really up for any more just now, he didn't want to show himself up in front of his new companion after all, because he had to admit that he was completely enraptured by her company. *'Come with me and I'll show you old Saltburn,* leading him towards the beer garden. *There are only a few buildings here now but if you look there you can still see the foundations of the houses that have been lost to the sea, I don't think anyone really knows how many there were in total but I do know that there was another pub called the Bounty after Captain Cooks ship, he only lived a few miles down that way at Staithes so I guess he was a bit of a celebrity in these parts in his day, then in between the two pubs people say there was what they called Gin houses, I guess that* apart from fishing and farming there wasn't a great deal else to do around here. Oh there's something I forgot, it's the newest part of our village, come see, she took him by the hand and led him over to an old mortuary across the road from the inn (FIG 3.) *This is it the newest property on the* block, 'look see', she pointed up above the door which stated built 1812.

1812 SALTBURNS COASTAL PATH

John had some quick thinking to do, not only had he killed two excise men who worked in essence for the king himself but was also in charge of two stolen horses, so that meant four hanging offences *and there's me with only one neck, I've only been in the business five bloody minutes and I'm already in bother.* Thankfully he was on the high road up on the cliff top and not on the lower road which would have brought him out into the village. That meant that he could dispose of the bodies farther around the cliffs where it was quieter and this far up he wouldn't even hear the splash. He quickly lashed the two bodies to the back of one of the horses using the reigns from the other and set off again towards Whitby, *'well at least I'm heading the right direction'.* After another three miles he stopped and looked over the edge, *'this'll do fine* he said, *c'mon you two it's time to leave the party',* he pulled and pushed the two bodies close to the edge at a particularly steep area, almost an overhang, he gathered up a few rocks, buttoned up their tunics and filled the pockets with what he had collected, then sat them both up so that they lent against each other, stuffed the gun back into its belt, stood half a pace behind them and kicked them both over the edge *'send my regards to Davy Jones y'orrible couple of bastards'.*

SALTBURN PRESENT DAY

'I hope there's no residents still in there? Ryan inquired, *no there's nothing in there and hasn't been since they built the road years back, hang on here I'll get the key and show you',* as she turned away he said *'does your dad*

own this as well'? 'Yep he owns everything down here'. While she was gone Ryan decided to have a look round back, but found that he couldn't because the building backed up into the hillside, curious he thought, why would they do that?, there's plenty of room at the front, just means more work for the builders. *'You still here'* he heard Vicky shout, *'yeh round the back'.*

She produced a key and Ryan noticed that it didn't seem very old, seeing his look Vicky said *'in the olden days they didn't bother locking it up, the threat of ghosts and zombies was enough to keep people out but these days it's more of a dare for the kids'.* As they pushed the door, the hinges gave a real old fashioned movie style creak *'I wouldn't want any of those kids to dare me'* he said smiling. Vicky was spot on about the interior it was as he imagined it to be, cold, dark and spooky as hell, in the middle of the floor was a waist height stone slab with a drainage hole and ditch below ready to take the fluids and gooey bits away *'I don't know when this place was last used but there's a definite smell in here from one of the last residents'.*

1812 SALTBURNS COASTAL PATH (FIG 4.)

'Right then what am I going to do with you two'? as if hoping that the horses might come up with an answer to the problem. He looked at them for a while then came up with a plan, he took all of the tack off both horses and threw it all over the edge having done that he looked both over for any distinguishing marks that would make them stand out in a crowd and apart from a white patch on the chestnut mares flank there was nothing dramatic, he walked back over to the cliff edge where erosion had left a bare area of brown clay, bent down and broke off a hand full, he returned to the mare and rubbed it over the tell-tale patch, that done he stood back and admired his handiwork just the job he thought even her mother wouldn't recognise her now. So off they set John riding bare back as he had done time and again on the old plough horses, with the mare following on behind, he knew that he had to be

careful and hoped beyond hope that no one spotted them, it wasn't that far to Sandsend now and he also knew that once he had crossed the ford there were stables at the back of the old coaching inn directly opposite and one seedy little stable hand who would love nothing more than to move a couple of nags to new owners and if that was the case then John could also profit from it. It was early afternoon now and the weather was closing in, there was a heavy sea fret covering the coast the kind that got you wetter than any rain could, but looking on the bright side it would keep people inside and even if it didn't visibility was poor. At the top of the bank John had to dismount and lead the horses down the steep dissent passed the castle gate house and down to the ford. Just inland from the coast were a couple of small wooded valleys with poor access all round, he led the horses into the first and into a little glade that he knew, and there he left them and travelled on alone he waded through the ford and onto the rear of the inn. It was quiet in the stables but he could see a dim light coming from the back, and as he neared he whispered *'Nathan are you in here?* which got a *'who's that?'* in return, as he got closer he could see the stable hand was sat on a pile of logs warming himself by a potbellied stove.

'Bloody hell John where have you been hiding? haven't seen you in the best part of two years what brings you a calling on such a wet day', well he said *as a starter I could do with bit off heat off that thing, aye on you go you look like a drowned rat, yeh I feel like one, you haven't got a nip have you to chase the cold away, d'you think I would be sitting here stone cold sober if I had, here ill pour you some tea, it'll be a bit stewed but at least it's hot'.* John took the cup gladly and took a big gulp, *bugger* he said, *that is hot.* Nathen chuckled and asked *'what are you doing here? I'm sure you haven't come all the way from Saltburn just to test my tea brewing abilities, so why are you really here'? Well I've got a little proposition for you. Do you still take the odd nag over to Yarm to find them a better home so to speak? I've never done that in my life and I'll kill anyone who says different, calm down don't be doing anything rash, it's just that if I could put my hands on a couple, ones wot the owners won't be looking for would you be interested? Why won't the owners be looking for them then? Because*

they're a little indisposed at present and won't be popping in here any time soon. Nicked are they? to be nicked they have to have owners which they don't, and so no one will be looking for them which means it will give you plenty of time to move them on. How much? Two guineas each, *The tea went everywhere,* where the bloody hell am I going to put my hands on four bloody guineas who do you think I am the Earl of bloody Winsor, keep your voice down John growled, I know you and the landlord have got a racket going so think carefully, this is the best offer you'll get this year, you can sell them on for five times that, I'm sure that will line your purse nicely, are they shoed? he asked, of course there bloody shoed you moron now do you want them or not, let me go and speak to the boss, you stay here out of sight. *Nathen headed in the direction of the inn so John waited and drew closer to the fire his coat steaming. After ten long minutes he was back,* you took your time, how do you know I wasn't setting a trap for you *Nathen said,* because you don't know where there hid daft lad, Oh yeh ok, the boss said if you can guarantee they can't be traced he'll think about it. Oh fuck this I'm out of here, see you later, wait, wait ok, ok we'll give you the four guineas, you can't blame a man for trying though. Ok show me the money then I'll walk you to where there hid and when you see them you hand over the cash and I'll leave you to it, *undoing the strings of his purse Nathen tipped the coins into his other hand and showed them to John,* good enough for you then, *John nodded and Nathen tipped them back into his purse retied the strings and tucked it back into his jacket pocket,* let's get going then, times a wasting, Oh and bring some rope with you you'll be needing it.

The sea fret was getting heavier as the two of them walked back across the ford, *couldn't you have left this for a brighter day? I didn't have a lot of choice in the matter, it was a case of now or never,* not another word was spoken between them until they turned left into the valley, *there they are over there in the clearing* John pointed forward, *now give me my money and I'll be off, not so quick, I need to see what I'm buying first, that wasn't the deal as well you know, it don't matter you won't see a ha'pney till I've checked them out, right as you wish let's get on with this sharpish I've got to be on me way',* Nathen tied two nooses and gathered the horses together however liking their new found freedom neither of the animals where keen on being tethered again and backed away from both men, snorting and pounding the ground, John managed to get a hold of the mare and threw a noose over her head just before she reared but he had her now and pulled her back into submission, he patted her neck and said a few calming words before tying the other end of the rope to a tree, Nathen wasn't doing quite as well, the colt was bucking and rearing every time he got near, *here give me that rope, we'll be hear all afternoon at this rate,* Nathen threw him the rope and John readied it he starting talking to the creature in soothing tones and told Nathen to back off, *steady lad* he kept repeating to it and after a short while the colt got the message and started to calm a little, still backing up it had found the edge of the glade and stopped and found it had nowhere else to run, it finally submitted and John very slowly and gently lifted the noose over its head and moved closer to him, he reached out and patted his neck to reassure him, and tied him to another tree, *well at least you know that neither of them are lame* he said turning to face Nathen, and found he was staring straight at the barrel of a pistol. *You bastard he growled, I should have known better than to trust a little shit bag like you. No need to be rude John, it looks like I'm holding all the cards now, producing another length of rope, you were right about needing this. I was right about a lot of things you most of all, how's* your *mother these days is she still tethered in the sty with the rest of the pigs, no wonder you turned out the way you did you arsehole, you leave her out of this she's got nothing to do with it, she's got everything to do with it the bitch should have drowned you at birth like every runt of the litter, I won't warn you again, one more word and you're a dead man, no not me, it takes balls to take a life and you haven't got any.* By this point Nathan was physically shaking with anger gesticulating with both hands and just as he was calling John all the bastards under the sun and how he was going to bury him over there, John leapt shoulder down and hit him square in the chest slamming his back into a tree, knocking all the wind out of his lungs temporarily stunned he still had enough wits about him to raise the pistol however John had a different idea, he lunged for the pistol himself and started to wrestle it from Nathans grip, still with his head on Nathans chest he dug in his heels, straitened his back and gave Nathan a huge upper cut with the back of his head, smashing his teeth and biting off the end of his tongue after that Nathan forgot all about the pistol and simply dropped it to the ground he fell back against the tree and gravity did the same to him. John staggered backwards rubbing the back of his head and watching the stars jump about his vision. Bloody hell that hurt he thought, but when he finally focussed on Nathan he smiled happily to himself. He reached down to retrieve his purse and picked up the pistol as well, he wasn't going to be caught out like that again. Having put both items into his own pockets he left the still unconscious Nathan and the horses and set off south again, *I will get to Whitby if it bloody kills me.*

SALTBURN PRESENT DAY

As they locked the morgue door Vicky, seeing Ryan being genuinely interested in the history of the place told him about the urn, '*what urn he said? The one that was bricked up inside the wall in one of the cottages. You see…about forty years ago the sea claimed more of the cottages and some were badly damaged so much so that they had to be demolished, so as they were pulling them down one of the workmen hit a wall with his hammer only to find that it was hollow so he pulled it apart and hidden in there was this old sealed urn with paperwork and a few gold coins inside, well it turned out that it was some sort of ledger from the early eighteen hundreds and better still it belonged to one of the smugglers that used to operate around these parts, well I guess it should really have gone to a museum but no one really thought that way back then. So what happened to it then? Well, see when Dad bought this place years ago, he was rummaging around in the loft and stumbled across it, he didn't know what it was at first until one night in the bar he happened to mention it to one of the local fishermen and the guy turned round and said Oh that's where it went did it. Well he filled my dad in about what it was and who it belonged to and that conversation brought forward all the old stories about smugglers and pirates. Well you can imagine me as a kid listening to all these stories about buried treasure and escape tunnels I was fascinated, but after twenty years of searching I guess that's all they were just stories. Has your dad still got it? Yeh it's in a cupboard in the back bedroom, come on I'll show you.* Vicky led him to a private staircase at the back of the bar which led up to the living quarters. Ryan felt a little uncomfortable being in this part of the inn, nervous about the possibility of bumping into Vicky's dad. Vicky noticed the expression on his face, and said *what's up? I don't know I just feel a little awkward being up here with you and your dad just down-stairs don't be silly this is my house too you know and I'm allowed to have friends up here,* she led him in to the bedroom and turned to face him, *still nervous* she said looking into his blue eyes *yeh a little he said well don't be* she lifted her hand and gently touched his face, she moved in a little closer and went up on tiptoes and kissed him for the first time. Ryan could smell her fragrance as they embraced and kissed her back, it started with just little pecks but both of them were taken up with passion of the moment and they fell onto the bed as one, they lay there lips together in each other's arms unable or not wanting to let go of each other. After some time Vicky said *'come on lover boy not on a first date'*, she gave him one last kiss and rolled up to sit on the edge of the bed Ryan did the same and sat next to her, *do all your customers get this kind of attention, only the handsome ones* she said back and playfully slapped him on the leg. They kissed again then Vicky stood and shook her head and teased her hair to look respectable again. *Do you want to see the urn then or are you going to sit there all day,* he gave her a cheeky smile and said *spoilsport.* She laughed and turned to opened the cupboard door and there tucked away at the back covered by a blanket was the urn, she leaned in and lifted it out, turned and placed it on the bedside table and removed the blanket, *it's certainly no Ming Vase is it, no but it's what it contains that's important not what it looks like,* she lifted the lid and retrieved the ledger, again he was a little disappointed, he was expecting it to be a big leather bound padlocked tome, instead he saw a scroll of papers tied up with string. Vicky untied the string and unveiled the dry and faded papers on the bed, as she had already explained these were lists of everything coming in, from whom, when and at what price, and everything going out and again to whom, when and at what profit, Ryan whistled *I bet these could have been lethal back in the day, yeh said*

Vicky we thought they must have been like an insurance policy, you know like if he got caught he could have bartered for his life in exchange for more smugglers names, not much good to us now though, apart from the historical value, look there she pointed *there's the guy's name* and sure enough at the bottom of one of the pages written in the hand of a three year old he could just make out the name John Andrew.

1812 WHITBY

John was almost there and he could just about see the remains of Whitby Abbey towering above the town, on a fine day you could see it from miles back, but the sea fret was determined to make everyone's life a misery before it was done. He walked down to the key side through the fish market, and onwards to the tannery, people were milling about going through their daily routines trying their very best to stay dry, but with weather like this every one seemed dower and miserable, even the gulls that plagued the area looking for a free meal didn't want to play today and so they also were subdued. He headed across the wooden bridge to the old part of town past the smoke houses and onto the Duke of York at the bottom of the steps that led to the Abbey. He walked in and headed straight for the fire, *'ere you carnt just come in ere off've the street expect'n a warm bo'ee moi fire you av't go'n order a drink first moi lad'.* Now there's a nice warm welcome for you, John thought. *'Is your old man about I'd like to speak with him if I could? e's took imsell upstairs for a loi down e as, why's you wantin im? Sorry luv that's between me an him, pull me a flagon and go fetch him down there's a good lass.* By the time he came down stairs John had finished half his ale and was feeling all the better for it.' *'Well I never did if it aint young Johnathon from over the cliffs, howya doin son, I'm good thanks Thomas how's yer'self? your good lady said you'd gone for a lie down, oh it's just this bloody weather I'm not as young as I was and this cold gets right into me bones these days'.* They shook and Thomas sat down. *'Look at the state of you all soakin wet through, you haven't come all this way from home on a day like this have you. I'm afraid I have Tom, but it wasn't like this when I set off.* *'Well lad what have you come all thisa ways for? Well it so happens that I've found myself in possession of four barrels of best brandy and I was wondering if they would be any good to you. Nicked are they? no I bought them fair an square and now I need to sell them on and low and behold you were the first name that came to mind, seeing as you've got your own berth on the river and all. 'Bloody useless it is too, I can only use it at high tide an folk watch it through the day so it seems. So you do still do a bit of free trade? only with folk I can trust, can I trust you John? How long have you known me Tom, and me dad before that? long enough I'spose, where's it come from and how much you lookin for? They were rescued off a sinking French merchant ship on its way back from the Caribbean it took a long time to go down and so most of the cargo was saved and is now safely stashed away from the excise men so there's plenty more to be had if you want. How many in total lad? three hundred. Bugger me that's a king's ransom, is that, an what you going to charge me for em lad, well we both know that a thirty gallon barrel costs just over 12 guineas after the tax man has his cut, well how does eight guineas a barrel sound and if you can't use that much in here you can always flog em on to other ale houses, listen Tom you're the only inn around these parts with your own berth, it would be far too risky to send them by cart, so what do you say? I say it's going to be very risky, aye but think of the profit Tom'.*

Saltburn Present Day

'Look at the figures he's written down, this fella was doing a rare old trade'! 'wasn't he just, he only starts off moving a few barrels of brandy but look at the amounts he's shifting as he goes on, ten and twenty at a time, and look at all the other stuff, gin, wine, tobacco, snuff, grog, what's grog?, I'm not sure ale maybe?, and look at the last few pages, rubies, emeralds, silks he was making a killing', let me see those last couple of pages again, hmm that's odd, 'what is?' 'well see where he's written down all the profit he's made up to this point here', 'yes', 'well look it just seems to stop there, 'maybe there's another ledger somewhere', 'maybe but it just seems a bit odd'.

1812 SALTBURN

Through the haze of the full moon john could just make out a sail on the horizon, and as the boat came closer to shore he could see it was sitting low in the water. From his vantage point on top of Blue Mountain he uncloaked the lamp he was carrying with the tiny candle flickering in the slight breeze and waved it from side to side. He hated these conditions why couldn't it be raining and blowing a tempest like it normally is, keeping onlookers indoors, I hate all this cloak and dagger business he thought to himself. He blew out the candle and started his dissent half walking, half falling on the damp grass. He stole passed the morgue and onto the beach and waited, he'd had to make a tactical decision for this load and he told Peter to land the craft straight up onto the beach just along from the village. There was so much cargo this time that he wouldn't have been able to transport it all across the sands in time, not on his own so it had to be a doorstep delivery. The boat slid to a stop on the beach and Peter jumped out to give John a hand. It took the two of them a good twenty minutes to offload the goods John turned to push the first barrel to the morgue closely followed by Peter, he opened the doors and pushed inside, when Peter had entered with the second barrel he closed the doors, and only when they were tight shut did he start to speak in whispers, *what you doing Peter you never leave the boat, what's going on mate?, message from the suppliers, they have noticed how much more your ordering these days and wanted to know if you would like any other items bringing over, what sort of items would they be then, anything you like, they reckon you're doing alright at this game and want to push more through, have they got any Gin, yeh they've got their own brewer over on one of the islands fella by the name of Ginger Steve, runs a compny by the name of liquorice tooth sez you can have as much as you like, bloody silly name if you ask me but ok let's start with half a dozen barrels next week and we'll see where we go from there'. 'Anyway how comes you're the messenger this time what's wrong with rider we normally use, excise man got him, beat him to death cause he wouldn't sprag, better than going to the hang man I'spose, no one will find your stash will they, not bloody likely its well hid, just be careful john those bastards are treating the caper like a* war now, they'll have a noose round all our necks given half a chance, do you want a hand with the rest of the stuff, no that's ok I'll manage, go get that boat off my beach its sticking out like a sore thumb, right you are see you next week and be careful'.

SALTBURN PRESENT DAY

As Vicky gathered up the papers the sun lit them up through the window and Ryan spotted a blemish on the last sheet. *'Can I see them again before you put them back, yeh sure why'?* as she handed them back and Ryan started to separate them again and quickly held each individual page up to the window, and on the very last page he saw it, not very clearly but there was definitely more writing on the reverse. *'Don't suppose you were ever a junior spy where you, a what'? She said, 'now don't laugh but when I was a kid about eight or nine my dad used to give me pocket money once a week and I used to go to the corner shop to spend it on sweets, anyway one week I walked in with my best friend Josh and in amongst the papers and magazines was a new publication for kids called action and adventure or some such, full of comic strips about action heroes and wars and the like, anyway because it was the first issue you got a free spy kit with it, it probably wasn't up to much in reality but when you and your best pal are eight years old it opened up all sorts of adventures, and one trick it taught us was how to make invisible ink with lemon juice, sugar and water, and I've got an idea that this is the same sort of thing',* 'Great we have a mystery and a clue but we can't read it, *not right now we can't but if you can put your hands on a candle then we should be able to.* Vicky reached over to the bedside cabinet, opened a draw and took out a large well used votive candle and a box of matches *'we keep them in every room'* she said *'you never know when the power is going to go off in here, yeh I can imagine in a place as old as this'* He put the candle down on the cabinet and struck a match, held it over the wick until it lit, then said *'watch this'* he held the lit match between his first and second fingers and flicked the wooden end with his thumb nail extinguishing the flame, *'I haven't done that for years nobody uses matches any more, very clever show off, now can we get to the main event, yeh sure'* he picked up the sheet and held it at distance over the flame. *'Is this safe it's not going to damage it at all is it? No but once it has shown us the hidden writing its back for good'.* He started to move the paper over the flame and slowly but surely the hidden text started to show itself until after a moment it was as prominent as the writing on the other side, and written by the same hand. Vicky lent over Ryan's shoulder to get a better look, they both started to read the text out loud, after a few seconds Vicky looked at Ryan and said… *'Bloody hell'*

1812 SALTBURN

Over the past two years John's business went from strength to strength so much so that he needed more hired help to transport stock to and from his hidden storage tunnels, which he and a few neighbours had enlarged and extended over the years, even the landlords of the Bounty and Ship inn wanted a piece of the action digging from their basements into the network, and in doing so they could be supplied with stock without it ever being seen above ground. It was now a vicious circle, the more stock he moved the more profit he made and the more the profit the more stock he could buy. So he now had just about the whole village willingly involved in the scam in fact the only villagers that weren't working in *'the trade'* were the very young and the old and infirm and they were far too busy getting drunk to care. A couple of other neighbours decided that they wanted a bit more of the profits and so they also joined the network and opened up as Gin houses. Just about all the farming and fishing activities had ceased they kept up a small amount to use as a smoke screen, but it was much more profitable to use boats and beasts as transportation, instead of fishing and ploughing.

John having waved off another supply boat and watched the villagers stash the last of the cargo into the morgue stood and took stock of what was happening, he smiled to himself and thought that this had to be a first, a whole village labouring to the same end and it had to be unique that just about all of them were working nightshift. He walked over to the morgue and saw the last of them off home to bed. He re-rigged the death stone as it had been nicknamed to the block and tackle hanging from the roof beam and hauled on the rope lifting the stone upwards, he caught hold of one of the corners and gently landed it on top of the stone framework, the rope went slack and he undid the hook from the stones drain hole, he stood on top of the death stone and lifted down the block and tackle and tidied it away into a wooden box in the corner, he was particularly proud of the adaptations he had made to the lifting assembly for its only reason for being there in the first place was to aid getting the deceased from the floor and onto the stone. He took one more look at the place and satisfied he walked out, closed the doors behind him and went for some well-earned rest.

Over in Hull the excise men were up and about early and arguing amongst themselves William Germain the chief excise man was not in a good mood and the six outriders were feeling the brunt of it. *'You killed another one what the hell were thinking of you couple of bloody idiots, don't you like money, do you come here just for the craic, something to do whilst your bank manager counts all your savings again'*. David the younger and dumber of the pair looked up at William and said *'we didn't do it on purpose boss'*. *'Oh well that makes everything alright then doesn't it if you didn't do on purpose you bloody moron'*. *'When will you get it in to your thick heads, if they don't go to the gallows we don't get paid'*, totally exasperated and just about out of steam he left the room and slammed the door behind him.

'Haven't seen the boss that mad since you killed the last one young David awe come on cut me a bit of slack I didn't mean to kill im, he just fought back that's all where about's did you do this one then? over Redcar way almost on the Tees. That far up?, rather you two than us aye but Jeffrey here is sweet on a girl up that way ain't yer mate, shut up gob shite you're not to tell anyone I said, sweet on a girl are you Jeffrey well I never did, what sort of lassy would look twice at an ugly bugger like you?, whats she like then David is she a sour faced auld trout with warts an all? Dunno he won't

let me meet her, sends me away when he wants to sow his oats he does says he's a better lover than a fighter, reckon that's how I get to kill more than him. When you've all finished ill have you know that my lady friend isn't just good in the sack but she's also very good for information as well. What d'you mean by that Jeffrey? what I mean is that she's one of the few people up that way that'll talk to us about the smuggling activities, that's what.

After ten minutes William had calmed down enough to re-enter the room this time carrying a hot cup of sweet tea, '*did I hear that right Jeffrey have you got yourself a girl up Redcar way?*', Jeffrey shot David a look that could kill but said '*aye*', *how long have you known her? Long enough to get her draws off eh Jeffrey lad said Frank. Pack that in the lot of you* growled Germain *this might just be the lead that I've been looking for.* He pulled up a chair and sat against the table in the middle of the room he produced a sheet of paper and told them *get all this shit off here were going to do a bit of work for a change,* as the cutlery and crockery were removed he put the paper down and flattened it with the palms of his hands, took a pencil from his top pocket and said *right lets draw up some plans and this time no fuck ups!.*

Saltburn Present Day

Gold does it say how much? well in a manner of speaking it gives a total of eighty thousand pounds worth but what that would be worth these days I wouldn't have the first idea but you can bet your bottom dollar that it will be into the millions

1812 Hull

With the five of them gathered around the table, William asked Jeffrey *what's this lass's name up in Redcar? 'she's called Nell and don't you be thinking off getting her into any bother, she's already got you for that Jeffrey',* which brought laughter around the table, *quiet the lot of you* snarled

19

Germain *just how reliable is she? Well that depends on what you've got planned?*

1812 RUSSIA

As *Le Grande Armée* prepared to march across the River Nieman into Lithuania Napoleon Bonaparte stood back and admired the half million strong force move forward across the pontoons. The Imperial leader was itching for a fight, for Tsar Alexander 1ˢᵗ of Russia had broken the continental system agreement by dealing in trade with his arch enemy the English. Riding with the imperial guard he moved to the front of the column acknowledging people as he rode by. At this point in time the Armée was in high spirits as never in the history of warfare had such a massive army been seen and under the leadership of such a brilliant commander who was looked upon as a hero, surely such a force could never be beaten.

Napoleon always the great tactician had personally organized all the logistics that such a large army would require for what he saw as being a four week campaign against Russia. His plan was a simple one insofar as he was intending to put the bulk of his army as a spear head against the enemy troops, at the same time he would encircle them and crush them completely if indeed it actually came to that for the emperor felt that with such a large army the Russians would simply lay down their arms and try to re-negotiate terms.

As part of the elite imperial guard Jean and Henry Verrel and Phillippé Oubre along with Adrien and Claude Deveraux were used to going into battle with Bonaparte for together they had several campaigns under their belts and as Napoleon respected their bravery so too did they respect his command they would have willingly entered the gates of hell on his orders. *Six francs to one says we won't even load muskets before the Russians surrender to us* Phillippé commented to his friends as they marched across the pontoon bridge *You getting tired of a fight Phillippé not likely but just look around you I've never seen as many men in my life, no one can stand against an army of this size they'd be completely mad, they've got to be mad to live in Russia in the first place, yes but honestly we'll be able to march straight through their ranks and pull their drawers down, well I hope it's going to be sometime soon I'm bloody sick of marching every day.* On the 26th of June a scout rode into camp and informed the emperor that the city of Vilna was not more than half a day's march away, this information went through the troops like wild fire and the mood was immediately full of expectation and high spirits, they were finally going to war against the Russians.

1812 HULL

Ok we've known that the whole area up there has been smuggling under our noses for years and we can't get near them, the whole lot of them are tighter than a ducks arse, this Nell is who I've been looking for, for an age, me too said a despondent Jeffrey, *don't you worry about her, if she can put us in a position so that we can nab a few of them, I will personally bring her down here myself and be best man at the wedd'n' hang on don't be getting ahead of yersell now, I've only known her a couple month. Right we all know the suspects names, what I want you and David to do is get your feet under the table up there, I take it she doesn't know what you do for a living? No she doesn't, her brothers would drown me in the Tees if they knew, Ok well I want you both to go up there and let them know that your actually batting for the other side, ere I'm not telling any bugger that I'm a queer said David, no for the smugglers you idiot, god give me strength, Tell them that you used to work for that fella wot we hung the other month, he was a Hull lad but did all his business south of the river so they might know his name but I doubt very much that they'll have ever met him. Frank, Wilf I want you two go up there as well not into Redcar that would be too suspicious by half, head over to Middlesbrough it's not ideal but you'll be close enough to help out when your needed, lie low for a while but keep in contact with these two. I want you to tell Nell that you need to open up the market again in Hull and ask her if she might know anyone to start tradin with and set up a meet, if it works we might have to set up some small deals and when they think we can be trusted we'll set up a sting. Got all that, yeh got it, right the four of you mount up and fuck off but take different routes we don't want this thing spoilin before it even gets start'd.*

1812 JUNE 27TH VILNA

The men were up before dawn keen to spill some Russian blood, they ate what meagre rations they had with them and on command fell in and marched north. The five friends marched side by side as they had done for the last six years sharing both laughter and tears. it looks like it's going to be another hot one boys Jean the younger of the two Verrel brothers said as the dust started to gag in the back of their throats. By a little after eleven the sky had clouded over and they were looking down on the city and were surprised to see… well nothing… the City was standing there in all its glory but of the expected Russian troops there was no sign. They marched into the city streets warily, *watch your backs boys I don't like the look of this at all, it's got all the trademarks of an ambush* Phillippé mused, no sooner than the words had left his mouth there was a great cry from their left and a mob of defiant armed men came rushing at them, my these guys have done their homework he thought drawing his sword, even after all the fighting and training he had been through he still struggled at times to use his left hand, his companions didn't seem to have the same disadvantage and drew their swords fast and smooth. Like a flash the enemy were on them in a great clash of steel one of the attackers was half way through a huge arc aiming for Jeans head but in a flash his brother Henri thrust his sword forward not to parry his opponent but with all of his might pushed the tip of his weapon straight into his eye socket burying it straight into his brain, as his opponent fell backwards Henri pulled back and the sword pulled out again this time dripping with blood, *'thanks'* his brother shouted as he gutted another one of the fore runners. As well trained as they were this was not an exercised fight, this was a brawl. Both sides simply hacking and slashing at each other, but as the initial surprised rush had lost its momentum the attackers were overwhelmed by sheer numbers and the last of them screamed in agony as he was dispatched. From start to finish the attack lasted no more than a hundred heart beats. As the Sergeant shouted the order sheath arms the men fell in and fell quite. Napoleon having been no more than two hundred yards behind the skirmish when it had started rode forward on his white stallion and in his calm fashion asked *Sergeant do we have casualties, four sir but not life threatening* he turned to face the troops and simply said '*bravo*' smiled and rode back to his generals. As the afternoon wore on there were skirmishes here and there, but of the army there was still no sign. That evening the skies darkened and a spectacular lightning storm erupted bringing pain and misery for anyone unfortunately caught up in it, Napoleon and his generals were safely tucked away in the city, but out in the countryside where there was little in the way of shelter from the rain, hail and high winds that were now beating down on the troops, it brought death and despair and for some enough was enough, they hadn't had a decent meal in days they were cold and desperate so they just gathered their belongings and walked away into the night.

The next morning word came from the war council that Napoleon and his generals were not going to take this cowardice from the Russians lying down, he had created the largest army ever seen and was not going home without a fight so the order was to reassemble and march forward if need be all the way to Moscow.

It's alright for them to say march it's not something I relish on an empty stomach, when are the supplies going to catch us up Sarge? Don't you worry your pretty head about that young Verrel it'll turn too soon enough just you wait and see. That's what I am afraid of the bloody wait. As the marching went on relentlessly day after day the weaker of the soldiers slipped away in two's and three's into the night in search of food and plunder never to return. *Some more left last night* whispered Adrien, *what do you say should we join them do you think, you stay where you are lad you'll have yourself a full belly tonight, oh I suppose the buffet cart is going to open at seven sharp and we'll be eating hors d' oeuvres and drinking best brandy from cut glass tumblers eh, oh and if your emperorship doesn't mind I'll have one of those big fat cigars as well thank you very much for asking. Calm down little brother I overheard the sergeant talking to one of the drovers when I went for a piss earlier he said one off his horse's has gone lame and he's going to have to put a bit of lead in its ear, well guess what? it appears that our sergeant is as worried about the lack of food as we are and he's only gone and bought it for us, he's going to lead it over here just after dark and it will be butchered five minutes later, so there you go Jean my boy you will eat well tonight after all, Err I can't guarantee the cigars though.* He said with a smile on his face, playfully punching his brother's shoulder.

1812 June 27th Coatham near Redcar

Having said their goodbyes to Frank and Wilf on the outskirts of Beverley and agreed to meet up with them later that week for an update, Jeffrey and David had taken the coast road via Whitby up to Redcar. They led their horses into the stables at Coatham on the edge of the beach next to the life boat hut, shook hands with the owner and paid for their livery, their own accommodation would be two hammock's at the back of the stable for an extra thruppence a night. Once the necessaries had been dealt with they closed the stable door and started to walk the mile or so into Redcar, it was now lunch time and the two of them hadn't had a scrap of food since they'd left Hull early that morning and Jeffrey's stomach was complaining loudly. It was a stunning day, bright blue skies and the sun warm on their backs, *d'you know I reckon I'm going to enjoy this caper d'you think we might be here a while Jeffrey? Dunno mate spose it all depends on Nell really, aye when am I going to get to meet the luvly lady then. After we've ad summet to eat, if I have to introduce the pair of you then I'm going to do it on a full stomach.* They found a small place in Redcar and ordered two mugs of tea and four portions of bread an dripping, *do you want egg with that fellas?, wot with bread an drippin?* asked David, *yeh its new we call it gypsy toast, Oh very lardy dah, aye go on luv give us four of them then before you piss off back to the palace. Oy you pack that in we're supposed to be under cover remember not making a show of our selves* Jeffrey whispered loudly. They sat down on a couple of tree stumps with their tea and waited for their breakfast, *where will we find Nell then? asked David, just at the back of town she's a cleaner over at the abattoir it's her job to try an keep the fly's down, very important job that is, yeh sounds it.* At that the cook brought over their food on wooden plates, not from round ere are you boys, bloody ell that's ot said David trying to suck in cold air and waving his hand up and down in front of his mouth, *no luv we're from Ull over ere on business like,* said Jeffrey staring at David like he was something he'd just stepped in, *oh aye wot sort of business is that then, well I'm here to see if I can find anyone who can knock some common sense into this bloody idiot,… tall order that one my luvley* she said laughing, *don't I just know it.* They finished their food in silence and David used his thumb to burst the blister on the roof of his mouth, and continued sucking it complaining all the while. *Come on you lets go and get this over with,* they gave their thanks to the cook and returned their plates. *Right you I want you on your best be'avier when you meet Nell, mind your language, I don't want to ere any cussin in her comp'ny.* It only took them ten minutes to find the abattoir, more by smell than by sight, come ere Jeffrey said as they walked up to the door he spat on his hand and started to smooth down David's hair *Oye give over who d'yeh think you are me mam?* Jeffrey turned the handle and walked in closely followed by David, looking like a naughty schoolboy, *bloody ell wot a stink,* for which he got a slap over the back of the head, *look there she is'* pointing over to the far corner, as Davids sight got accustomed to the relative darkness inside the building he could see a woman arm wrestling some bloke over a small wooden table in the corner, as the pair got closer the woman looked up and shouted *'Jeffrey'* pushing the blokes arm onto the table with a bang she jumped up and ran over to the pair picking up Jeffrey and swinging him about in circles, well to say that David was impressed didn't do it justice he was totally besotted by the woman. When Nell had finally put Jeffrey down his legs didn't work anymore and he fell to the ground amongst the blood and the flies

Well who's this with you Jeffrey ee's a strappin young lad ain't he, *David he said* as he pulled himself back off the floor to a sitting position *David meet Nelly Basham*, David held out his hand and she took it with both of hers and shook it for all she was worth, David was sure he felt a knuckle pop and when he finally managed to speak he said *me mam used to arm wrestle down in Ull for extra money so she could feed us kids*, with his eyes brimming with tears, Nell rolled down her blood stained sleeve and wiped them away then gave him a hug like a grizzly bear, she said in a comforting voice *there, there David don't go getting all upset now*, she turned and picked Jeffrey up off the floor and the three of them walked carried and sobbed their way out of the building.

1812 VILNA TO VITEBSK LATE JULY

Napoleon undeterred by the abandoning troops was still upbeat, his determination still strong and quoted by one of the war council later he said *I have come once and for all to finish off these barbarians of the north, the sword is now drawn. They must be pushed back into their ice, so that for the next twenty five years they no longer come to busy themselves with the affairs of civilized Europe*

The Russians had different ideas and before the Grande Armée arrived on the doorsteps of Vitebsk they abandoned the city setting fire to military stores and a bridge on their way out. *How much more of this are we to endure Phillippé*, Jean asked. They had now been living on horse meat for the last month and scrounging bits and pieces from the fields, they would butcher the horses, themselves just skin and bone collecting their blood to drink straight from the pail. As they descended upon Smolensk in mid-August they found that the city was not only abandoned but the Russians had put it to the torch, many peasants meanwhile had burned their crops to prevent them falling into French hands. The scorched earth policy successfully denying the troops of any sustenance. The summer heat had likewise become oppressive, and the soldiers were now suffering from insect-borne diseases such as typhoid and water related diseases like dysentery. There was still the odd skirmish here and there usually around the towns and cities but with the general condition of the Grande Armée thousands were lost to the enemy. *Jean, Jean wake up Jean please wake up Henri leave me be I don't want to march any more I'm hungry and tired and I feel like shit, please Jean sit up look I've got you some food, what, where, where did you get it? I went back through the ranks last night and went through the bags and pockets of the dead, I also got a chunk of horse meat from a dead one some guy found from way off the road, he was just coming back from the carcass when I spotted him, did he put up a fight? Not in the end he didn't no. Oh Henri what have we become.* Henri held his brother while he wept.

Phillippé and the Deveraux's unaware of Jeans mental condition awoke and accepted the offered food gratefully, they ate their fill and saved the rest for the journey. Moments later they were back on their feet and marching deeper into Russia. It was on September the sixth when they finally found the Russian army about seventy five miles south of Moscow. At a place that would go down in history as the Battle of Borodino. On the morning of September the seventh as the Russians dug in, the French lined up to face them, when the fighting started the two sides pounded each other relentlessly giving charge and counter charge, the Imperial guard however were not to be a part of this battle on Bonaparte's orders they were to ride it out in camp cleaning their weapons and cutting bandages for the injured. *Why is he keeping us here Phillippé, I don't understand? I don't think he wants us out there to be used as cannon fodder Adrien my boy, we are supposed to be the elite, I guess he wants to wear them down first before we'll be invited to the party.* In the distance they could hear the battle intensify.

It was said that at its height three cannon booms and seven musket shots were heard every second the losses on both sides were enormous with total casualties in the region of seventy thousand men.

After the appalling loss of life, and not wanting to lose any more, the Russians decided to withdraw from the field that evening, and left the road open to Moscow.

There you go Jean that wasn't so bad after all was it, Henri said to his brother patting him on the back, Dear god I've never seen so many dead in my life, and you won't again my lad, no country can justify that amount of loss of life. No matter how important the cause, don't ever forget what you have seen on this field today boys, I think it's time we revaluated our lives, Phillippé, what's your thoughts on the matter, the same as you four I think I've had enough of death and war, the question is how do we escape it I don't know anything else, how would I earn a living, I don't have the answer to that one my friend but I'll tell you this, at the first opportunity we're off.

Napoleon decided that the only way forward now was to march onwards to Moscow and once there wait for Alexander to negotiate terms for their loss. He gave the order to march, *leave a battalion behind to bury our dead they can follow on later when they have finished the task. They'll be lucky to finish by Christmas* whispered one of the generals.

On September the fourteenth the Grande Armée entered the ancient capital only to see it engulfed in flames. The prisoners of Moscow's jails had been freed and told if they torched the city they would be given their freedom and they did this with reckless abandon. It was reported to the emperor that one individual when ordered to stop what he was doing, ignored the order and kept trying to start another blaze, and when a sword had been drawn and the hand that held the torch removed the criminal bent down, picked up the torch with the other hand and attempted to light the fire anew. With other reports of a similar nature the order was given to shoot and kill any arsonists found in the act, and so the order was carried out and the hapless victims left to rot still tied to the trees on which they died.

The next morning the damage to the city albeit extensive had only destroyed about one third of the buildings and so two thirds were still habitable and were done so by Napoleon and his troops. When the Russians had fled they had taken all the food they could carry but what was left behind were huge quantities of vodka and so the French did what any army would have done….got absolutely plastered and ate any animal left in the city including the rats. Hey boys look at this, Phillippé slurred, he had created rat kebabs on the end of his sword and was turning them haphazardly over the remnants of one of the fires, 'ratatouille' he shouted and fell over in hysterics as did his four comrades.

The next morning hurt, everything hurt, throwing up hurt, and not throwing up hurt as well, Henri pronounced in a slurred voice *hey do you know the best way to avoid a hangover* which was met by pale shaking heads *no do tell us, stay drunk he said taking a slug of vodka*, he giggled at his own joke then collapsed and went back to sleep.

1812 COATHAM

Nell introduced Jeffrey and David to her family and were asked if they would like to eat with them, just a plain fair of fish, potatoes and bread but considering the company a veritable feast for the two men, poor Nell couldn't stir without David following and hanging onto her every word, *I'm just gunna pop out back, David luv you just sit yersell there an please don't follow me pet*. He stared at her with a wounded look on his face sucking his thumb, 'acudelp' he said *not this time luv I'm goin for a piss*, David went as red as Nell's hair and stared at his feet to everyone's amusement. *So Jeffrey, from Hull yeh say, aye, man and boy and in David's case just boy*. He was getting on well with Samson Nell's brother and they were shooting the breeze most of the afternoon it was only at the point where Samson asked, *so wots it yous two do for a livin then*, that it got a little awkward, *we used to work for a fella down in Ull by the name 'o' Fletcher. Thomas Fletcher by any chance? aye that's right did you know im, no we erd his name mentioned a few times before them bastards got im......aye the bastards.....so wot'r yer doin now then, spendin our savins or wot we got left of em, to be honest with yer I was thinkin of tryin to trade again now the dusts settled so to speak, but Fletcher kept is suppliers to im sel, right to the end, but if I'm gunna make an honest woman of your Nell I'm gunna aft'r think of summet, gimme a mo I need to go water the weeds*, and at that Jeffrey stood and walked down the lane. He'd just unbuttoned his pants when he was grabbed from behind by Samson and his older brother Danniel, *right you bastard wots goin on why are you really ere, to see Nell he screamed don't be givin us any o'that bollocks, tell you sumthin Samson its makes our work easier when they send excise men daft as these two, aye yer right there Danny, excise man, EXCISE MAN I'm NOT A BLOODY EXCISE MAN, IM HERE TO SEE NELL, why, tell us why,…. because.…. I luv her, because I luv her and I want her to luv me that's why I'm ere.* At that revelation the brothers let him go studied him a while, turned and walked away. After Jeffrey wiped himself down he followed them back to the front of the house, *come and sit here in the sun and dry yourself off a bit* said Samson smiling, *now tell me all about Hull.* As the afternoon turned into evening David started to yawn and suck his thumb again, Jeffrey realizing that they had been up since half four that morning made his excuses kissed Nell to a great cheer and said their goodbyes promising to meet them again in the morning, *c'mon son let's get you t'bed.*

1812 MOSCOW SEPT 17TH

After days of drinking vodka three of the friends decided it might be a good idea to go and find something to eat and sober up for a change, as Henri tried to awaken Adrien and Claude he got nothing but abuse from the young soldiers, go away and leave us be Henri, Phillipé had the right idea stay pissed it staves away the hunger, so they split up and left the Deveraux's to sleep it off. Phillipé, Henri and Jean started to search every building that wasn't already occupied and after an hour or two they met back at their lodgings and amassed what they had found. *Not a bad haul Phillippé* admitted Henri, they had three huge cheese rounds a bag of dried corn a dozen or so small apples two bags of salt, one of sugar four bottles of red wine and a small tin of snuff that was left in a gate house belonging to one of the mansions, *that'll keep us going for a while boys*, they had finished dividing the food and eaten a hearty meal when their Sergeant knocked on the door frame and walked in, *morning gentlemen do I find you three sober this fine day, yes sir sober as judges as it happens, excellent, well I'm here on business, I've been charged with finding any of the imperial guard that can stand up on their own, and put a sentence together without slurring. That will be us three Sarge, good I want you to gather your gear and follow me over to the Kremlin and try and clean yourselves up a bit, your about to meet with the grown-ups, what about Claude and Adrien? Asked Jean, are they sober the two of them? Well not as much as we are Sarge but I'm sure they'll soon pull round, no leave them be they are no use to me being drunk.* So Jean quickly ran to where they were sleeping and shook Claude awake. Claude, Claude, we're just off with the Sergeant, does he want us too? No he says your too drunk, he's not wrong there mate, here tuck this under your arm and he gave him half a cheese round, for you and Adrien when you wake, we won't be long, and don't let anyone steel that from you. He patted his shoulder and ran back to the Sergeant as fast as he could. As they followed their leader through the streets and up the steps into the Kremlin itself they were met by other puzzled faces, they were all left there while the Sergeant knocked on a door at the far side of the room and entered, he saluted and said *sir may I bring in the volunteers,* he beckoned for them to enter and they were surprised to see that he wasn't joking, there stood in front of them was the Emperor himself complete with his war council each one stooped over a large map that was opened on a marble table. *Ah Sergeant McAllister you found a few sober ones then, yes sir eleven in all, eleven is that all? You have over a thousand men, begging your pardon sir but it was a lot of vodka, yes yes well eleven sober men are far better than four dozen drunks I suppose, and this matter is rather delicate. Gentlemen you are in this unit because you have all proven your loyalty and courage time and time again to your Emperor. He will now address you all and tell you of the mission he has planned.* Napoleon stood and turned to them, and in a quiet but firm voice said *as I'm sure you are all aware this campaign was only to have been of a short duration a matter of weeks in fact but because of the cowardice of the Russian army we have been in this god forsaken country for many months, I will not toy with you gentlemen my intensions were from the outset to feed all my troops for the duration of the siege however as a fall back I brought monies to deal with the locals for provisions as we advanced, as I did not intend to alienate the locals, just* their armies. *This however never came to pass as the locals sort to toy with us destroying their own crops as we advanced and so I am now left with a predicament, I need to transport the monies back to Paris and for this task you have been volunteered by your good sergeant who will lead the mission. You will gather the strongest horses and wagons and drive the money chests to St Petersburg, here you see* he said pointing to the map *it is the shortest route out of this country, I have a ship that is at anchor in the port named Les Contrebandiére flying Finnish colours, once safely on board it will sail to the North Sea and from there to Le Havre. You will stay with the chests and transport them to the imperial embassy in Paris for this you all will be greatly rewarded and honoured. I cannot impress on you just how important this mission is and how much you are trusted to carry out these duties to the best of your abilities. Questions? no then on your way* he turned his back to them and conferred with his council.

1812 COATHAM

The next morning dawned bright and cheerful as did Jeffrey and David. The two walked back into Redcar to entertain some more gypsy toast and tea, *now blow the bugger this time and don't be in such a rush were not meetin Nell till after her shift this afternoon, wot was it wot you was talkin to Sammy n Danny about yesterday then? Just gainin their trust that's all, did they believe us dy'think, oh aye I told em how it is, even convinced me self I think.* Passing by Danniel spotted the two of them and walked over, *hiya Danny, its Danniel 'Oh' yes of course it is sorry Danniel. Listen our Sammy was wantin to talk to yer this morning before our Nell gets back from work, when your done ere ave yersel's a walk over to ours right, I'll see yer later I've got to go see a man about a dog,* And walked into town. *Well David that sounds a bit promis'n don't it, dunno spose, well you can eat yer posh toast as quick as yer like now an then we'll take a walk an see wot Sammy's got up his sleeve…* As they reached the cottage they rapped on the door and heard Samsons voice from round the back, *who's that? it's us Jeffrey and David, come on through the pair of yer's.* Samson was up to his armpits in rabbit guts in the tin bath, *pass us that rag over there will yer, ta,* he wiped his hands and threw the cloth back *they'll make some good bangers they will our Nell can mek bangers owt of anythin she can,* they both eye'd up the bloody soup mixture in the bath tub dubiously and thought aye I bet she can. *Er we bumpt into Dannyyy..iiiel a bit back an he said you wanted to see us, aye I did, just summet yer said last night about tradin in Hull, 'Ull', 'Ull' yeh wotever, well after you's two buggered off I sat with our Nell and told her wot you said about luv an all that shite, luv? shut up David, aye go on, well it appears she's got asper, asp, hope as well for the future like and says that I should trust yer cause she does, so I wanted to ask just how serious are yer, about dealin I mean, well like I told yer last night we avent got a lot of savins left but I'd like to see if we can mek it work, ok I'm not promisin owt mind but if I could, wot would yer want an how much, well I know gin is always a good seller an backy, but wotever the price I reckon we can only afford maybe three or four barrels an may'be a bale of backy, ok leave it with me an I'll see wot I can do.* Just then Nell walked in and David started sucking his thumb again.

1812 MOSCOW SEPT 17TH

Well boys what do you make of that, eleven blank faces looked back at him, not sure of what they felt, dumbstruck mainly. Well when it's sunk in that we're not just getting out of this country and the war, we are also doing it in style, we'll be home before the end of next month and we'll all be rich and sporting medals as well. Will he keep his word Sarge, he will indeed and as proof I have his signature on the bottom of these orders. *Well Phillippé God is smiling down on us today, we were looking for a miracle and hey presto we've got one.*

For the rest of the day the twelve men went foraging, gathering muskets, powder and shot, enough to start their own little war, they found the fittest well fed horses they could, wagons, provisions everything they could think of, and every time that anyone resisted sergeant McCalister waved the signed orders under their noses like a magic wand, and nothing was too much trouble. By the end of that day they had everything they needed for the journey including Russian uniforms which didn't go down very well as they were all fully aware that if they were seized they would be shot as spies but after a quick discussion they decided that the rewards were well worth the risk.

The next morning they rode their wagons over to the Kremlin and were told to take them around the back and wait, after ten minutes the yard gates opened and a guard told them to uncouple the horses and push the wagons backwards to the rear doors, this done they were left to wait another hour *what's keeping them Sarge? they'll be doing a final count before we load up that's all*, after what seemed like an eternity they heard the doors being unlocked, they were pushed out wards by two more guards, *bring the wagons right up to the doors* one of them barked, this done they were ordered to pick up and carry four chained and padlocked chest's onto the back of the wagons, two on each *hope you two are feeling strong boys* said Phillippé as they bent to pick up the first chest, *Christ almighty that's heavy* jean said through gritted teeth as all four strained to lift it, they fumbled it up to waiting hands on the back of the first wagon, *Jesus, it feels like it's full of lead, I'm pleased it's not any bigger*. After stowing all four chests they through blankets over them and re-hitched the horses. McAllister signed for the consignment, the six out riders saddled up, Phillippé and the Verrel brothers took the rear wagon, McAllister and two others the lead, *Ready boys, let's go home*, and at that all hearts lifted, they were off to fame and glory.

1812 COATHAM SEPT 17TH

Unbeknown to Jeffrey when Danniel had left earlier that morning he had walked to Saltburn to meet up with John Andrew, when he had told him of the possible connection to Hull, Johns ears pricked up, ever keen to expand his empire he had asked to meet with the two newcomers, and so the pair had rode back along the beach. all four of them were sitting in the sun when John and Danniel got back and dismounted, Danniel did the introductions and when John's name was mentioned Jeffrey's heart quickened *very pleased to meet you too John* said Jeffrey trying to keep the tremble out of his voice, *I hear you might be in the market for some goods.* Jeffrey told John the full story and why they would have to start small at first. *OK I've a boat due in on Friday can you arrange transport? yeh sure, any particular time, you ask a lot of questions Jeffrey, oh don't worry about me it's just that this will be the first time me and the lad'll have run solo and I don't want to screw it up. I'll let you know time and place just before delivery, and it will be cash up front. But how will I kno.....Ok cash up front. Hand me the purse David*, he went into his trouser pocket and produced a small bag he tossed it over, Jeffrey caught it single handed and tipped the contents into Johns open hand, *will that be enough?* He asked, *under the circumstance aye it will, this time.* At that he walked over to the horses and started to untie them from the post, he turned back to Danniel said his goodbyes and shook him by the hand, he mounted up, tied the spare leash to his saddle and trotted off back to Saltburn. *You were a bit jittery in Johns company there Jeffrey, was I, aye yer were, not getting cold feet now are yer, no not at all it's just that Tom Fletcher mentioned his name once or twice in passin like, did they ever meet the two of them, not that I know of but I couldn't tell yer for sure,* hmmm…

The next day Jeffrey and David rode into Middlesbrough, David had his guard up straight away, having the locals down as *'nowt but bother' where are they stopping Jeffrey* he asked, *at an Inn called the Dick Turpin down by the river, Oh great we'll be well safe in some place called that I'm sure, let's just save our opinions till we get there shall we.* They spotted the inn up a side street a little further on, they rode passed the front door and out back, where a stable hand was given a few pennies and instructed to rub the horses down. They walked in through the rear door straight into the bar, the conversation suddenly stopped as they ordered two ales and every one's eyes were upon them it stayed that way until they heard a familiar voice from the back of the room shout *hiya fella's get one in for me while your standin.* Drinks in hand they maneuvered through the silent crowd and sat at the table that Frank had commandeered they shook hands and only then did the conversation start up again it was at this point that Jeffrey finally breathed out, *bloody hell frank couldn't you have found some place better than this to hang out, they'd have the shirt off your back in a flash, no their fine when you get to know them, trust me that aint gonna happen any time soon, anyway where's Wilf? he's in the bog cleanin the blood from his nose 'Wot' yeh it started to bleed again when he sneezed, a sneeze made his nose bleed? No an axe handle made his nose bleed the sneeze just set it off again, an axe handle are you kiddin me, no no it was just a bit of fun, if the fella had of been serious he'd of hit him with tuther end. Anyhow wot brings you round these parts? Have you forgot why your ere? sfunnything about the Boro after a while you just kinda forget everything, couldn't even tell yer wot day it is, its Wednesday you pillock and you's two aint on holiday, now listen sharp, we got a deal set up in Redcar this Friday and I reckon you had better be there just to get your faces seen more than owt else, can you put your hands on a wagon, aye the landlords got one we could borrow that. Right I want the two of yer to ride the wagon over to Redcar sands and just enjoy the view, me an David'll catch up with yer on the beach an let you know wots appn'in and when, you'll best tell the landlord you'll be away a couple of days cause you'll be going straight back to Ull. Wot if we get stopped on the way, you're a bloody excise man for heaven's sake, shhh not so loud, listen you work for the king right, if anyone questions that then show the buggers yer papers an tell em to piss off. Right you good with all that, yeh spose, just then Wilf appeared and sat down, ullo ow ar yu Dabid a carn talk proper coz a got te keep deez carrots up be dose te stop bleed'n drip'n out, David seemed to understand every syllable and asked if he was enjoyin im'sell, Oh aye bart from carrots, Wilf why carrots? cause they ad no sausages....ohhhkay, will yer be good for Friday? oh aye no problub. They shook hands and made to leave and as an afterthought Jeffrey said Oh an Wilf don't bleed all over the merchandise. Right we're off now don't forget, Redcar beach Friday, ok ok.* They returned to the stables ready to mount up and David said, *Jeffrey were did your shirt go...* He looked down and said '*Bugger*'.

Friday turned and as promised Frank and Wilf were on Redcar beach with knotted hankies on heads and trousers rolled up having a splodge, the wagon was old but serviceable and their two horses were having a go at the dune grass. *Oye you two get out of that water n come ere.* Frank came over straight away but Wilf was having far too much fun. *Wot did I tell you about not being on olidays, or away man we've been ere hours an it were red ot sittin on that wagon so we thought we'd blend in a bit an take to the waters.* While the two of them were talking David was jealously eyeing up Wilf until the urge got the better of him, he whipped off his boots and ran headlong into the sea kicking and splashing water all over his friend, well not one to refuse a challenge he started to fire back at him giggling like a six year old, David acting like the six year olds baby brother started to pick up stones and tossed them in to the water to soak him even more. *I don't bloody believe it wot on earth do those two idiots think their playin at, d'yer know I worry about them I really do…. anyway…. Frank I've had word that there's a boat cumin in after dark tonight around half ten or eleven'ish its gunna land about half way down the beach at Marske, seems that there's a landlord over there that runs another inn called the ship an he don't like payin full whack for his drink 'n' backy, so rather than the boat offloading at Saltburn its gunna drop off right on his door step so to speak, so what Samson told me is that the landlord'll get his fill first and then we get the rest so you two need to be tucked up in the sand dunes right underneath that mansion wots on the cliff top, wot if we're seen from there, you won't be cause it turns out that they're in on the same racket, Pease they call the family or some such, anyway they've been told to snuff all the candles and close the drapes by ten o'clock so the whole place will be in darkness by the time you turn up. So when your loaded I want yer to come back this way, and pull off the beach at Coatham then take the track to Guisbrough from there the roads are much better and you'll have a clear run all the way back to Ull. Wot do we do when we get back? I want you to stash the load in that lock up at the back of the station and when you've done that tell William the full story and ask im for more cash, wot for? cause were gunna do the same thing all over again next week, that's wot for.* While the two of them were making their plans Wilf and David were sat on their backsides chest deep in water still trying their damnedest to soak each other when all of a sudden Wilf cried out, he leapt up and tried running on top of the water, David thinking this was great fun jumped up and ran after him. It wasn't until they were both about knee deep that panick set in, the initial cry had become a howl sounding something like getitthefuckoffovmejewels, when he finally reached the dry sand he fell over in a foetal position and when he removed his hand from his crotch there was a large brown crab hanging from his thumb David who could barely stand for laughing said *don't chuck it back Wilf thems good eatin them is.* All the while Jeffrey was stood with shoulders slumped and his head in his hands.

That evening when all the sand and seaweed had been swept up and clothing dried, Frank and Jeffrey went over things one last time, *right you ok with it all, for heaven's sake aye we'll be fine, so your gunna take David along with yer too, that auld wagon can take one more passenger and with shoulders as broad as his he'll be a big help, that aside, him an John Andrew have been introduced so it will be less suspicious if he sees a face that he recognises. Wot about you how come you aint coming along for the ride, Nah threes company fours definitely a crowd I'll wait here till yer get back you can drop David off and then I want to look the goods over, if he's short changin us I want to know. Right'o boys it's just about full dark, time to go to work I'll catch up with yer on the way back, good luck.* The three of them on board Frank pulled at the reigns and trotted down the beach, after a few minutes their silhouette faded from sight. Jeffrey walked back upto the village knocked quietly on the back door and whispered *Nell you in here? come here lover boy* came the reply.

Over at Marske john was already in place with his trusty signal lamp, the same one he'd used when he first started, it had never let him down and he was always comforted by its company, albeit he wasn't superstitious by nature he thought of it as his lucky charm. He was looking out to sea, looking for any sign of the boat that was due, and then he saw it, very faint in the distance but there never the less, he lifted the lamps blackout screen and clicked it in place then he lifted the lamp to head height and waved it side to side three times which was the agreed signal, he muted the lamp back into darkness and watched, there it was the three return waves of the lamp and then extinguished.... It was on! The signals exchanged he gave a low whistle and the inn's landlord emerged out of the darkness with two of his men pulling a hand cart.

As they approached they nodded to each other in recognition, and then they settled in to wait at the same time Frank's wagon pulled into the dunes and stopped, John acknowledged their arrival and the three men also sat and waited. Soon enough the boat rose from the water onto the beach and scraped noisily across the pebbles, the sailor jumped from the boat and pulled it inch's further up onto the sand, all seven men ran to assist him, *hello John the sailor said in hushed tones, hello Pete how was the trip, steady away mate, ok lads let's see if we can get this over with as quickly as possible so Peter can get himself away. You three get your cart and start loading,* they soon had five barrels and three bales on the cart and with one pulling and two pushing they slowly transported it up the beach and into Marske. Once they were out of the way John beckoned Frank to bring their wagon down to the water's edge both men shook hands and the three excise men started lifting contraband barrels from the boat and onto the back of the wagon David was lifting them with ease which brought a hushed comment from John, *bloody hell he's a strong bugger, aye he is that, nutty as a four tiered fruit cake but as strong as an ox.* Minutes later and beaded with sweat everything was loaded and the four men helped push the boat back out into the water with a thumbs up from Peter he raised the sail and was gone. John turned to David and said 'Where's Jeffrey Oh he's on a hot date he is, is he now, he's a cool customer', which got him a tick in the right box. As Frank turned the wagon around John fetched his horse from the dunes saddled up and with a wave rode back to Saltburn, and with a flick of the reigns the excise men headed back to Coatham with a wagon load of illegal contraband.

Jeffrey was on the beach by the time they got back and as Frank slowed the wagon David jumped down. *'How did it go boys? Better than ex-pected, no hiccups at all, good I knew I could trust yer's'* he said jumping onto the back of the wagon, he moved the hastily thrown sheets away and examined the load, 'well' he said mainly to himself *'none of the bales are torn, seals all waxed up on the barrels yep I reckon we will do business with Mr Andrew again, it would appear for a smugglin murderin bastard he's actually quite trustworthy'.*

1812 The road to St Petersburg Sept 17th

The twelve men were in good spirits as they rode away from Moscow and headed North West, McCalister put two outriders ahead of the wagons at a distance of four to five miles and another two behind at the same distance, this he had said would give the main party plenty of time to deviate or hide from any potential trouble from the Russians. Unbeknown to the whole party was that the bulk of the Russian army had in fact moved south of Moscow, which would make the journey a whole lot safer, but not completely. *'Here Sarge what are you going to do when you get home then, you being a celebrity and all, me I'm going to head back to Chaponnay my village, I'm going to find a good woman, settle down, grow some crops and shout at my fourteen children, fourteen Sarge is that all, yes I'm not a greedy man fourteen will do, she'll have to be a good woman the poor soul. What about you two he shouted back to the Verrels where are you from, we are from Le Breil-sur-Mérize near Le Mans, Le Mérize you say, yes that's our home, there is one fine bridge that spans the river and in the height of summer when the sun is warm we gather there to dive and swim in the waters, my heart aches for it now. And what of you Phillippé how come you ended up with those two reprobates, Oh these two, well there I was one fine day just sitting in a trench close to a lovely little village called Marengo when these two lunatics decided to drop in for a visit, well myself and Henri here collided heads and I can tell you his head is as hard as an unripe turnip and about just as clever* chipped in Jean receiving a slap himself, *and that's it Sarge we've been friends ever since, Marengo you say, yes Sarge, were you there? I was indeed young Jean, a great victory it was, twelve years ago now can you believe it, we've all seen some sights since then and I for one am sick to the stomach of it all, same here Sarge, this will be the last war that will see my musket, amen to that.* The wagons rolled on wards mile after mile and the farther away from Moscow they travelled the less comfortable and more observant they became. *Hey Sarge see us all dressed up in Russian uniforms, well what if we come across any of them what will we do? You will do nothing, I on the other hand, will do the talking for you all, do you speak a bit of Rusky then Sarge, I do indeed that is why I was picked for the mission, say something then Sarge, what would you like me to say? Say we are coming home!... МЫ ПРИХОДИМ ДОМОЙ... wow that sounded great, do you know any more? what Russian or other languages well either, both, well how about, Wir sind nach Hause komman or Estamos llegando a su casa, or how about a little Finnish, Olemme tulossa kotiin.....I am very impressed Sarge, how many languages do you speak in total? well my main two are French obviously and English then maybe another six on top of them, English Sarge how come? because my father was Irish, he came to France long ago looking for work, he met my mother in Paris, got married and hey presto I turned up that's how I got this bloody silly name I doubt very much that there will be many more McAllisters living in France. Mind you never know people did say that he had a bike that's how he got to learn so many languages himself. Sarge if your that clever with languages and all how is it that your still a sergeant, you could have been shaking hands with the top brass. Well there's a very simple answer to that, I didn't want the pressure! What do you mean? well imagine were all sitting around a table negotiating terms and I mispronounce a couple of words here and there I could start another bloody war I didn't want that on my shoulders, people dying because of me, and anyway if I had gone up in the ranks I would have missed your stimulating company* after a while they all went quiet lost in their own thoughts. Presently Phillippés thoughts turn back to the present and asked *Sarge it'll be getting dark soon what are your plans? I was just thinking the same thing myself Phillippé, see that outcrop of rocks over there in the distance, I would say that they are about five or six kilometres off the road, we'll head for them, if we make camp on the lea side they should be enough cover to hide us from the any onlookers throughout the night.* Ordering one of the out riders to stand firm and wait for the scouts to return, they pulled off the road and onto the scrub, it turned out that the outcrop was farther that they first thought and it took them a good three quarters of a hour to reach it, and when the well shaken wagons pulled to a halt they found themselves in an almost perfect hide away, they were in an a horse shoe shaped gully, as they dismounted and stretched their legs McAllister started giving out orders, the four wagon passengers were to take watch through the night, three hours each then Phillippé was tasked to gather wood and start a fire up against the rocks to shade it from the road, *not too big now we don't want to give away our position* the rest were to pitch the field tents and feed and settle the horses. Just after dark the four scouts and the out rider rode into camp and were handed hot tea for which they were truly grateful, they soon had their horses fed and tethered with the others. All tasks complete the weary men sat around the camp fire while Phillippé prepared salted beef with corn and potatoes, once cooked it was divided equally between them and Oh what a meal, with satisfied belly's they started to talk about the mission and what might lay before them, none of the discourse dwelt on any of the difficulty's they may endure but of much happier times that lay ahead, going home meeting friends and family, McAllister was half way through the fourteen children again when a small terrier crept up to the fire and sat by Jean, now Jean being Jean picked up a small scrap of salted beef and offered to the scruffy little mongrel it snapped it up and took its time chewing the tough morsel, he then offered it the left overs of corn and potatoes which it greedily demolished. By this time everyone was comfortably tired and started to disperse into the field tents to sleep. As Jean crawled into his the little terrier crept in after him and settled in to sleep by his feet, Jean smiled, yawned, and the new found friends fell soundlessly to sleep.

The next morning, the lookout woke McAllister as instructed and raised the fire for morning tea, the tea leaves were the reincarnated ones from the night before and so not very strong but at least it was hot. When all were awake McAllister gathered the lookouts and asked of any sightings through the night, two of them reported seeing Russian troops heading south, cheered slightly by this news he ordered break camp and within twenty minutes they were on the move, breakfast was salted beef on the hoof and Jean shared his with his new found friend. Henri teased his little brother saying *I see you've still got your new girlfriend then and a lot prettier than some you've had in the past. She isn't a she, she's actually a he and his new name is Mac, I heard that young Jean* said McAllister with a smile on his face.

As the convoy rolled on the weather started to change for the worse, a stiff breeze started to blow into their faces and with it came the first drops of rain both McAllister and Phillippé donned their drovers coats and pulled their Russian caps low over their noses to try and keep the worst of the weather out of their eyes after about an hour the four passengers had decided that enough was enough and all four climbed into the rear of the wagons and tried to shelter under the concealing sheets, for Mac it was easy finding a dry spot him being so small for the rest however it wasn't quite that simple and without any physical exercise to keep them warm they were all suffering from the cold Mac was most put out when Jean picked him up and shoved him inside his jacket for warmth but he soon got the message and stayed put. Henri after about four hours of suffering jumped out of the wagon with a splash and jogged alongside and after the initial discomfort, he very slowly started to warm his muscles, after marching to nearly every point in Europe at one time or another he was well versed in warming himself up so much so that Phillippé saw what he was doing and asked if he would like to take the reins for a while, hang fire for another ten minutes my friend and then I will ease your suffering. Visibility was dreadful it was a full time job just trying to keep the wagons on the road, but out of the rain suddenly appeared the two forward scouts. McAllister slowed the lead wagon to a stop and spoke with them, Sir I have to report a Russian company about eight kilometres ahead and marching this way, ok thanks for the warning, now ride to tell the rear scouts tell them that you must avoid contact with them, go off road and circle around them we'll meet up with you ten kilometres ahead, will you not go around as well sir, no I daren't take the wagons off the road in this weather I'm going to try and bluff our way passed.

What with the weather being as fierce as it was and the possibility of impending doom up ahead it had turned out to be the longest loneliest journey that McAllister had ever endured, minute after minute seemed like a lifetime but in time sure enough the Russians appeared out of the squall, at first it was just their scouts who had to shout out their questions to be heard over the noise of the storm 'Здравствуйте,

Здравствуйте, Были вы, Санкт-Петербург, Как дорога, ОК, если ваше пристальное, поблагодарить Вас, удачи'. *With a wave both parties moved on, what was all that about Sarge? nothing much they just asked where we were going so I told them the truth I told them we are going to St Petersburg oh and I asked what the road is like ahead and they reckon its fine if were careful I reckon this weather is going to save our bacon you know* two more kilometres and they came across the main company of soldiers as soon as he spotted them he did the polite thing and pulled off the road to let them pass, the few men who looked up, looked despairingly cold and downtrodden it looked like all they wanted in life was to sit by a roaring fire and rest. When the last of them had past McAllister pulled back onto the road and kept on going they travelled for another ten kilometre's as promised and decided to take as much shelter as they could find by the side of the road the two wagons were backed up to each other and the order was given to gather as many rocks as they could find and create a wall to take the brunt of the wind and rain once this was done with a struggle four field tents were dropped over the windward side of the wagons and bricked in place this did a very reasonable job of keeping the worst of the weather at bay, there was no chance of them lighting a fire to warm up any meal so it would have to be salted beef and for those who could tolerate the taste raw potatoes. Three more field tents were with a struggle erected downwind of the wagons and so all fed they crawled into the tents to wait out a very uncomfortable night.

The next day was somewhat brighter than the day before, the wind was gusting every now and then but the rain had stopped completely so it was possible to dry their clothes while still wearing them not ideal but by midmorning they were all reasonably dry. The scouts joined them at around midday, they had faired a little better than the main party insofar as when they went off road to bypass the Russians they had stumbled upon an old shepherds hut in the middle of nowhere and as dilapidated as it was it gave shelter to the men and their horses unfortunately when they set off this morning they got a little lost and couldn't locate the road at first but they finally found it and it was good to have the whole squad back together again. The rest of the day was pretty uneventful but as darkness drew again the order was to make camp and this time they found a small wood which fit the bill suitably there was plenty of cover and food for the horses and a large pool of water had been created by the rains of yesterday so all thirsts were quenched. McAllister told the men to break out the tents not for sleeping in this time he had them all strung between the trees to create a shelter from the elements with having the benefit of them all drying out overnight once the shelter was built he told everyone present to try and gather as much dead timber as they could find and with great difficulty managed to start a fire using it to dry the sodden branches which would be the next to burn, the cooking implements were brought out and Phillippé started work on their dinner, a task he relished simply because he was warmer now that he had been in the last twenty four hours McCalister reasoned that because no one had eaten any of their rations over the last day or so Phillippé should make double rations tonight, and no one could seem to find an argument good enough to go against the order. Sentries were allocated the same as before but this time they were also tasked to keep the fire topped up because it was reasoned that to try and start another in the morning would be too time consuming and McAllister wanted everyone to set off with at the very least a warm drink inside them. The team spread out sitting with backs to trees feeling the warmth of the fire, Jean rested his head against one of the trees and Mac rolled on his back between his legs burped loudly and started to snore with his legs in the air twitching now and then chasing imaginary rabbits.

The next morning dawned bright and fresh and although their sleep was very intermittent throughout the night, enough was had to put a spring in their step even more so when the morning brews were handed out with a bowl of steaming oats. *Ah this is the way to start a morning mused Henri I think I'll have the same tomorrow with a glass of port and a read of the morning papers... just think Henri this time next month you'll be able to do that very thing, bring it on I say the sooner the better, right'o' boys lets up camp and get back on the road, the sooner we leave the sooner we'll be home.* The dried tents were wrapped up and stowed, the horses fed, watered and saddled the fire that had been burning all night extinguished….eventually….even Mac felt the high spirits amongst the men and as a celebration he rolled in a big dollop of horse muck and jumped into Phillippés lap, *'GET OFF ME YOU SMELLY LITTLE BASTARD'* he yelled and at that the little dog jumped into the back of the wagon with an smug grin on its face, *if he does that again I'm going to kick him all the way to St Petersburg just you watch if I don't awe pillippé he's only showing his affection, well he can show it to somebody else the horrible little sod.*

The next few days passed uneventfully enough the few towns that they did pass through hardly acknowledged them, a quick stop in Valday replenished their food stocks both man and beast, all the negotiations dealt with by McAllister, the only hiccup was when Jean asked *how long they were stopping for?…..*in French whilst McAllister was trading with one of the locals, the Russian looked over when Jean spoke but the quick thinking sergeant casually said *you'll have to keep practising karlof or you'll never get it right,* Jean didn't understand a single word but was bright enough to catch on, he shrugged his shoulders silently and turned away from them and jumped up onto the wagon, McAllister told the woman that he was trying to learn French in case they happened upon any on their journey *you won't find any around here she said their all over in Moscow lording it up* and at that she spat as if just speaking the words left a sour taste in her mouth, they spoke a little longer then he wished her well and made his leave. When they were back on the road and out of earshot he reprimanded Jean severely saying that *if your stupid enough to do anything that again I'll personally kick you to the road side and leave you there and let the locals deal with you* but when he had calmed down he regretted being quite so tough with him as he could tell by the look on his face it said it all, he knew he had done wrong and jeopardised the mission, and it would most definitely not happen again, to add insult to injury Mac told him off also the only way he knew how and lifting his hind leg piddled on his boots.

It was on their approach to Chudovo that their good fortune finally ran out, they were about ten kilometres from the town when the lead wagon hit a particularly large rut and when the left front wheel fell into it, it collapsed completely and with the combined weight of the three passengers and the freight sliding forward the horses took all the weight on their rear legs but because they were out of step with each other the horse on the left took the majority of the combined weight and its leg simply snapped like a branch. The poor animal screamed in agony as its bone pushed out through muscle and skin to protrude at an obscene angle, the poor horse tried to run from the pain partly dragging its partner with it, this movement and the howls its stable mate was creating panicked the creature and it tried to run from the immediate danger, it jumped forward snapping the old leather bindings straps and yolk, once free it ran it didn't care where, it just ran as quickly as it could, by now the injured horse had collapsed in a writhing heap on the floor the initial adrenalin wearing off, now the pain really fired and the screams got even louder, the poor animal still thought flight was the best option an so it kept on trying to stand without success. McAllister yelled at the rear wagon, get a bloody musket loaded NOW! Henri was the first to arms and ran over to the fallen animal, Shoot the poor creature he shouted over the noise, Henri never heard a word his sergeant said but he knew exactly what to do, he took aim at the beasts head and for a brief moment looked into its eyes, he could see the despair and the pleading to stop the pain, he cocked the hammer aimed between its eyes, and quietly whispered 'sorry friend' he pulled the trigger. The noise abruptly stopped. The dead silence was tangible you could taste it, you could smell it, something had changed, all of the high spirits had completely gone. It was only an accident something that happens time and time again on badly maintained roads but this time it had happened to them and it had left everyone subdued even little Mac hid his head, who knew his thoughts? He did, and for him that was enough.

Phillippé put away his musket while McAllister assessed the damage, well the wheel was a complete right off as was all of the tack the first issue that they had though was to get the wagon and dead horse off the road and as Henri pointed out a dead horse is a lot heavier than a live one, they needed equipment rope, timber all manner of gear so it was decided that McAlister would take the good wagon and ride into town and gather what they required he would take two out riders with him as guards but this decision left him with another problem what if someone were to pass this way and get curious asking questions that the team couldn't answer and so the orders were to shoot anyone that came close and shoot to kill, once dead they were to drag the corpse into the scrub and leave them to rot, under no circumstance was anybody to be left alive, they were told if any escape you might as well shoot yourselves because the mission would be over. So McAllister set off and left them to it. The first job was to load the muskets they had brought with them, so they set to work and lined each one up against the wagon when loaded, forty two in total which amounted to forty two shots before having to reload, once this was done, Phillippé came up with a simple but ingenious idea he said can any of you pick up and move a dead horse and carry it off, don't be daft it's impossible came the reply, not if it's in bits it isn't, what a great idea said Henri why didn't we think of that sooner, well that would be because your all thick and I'm not which got him a punch on the arm, a sabre was pulled from the wagon and the grisly task undertaken. Because the animal had been dead a while its blood had already begun to congeal and so little was spilled. Piece by piece the animal was butchered and carried out into the scrubland to be dumped. On consideration the two hind quarters were saved, waste not want not said Henri. Once the horse had been moved off the road the problem with the wagon didn't seem quite so bad it was still a mess granted but it no longer seemed insurmountable. We can move it Henri stated there's enough of us we can push the bugger off the road, if it's not blocking anyone's way then it's less likely for anybody to stop and ask silly questions, ok let's give it a go. They all gathered around it and grabbed a hand hold, right is everyone ready, after three, one two three lift, no good, ok let's try again one two three lift, still it was too heavy. Right let's make it lighter, let's take everything off it, so they laboured hard and completely stripped it including the two money chests, once done they tried again, every one took hold and after a count of three they managed to lift it but it still didn't move anywhere right one more time but this time lets have some of you push instead of lifting, so everyone got into position and Henri started the count, three, two, one lift and this time the stubborn thing moved don't stop, don't stop he shouted as it rolled off the road and onto the scrub they kept pushing and with their momentum got it twenty metres away before it stopped and everyone collapsed in a heap.

Once they had recovered they decided to gather wood for a fire and cook the horse steaks. As they were cooking Phillippé had resigned himself to the fact that it was only meat and not the terrified animal he shot earlier that day and so joined the rest in enjoying their wind fall. Mac was thrown a steak that was bigger than he was but he managed to drag it away so that they wouldn't ask for it back.

As the afternoon led into evening the question was asked do we make camp, well I guess so there's not much we can do in the dark, so field tents were pitched around the fire and money chests, the muskets were wrapped so that they wouldn't sweat in the cool evening air. When they were all settled around the fire the conversation again turned to what they all would do when they got home, after a disastrous day was saved through team work their spirits were rallied again.

At about one o'clock in the morning Mac started to growl waking Jean, as he rubbed his eyes the little dog started to bark which had the desired effect everyone was awake guns in hands, the fire had died some time ago and it was a dark night with a lot of cloud cover, Jean reprimanded Mac and stopped him barking with a tap on the snout, the dog stared at him with a look that said you're going to regret that mate. Once everything went quite the group listened and in the distance there were men speaking in Russian, no one could understand them but they sounded cheerful enough, as they got closer they figured that there were about twenty strong. With McAllister still not back Phillippé took charge, and the first command was to spread out along the road side and take cover, he told them to cock their weapons before they left as if they did it when the Russians got closer they would surely hear them and give away the element of surprise, he told them to stay back from the road, keep ten paces apart and await his signal his final order was if they had to shoot then shoot to kill. As the French settled in the Russians got closer and a couple of them took an interest in the shapes in the distance. The French didn't know what was being said but there were definitely questions in their voices, two of them crossed over to the French side of the road and the first pointed over to where the tents had been pitched, turned back to his partner and whispered Shhh. They both slowed which in turn piqued the interest in the rest of the troop and one by one they all followed, when they were about ten paces away the order was given….'FIRE' and as one nine muskets blasted into the Russians. The Enemy dropped to the floor either dead or in fear, the nine guns were thrown to one side and fresh loaded ones gathered up. After the initial volley the Russians started to shout to one another fear and pain in their voices. The lucky ones were starting to regroup crawling along the ground to each other. A second order was given 'STAND' the French stood creating a better angle for the guns and as Phillippé shouted the order another volley thumped into the Russians and as soon as it did the third and last order was given, 'BAYONETS' the Russians didn't need to speak French to know what was coming and the hand full that were left unscathed got to their feet and tried to run but the French charge had already gained momentum and so they didn't stand a chance, a couple of them dug their heels in and turned to fight one even tried to load his pistol but the attack was so fast and so vicious all was lost, as Henri ran past one of the fallen the Russians his eyes opened and he grabbed at his leg mid stride tripping him, with his weapon still in hand he couldn't arrest his fall and he hit the ground head first bringing stars to his vision at once the Russian was on top of him wrestling the gun from his unresisting hands he then had his own hands around Henri's throat Henri could do nothing to stop him as he passed out, he was totally helpless but his little brother certainly wasn't Jean ran up behind the attacker and screamed at him get your filthy hands off my brother the Russian didn't have a clue about what he said but he knew Jeans intentions he went to grab at Henri's weapon but

Jean kicked it aside knowing he was doomed he did the only thing that was left, he lifted his arms and surrendered at the same time turning to face him, Jean didn't stop for a heartbeat he pushed the weapon straight into his ribcage and into his heart he was dead before he hit the ground so the next fourteen stabs were completely un necessary. As Henri came to he saw what Jean was doing he rose from the ground and put a hand on his shoulder whispering that'll do Jean that'll do, he took his weapon from him and drew him into an embrace until he could feel him calm, c'mon little brother let's see if they've left us any. They hadn't, a total of twenty six bodies lay dead or near as damn it. Well done boys Phillippé said, now let's get rid of the evidence as quick we can, so they all started to drag the bodies into the scrub. They were all so busy cleaning up the mess that they didn't notice the one injured Russian crawl off into the darkness and away from the blood stained road.

Everyone was far too worked up to sleep and so the fire was resurrected and water boiled for a brew of tea. Very little was said between the men they just stared into the flames lost in their own thoughts.

It was about three thirty in the morning when McAllister returned to the camp in a new wagon pulled along by stolen horses and was surprised to see everyone wide awake drinking tea. *Have I missed something?* he asked and Phillippé answered *no nothing much, pretty quiet evening really*, which had the rest of them rolling about the floor laughing, the tension finally broken. Once he had been brought up to speed with what had happened, he said *right let's go, get everything loaded up and we'll make an early start.* Thirty minutes later everything was loaded and they were back on the road. After maybe five or six kilometres a lone figure was spotted on the road and as they closed upon him he started to wave his arms to get their attention and pleaded to them in Russian McAllister had taken the lead again, he listened to what the man had to say for himself then reached into his coat and pulled out a pistol, aimed it at the man's head and shot him dead he jumped down from the wagon and dragged him by the collar off the road once done he climbed back onto the wagon, shouting back to Phillippé *it appears you missed one*, and that said he urged the horses onwards.

It was decided that to skirt the next town would be the better option than the more direct route as even if the owner of the wagon and horses hadn't gotten out of his chains there may be other people that would recognise them as they passed by.

So Sarge how did the previous owner of this fine vehicle end up in chains? Andrei he's called we had a few quiet drinks together last night, these Russians think there all heavy drinkers but not against me they're not, especially when every time it was my round I swapped my Vodka for water, so by the end of the night he figured he'd been duped but he wasn't quite sure how so when I walked him home and he wanted to show me the new wagon he had been bragging about all night then the rest was easy, he was virtually unconscious when I wrapped him in the chains and clicked the lock then I simply hitched up the horses and rode straight out, all I know is he will have one bitch of a hangover when he finally wakes up and this contraption will be the last thing on his mind.

As the sun rose the clouds parted and the men were treated to a glorious sunrise that warmed their hearts as well as their bodies, *has anyone seen Mac this morning?* Enquired Jean he wasn't sitting up front like he normally would, *last time I saw him he was in the back ripping your bivvy to shreds, he what? Didn't you try and stop him? not likely he's like a wild tiger when he's got his temper up anyway he's yours you do it, I'm kind of surprised he picked on you though man's best friend and all that crap,* at the sound of his name the little dog climbed out from under the pile of tents, sat on top of them and in the morning sunshine grinned at him in a way that emanated told you so, Jean pointed at him and said '*bad dog*' which made his grin even wider.

Towards the end of the day they had made good progress and found that they were not far from the town of Tosno. Being close to the outskirts of St Petersburg there was more and more traffic on the road including

Russian soldiers, McAllister decided that this would be a good place to pull over and make camp so he pulled on the reins and rattled a good hundred paces away from the road. It was now twilight and so the field tents were quickly pitched in a circle around the wagons and horses he was asked if they would be safe tonight, *yes I should think so there's been plenty of tradesmen camped by the road side on our way through, so we should blend in no problem and at least the wagons don't look abandoned this time. Just to be on the safe side we'll do a three hour sentry rota.* So that was it camp made, fire lit and evening meal on the go they all got their sleeping sacks into their tents before settling down by the fire, then through the silence came a loud you dirty little.....as Mac sloped back into the shadows. When everyone was seated the meal was served. Through the conversation McAllister was asked *how and when they reached St Petersburg they were to find and reach the ship? I haven't got the first idea but I'm sure I'll think of something, a good night's sleep will clear the mind and set us all up for the next part of our journey,* at that they all turned in and as the last one drifted off a voice was heard saying and you can bugger off you cheeky little sod.

As McAllister had predicted the whole party were unmolested though out the night and woke bright and early the next morning. The first up got the fire going and a pot of water on to boil for a brew and the morning oats. Mac was especially grateful for the warmth of the fire as the temperature had dropped with the ebbing fire through the early hours and with no one willing to share a tent with him the cold had knocked the devilment out of him, so as soon as Jean had risen and claimed a place by the fire, he crept over to him and tentatively licked the back of his hand and gave him the best puppy dog eyes he could muster, and after the performance Jean picked him up and dropped him into his lap.

McAllister had decided it was time to get serious with the men so as they were eating their breakfasts he told them all to listen closely. *Right the lot of you, the fun and games are now over until we make contact with the ship, we are no more than a day or two's march from St Petersburg and it is now when it gets serious, under no circumstance are any of you to speak*

French within earshot of any Russians until we are all safely on the ship and out of the harbour. I don't know what adversities we may encounter once were in the city, but believe this if the locals suspect anything at all it will be the death sentence for us all, so as a starter for ten I want you to learn six phrases in Russian that may very well save your miserable lives, so learn them and learn them good. What are they sarge? ok the first one is hello…Здравствуйте, the second one is goodbye… До свидания, three, yes… Да, four is no… Нет, five is please… Просьба, and finally, thank you…поблагодарить Вас. With these in your vocabulary you can go a long way, with other bits and pieces that you'll pick up along the road you won't go far wrong. And so with all of them practising, he walked over to the road side and asked a passing tradesman how far it was to St Petersburg. The whole gang started to up camp still muttering Russian to themselves, if things hadn't been so serious it would have been comical. Once they were all packed away, McAllister again took the lead with all the out riders in close formation. By mid-afternoon they had reached Pushkin in the suburbs of St Petersburg and rolled on through the hustle and bustle of the capital. Now whilst McAllister was fluent in many languages he couldn't read or write in any of them so none of the sign posts made any sense whatsoever, so whenever they hit a junction he had to ask directions from one of the locals, which he realised would make people suspicious so again he told everyone the truth, *sorry I can't read*, which worked a dream with them and they were only too happy to help, so each time he was pointed in the right direction he had a team behind him that shouted '*поблагодарить Вас*,' waved and barked to them, he smiled every time.

By late afternoon they had reached the harbour where things were winding down for the day, there were still a few fishermen mending nets and baiting lobsterpots all but one of the fish stalls had closed. McAllister strolled over to it and spoke with the stall holder about the ships that were anchored in the harbour at the same time buying what he had left for sale. When he came back he gathered the men together. Right he said we can't stop here tonight it's too conspicuous you will have to turn about and head back into the suburbs and find a suitable camp site back there, which meant at least another hour on their journey. McAllister had been drawing up a simple map each time they changed direction on the way here and in doing so he had marked four campsites that they could possibly use, just waste land really but quiet and deserted. He gave the map to Phillippé and told him to take the lead and direct all of them back out of the city. I know it will be dark by the time you make camp but do the best you can and stay out of trouble. What are you going to do? I'm going to take one of the horses and stay by the harbour tonight, the fish seller told me that there is a ship moored out there by the name of Les Contrebandiére but he knows nothing of the captain or crew, so I'm going to stay and find out what I can. Now off you go and don't wait up. So they turned the carts around and in a solemn mood set off back through the same streets they had arrived through not half an hour ago. Meanwhile McAllister found a coaching inn and settled the horse in for the night.

McAllister might not have worried about his men talking French in the open because none of them wanted to talk at all they were all so subdued they felt like they'd climbed the mountain and now there was only one way left to go. Just over an hour later they had found the first of the possible camp sites but dismissed it out of hand because of a couple of nearby taverns that seemed very popular with the locals so on they travelled for another forty minutes till they found the second possible site and this one was much quieter so when Phillippé had asked if it would suffice there was a unanimous '*Да*' so they pulled off the road and made camp in the normal ring formation with a fire in the very centre and again sentries were allotted for the night watch. Henri was given the position of cook for the night and in typical Henri style everything went into the pot, his argument was that they wouldn't need any of it tomorrow because they would be on the ship so in it went, what was left of the salted beef, the fish that McAllister had given them, the last of the potatoes a half bottle of wine that was too sour to drink, a few random vegetables and a half bag of sugar. *You sure about this Henri yes it'll be fine just take out the bits you don't like, if I did that I'd end up with an empty bowl my friend, you'll love it just you wait and see, old family recipe, is that right Jean? not that I'm aware of but Henri's a lot older than me, do you lot want to be fed or not.* Bowls filled and spoons in hand, no one wanted to go first, *go on you try it, not on your life I've had a jippy tummy all day I'm sure this isn't going to be the cure. Oh sod it here goes nothing........I'll tell you what its actually not that bad said one, needs a little salt* said another, *woof* said a third. Once fed the team retired to their respective tents and sentry duty started. Because Jean and Mac had made up the little dog was allowed back in the tent and everyone hunkered down to sleep.

Back at the harbour McAllister had sauntered into one of the taverns that looked out to sea, his thinking was that if he had a ship at anchor he would want to keep an eye on it even when he wasn't on board and everyone needed a little shore leave now and again, he was looking for a certain type, a seaman through and through, hard, tanned, tattooed but above all watchful, wary, and suspicious. He had no name, no description and he didn't even know what language he spoke. The man would have to be able to speak basic Russian at least so the plan was to visit all the seaward facing taverns have an ale in each and see if he could spot anyone who stood out, and if he did he would ask the bar tender if he knew the captain of Les Cotrabandiére the answer would always be an outstanding no of course because you would tend to lose customers rather rapidly otherwise. So away he went, he counted nine such inns in total, which meant his constitution wouldn't be compromised. Running from East to West the last of which was where he had stabled his horse. It was a no brainer, start at the farthest East and just keep going. In the first three he got what he expected a resounding no, numbers four and five were the same, and he started to think what if he isn't even on shore, what if he was still on board the ship waiting for someone to row out to him and make contact. He knew that this was going to be difficult but...Hay ho on we go, he walked into number six ordered another ale and waited for a lull in the conversation then hit the bar man with the same question, and in return received the same old answer, *sorry friend I don't know the man. Ok* he said, *cheers anyway,* finished his drink and left. He was about half way to number seven, when two men grabbed him from behind and dragged him down a dark alleyway. Of course he was expecting something like this to happen and so didn't put up a fight. The first man asked him in terrible Russian *who you, what you ship for asking?* it took him a second or two to figure out what he'd said and in that moment number two punched him twice in the stomach now the man was well built, but McAllister was six foot four and as hard as a tree, however he played along and feigned the pain, number two then grabbed him by the throat and said '*well*' McAllister had just about had enough of these two idiots by this time and turned the tables, number two had his arm pushed aside and a punch like a hammer blow hit his gut, he doubled up immediately and fell to the floor, number one was then grabbed by the wrist, he punched him on the opposite shoulder spinning him around and pushing his arm up his back, he kicked him in the back of his knee and he dropped into a kneeling position making him cry out with pain, when the cry died he got real close to the back of his head and said in Finnish *right bollocks, I need to get on a ship and get to France, now you either know this to be the truth or you don't care I'm hoping it's the former, yeh yeh we know, right where can I meet the captain,* and with his other arm he pointed *he's in there* he said just as McAllister said '*whoops*' and broke his arm. He left the alley and casually walked into the inn. He walked to the bar and turned to view the room and spotted him immediately, a big calloused man hard as a brick but not quite as pretty, standing by the window staring at his ship, McAllister walked over to him and face to face said in Finnish *we need to talk* the captain looked straight into his eyes and said yes we do. He swallowed what was left of his drink and followed McAllister outside he followed him to the harbour wall where he pointed seaward and said *that yours? Yes it is the names Kristian....McAllister* he said in return and shook his offered hand. *Sorry Kristian but you might need a couple of new deck hands* he smiled *I never liked those two dogs anyway reckoned they were hard as nails but chins like glass* McAllister then smiled liking Kristian immediately my kind of guy he thought. *Right he said what time is the tide tomorrow? Its half eleven can you be ready by then? We can yes, do you have transport to the ship? Yes I have a barge to take you from here and an on-board davit to lift your cargo. Ok he said I'll be away, see you tomorrow.*

He rode through the night trying to remember the camp sites that he had scribbled down that day, hoping that he would recognise them in the dark, he wanted to get there as quickly as possible but at the same time he didn't want to injure the horse so the best he could ask was a steady canter. The way he saw it was that if the journey was going to take two hours in the morning he was going to have everyone up and fully loaded by nine thirty but he wanted to get there at least an hour before high tide so that meant that the latest they could set off would be eight thirty add half an hours grace, and there you have it everyone away by eight.

there were of course noticeable land marks that showed themselves even in the gloom of the night and one was just ahead, the spire of an old church that he could swear left him no more than twenty minutes from the first of the possible camp sites and he was bolstered by that thought. As he turned a corner he slowed his horse to take a better look the site in daylight was just an ordinary wasteland but in the dark it was just a void and he certainly wasn't going to chance the horse over that, it was always taught to every soldier that if you are approaching a hidden camp then whistle and if you didn't get shot, then you would get a whistle in return so he whistled, nothing he tried again and this time he got a slurring voice from somewhere behind him saying *'Снизить уровень шума',* *sorry* he whispered back and rode on he smiled to himself thinking I know I taught them some Russian but none of them are that good just yet, so on he rode he figured the next site to be just over half an hour away then the thought struck him that conceivably they could have gone all the way back to the camp they used the night before, god don't let that be case, he thought. Half an hour came and went and he didn't recognise anything so he rode for another fifteen minutes and stopped, panic started to grow so he dismounted and walked around in a circle thinking, why did he not recognise the area then he looked back at the way he'd come, *that's it* he looked at a tree in front of him that he had noticed on the way to St Petersburg yesterday with a lightning strike down this side, that's why he didn't recognise the road because he had never ridden it in this direction before. He remounted turned about and rode on and sure enough after ten minutes he knew exactly where he was and just up in front he could make out the second camp site. He dismounted again and gave a whistle, nothing, he tried a second time and this time the sentry heard him and whistled back, the relief was all consuming never was a sweeter sound heard. He led the horse slowly over the dark ground feeling for any tripping hazards and soon he saw the dull shapes of a camp and as he got to the tents he heard a familiar voice say hiya Sarge where've you been, over here I've got some tea for you and he produced a luke warm mug and offered it to him thanks Jean, he took a mouthful and said can I borrow your tent for a couple of hours I'm dead beat wake me at seven will you and he crawled into the sleeping sack, turned over and Jean heard 'Oy pack that in you dirty little bugger'

As instructed McAllister was woken bang on seven o'clock he was handed a hot mug of tea this time and his first order of the day was get everyone else up. When they were all assembled he told them *you've got twenty minutes to pack everything away and mount up, we have got a ship to catch*

The mood that morning couldn't have been better you could feel the excitement in the air, the journey yesterday down this same stretch of road a long forgotten memory, it was difficult for the men not to speak at times but the order still stood firm only speak when it's absolutely necessary and not within earshot of any of the locals.

By the time they pulled up to the harbour wall the men were like kids on Christmas Eve, it was a little after ten in the morning and a bright and fresh day, they all dismounted to stretch their aching limbs and McAllister gathered them all together on the slipway so that they couldn't be heard by the locals. *Right he said this will be the most diffi-cult part of the whole mission for the lot of you, your uniforms might keep prying eyes away for most but whatever happens don't talk to anyone, I'm going to that Inn over there to try and find the captain and while I'm away I want you lot to guard the wagons so put your muskets on show and look as intimidating as you possibly can*, he walked over the road and entered the building. At first glance he couldn't see Kristian so he walked up to the bar and ordered an ale. As it was handed over he asked the bar tender *have you seen Captain Kristian this morning? Who? give over, the man I was talking to in here last night big fellow ugly as sin, we get a lot of customers that fit that description sir.* This was getting him nowhere so he took his drink over to the window and sat down facing the slipway so that he could keep an eye on his men. He had sat for maybe fifteen minutes when out in the harbour he noticed movement a row boat was being lowered into the water from Kristian's ship. He spent a while longer watching the boats progress and when Kristian didn't show he finished his ale and walked back over to the slipway, as the boat neared he could see that it was pulling a large raft behind it. When it was close enough he shouted to the four oarsmen in Finnish, *where's the Captain? We don't know came the reply we have orders to pick up you and your cargo and deliver you to the ship we thought he must be here with you. Hmm… ok boy's somethings not right here, so I need you all to be extra vigilant he said in a whisper, I want these wagons guarded constantly, I'm not so bothered about the horses we can always get fresh back in France. But see those chests I want them on board complete with you lot, so load your guns now and let them see you do it, I want five of you to go with the first load and five with the second Phillippé you stay here with me, we will go last and hopefully with the captain.* He walked down the slipway and spoke with the oars-men. He found out that they were as concerned about Kristian as he was which oddly made him feel a little better about the whole business. They told him that the captain hadn't return to the ship last night, which they said was very unlike him. *Ok I'll try and find him and travel to the ship on the third crossing,* they passed on their thanks and started to load the barge. *Phillippé grab four muskets and load them, me and you are going on a pub crawl.* Two muskets each one on each shoulder McAllister also had his trusted pistol and they both had a sabre each, if they were going in then they were going in packing. The pair walked purposely over to the Inn and straight to the bar, the bar tender had just started to reprimand the two for coming in armed when two musket barrels were pointed at his chest, and this time he was a little more cooperative. *Right friend we'll try this one more time, where the hell is Captain Kristian, look there's no need for guns I was just being careful that's all, comes with the job, bugger the job where is he. Ok, ok after you left last night he came back in here and was followed by two others, one with a bust arm, well they argued a while and he told them to piss off, and they left full of hell. After that he had a couple more drinks then he left, that's all I saw, maybe but that's not all you know is it… Where will I find the two of them? He said clicking back his hammer. Oh sweet Jesus, three streets back, white fronted building, lobster pots stacked out front, thanks friend,* and he clicked the hammer back off, *you keep a good ale here by the way* he said as they left. McAllister explained to Phillippé just what had happened the night before as they made their way up the street, *I should have known they'd want revenge.* He figured that they probably wouldn't kill him but it wouldn't surprise him if they tried to muscle in on the act and try and find out what his cargo was and where it was headed, so to kidnap him and make him talk made perfect sense to a couple of thugs like them. As they walked silently through the streets they spotted the house up ahead and snuck up to it. From an upstairs window they could hear deep groans, using mostly hand signals Phillippé was instructed to go around the back and wait, he held up one finger meaning one minute and mimed kicking the door in, Phillippé nodded and disappeared, McAllister counted the minute off in his head, he took two steps back, shouted *are there two fucking idiots in there,* and threw himself at the old timber door, it fell off its hinges and clattered against the wall. He heard the rear door go the same way and as his momentum carried him forward, he collided with the guy whose arm he'd broken the night before sending him screaming to the floor clutching at his useless appendage McAllister ran up the stairs, closely followed by Phillippé, they barged into the room and found Kristian bound and bruised on the floor, and his captor standing over him with a large fish filleting knife held close to his throat. Phillippé already had his gun cocked and put his musket barrel onto McAllister's shoulder aimed and fired in one smooth motion, the noise was incredible in the small room, but his aim was true and the lead ball hit him in the centre of his chest breaking ribs and ripping through his spine as it left, he fell to the floor in a seated position still conscious but only just.

McAllister bend down and untied Kristian's bond's his face was full of fire and brimstone, you better not have killed the bastard! he yelled, he crouched down in front of his captor and lifted his head there was still life in his eyes but not for long, he took the knife from his dying hand and dug it into his crotch, he opened his mouth and shoved his genitals down his throat and with that last look of agony on his face Kristian was satisfied with what he had done. *Where's the other bastard? Down stairs in the passage way, right he's next* and he stomped out of the room to be followed by Phillippé, a hand grabbed his arm and he turned around, *leave him mate it's his fight not ours.* Twenty seconds later there was the most horrific scream, after what seemed like an eternity the screaming stopped and the pair walked down stairs, there was blood everywhere and the man's heart was sat on the bottom step with a bite out of it. Kristian was outside covered in blood, McAllister slapped him on the shoulder and said *come on let's get you cleaned up you've got a ship to sail.*

When his men saw him they drew away in disbelief with a look of horror on their faces, he walked straight passed them and flung himself fully clothed into the sea. He stayed underwater for so long they feared he might drown but he eventually resurfaced walked back up the slipway where they were waiting and said *come on let's get going.* They all jumped aboard and the four oars men took them over to the waiting ship. They climbed aboard and McAllister went to inspect the cargo. The men had done well, everything they owned was aboard and lashed down securely and they had also managed to load four of the horses. Mac was barking his head off playing chase with rats in the bilges, he spotted McAllister jumped into his arms, licked his face and in a flash was gone again chasing another quarry.

The Captain went below to change out of his wet clothes and returned ten minutes later, he walked straight over to McAllister offered him his hand and said one unbreakable word… 'Thanks'.

Captain Kristian, barked orders to his crew and the men started to unfurl the sails and lift the anchor. McAllister sat with his men and looked at each one of them, he felt nothing but pride, *well boys it's over, we did it, those medals that the Emperor offered you have been earned fair and square, you should be very proud of yourselves you are all true heroes and I will tell anyone who cares to listen.*

As the sails filled and the ship slowly gathered speed they headed for the harbour mouth and out of Russia.

COATHAM 1812 SEPTEMBER 22ND

Jeffrey was sat on the garden wall enjoying a mug of tea with Nell when the wagon turned up *Hiya Fella's how you doin, Nell this is Frank 'n' Wilf, boys this is Nell, these two are our partners in crime so to speak,* she beamed at them showing off her three good teeth, *would you mind if I go an talk business with em luv, aye go on Dy'er want me to shout David for yer, aye if yer would, nice to meet yer lads,* and she disappeared into the house to be quickly replaced by David who came running out across the garden and leaped straight onto the back of the wagon, *wotcha lads ows it hanging.* Jeffrey climbed up behind him and told Frank to head for the beach. Only when they got there did he begin to talk. *Right lads ow did it go. It went good I reckon, right then tell me everything, well we did wot yer said and went straight to the station but Germain weren't there so we nicked the keys for the lock up an stashed all the gear in there, we were just about done when he tuned up like, he ad a quick butcha,s but he didn't seem too bothered about it, good did yer tell im that it was evidence like I told yer to, aye we did, good so wot else did he say, not much he asked how things went up ere an we told im it went a dream an we needed more money for another deal this week, and was he ok with that? Aye eventually, wot d'yeh mean eventually? Well first we told im that none of us ave ad our wages this month so we kinda leant on im a bit about that until he paid us, an then we told im wot you said about needin more tradin money, I thought he was goin to swallow is tongue when we said that, anyway he asked how much an we said the same as last time an then he stopped breathin for a bit, then he filled this purse an told us to give it yeh, so ere yeh go, one tradin purse an two sets of wages. Woohoo shouted David, let's all go on the piss, we'll do nothing of the sort David we've got plans to draw up, well bring your chalk to the pub with yer then, no David no pub. See when I get as old as you im not gunna be a misery guts like you are, what d'you mean 'when' from where I'm standin I'd say 'if'.*

Right boys I've been talkin to john Andrew and he's arranged a drop the day after tomorrow it'll be back over in Saltburn cause it's gunna be a bigger haul this time an he ses he wants to stash his share, but I'll be buggered if I know where he keeps it all. Right so apart from the location everything is the same as last time, you ok with that, oh aye no bother, right drop us two off back at the house and piss off back to Middlesbrough, you can go on the lash tonight but leave it alone tomorrow you need to ave your wits about yer for the drop. Can I go wivem Jeffery can I, can I, I'll be dead good an everythin w.....ell, or go on Jeffrey I'd luv a night out in Middlesbrough, well it's up to these two, wot d'you think Frank can yer keep im out of bother over there, yeh why not we'll burn the house down.....No not literally we'll have a great time is wot I meant. All right you can go but I want you in bed by midnight, and no bother or I'll tell Nell. Oh no bother at all Jeffrey I wouldn't want to upset our Nell, Frank nodded to Jeffrey and turned the wagon around then drove back to the house, once there Jeffrey jumped out and said, I mean it Frank watch out for im. David jumped down gave Jeffrey a hug like a grizzly bear, kissed him on the forehead and jumped back up on board, he waved them off, wiped a tear from his eyes and went into the house, *'silly bugger'* he said to himself.

As the trio rode the ten or so miles to Middlesbrough David got bored so he invented the clapping game which kept him amused for about ten minutes and then he invented the slapping game which Wilf wasn't very keen on and Frank couldn't play because as he said I'm driving then Wilf came up with a game that didn't hurt as much and he called it the what are you gunna spend your wages on game which everyone liked and as imaginative as they all were seemed to always come back round to beer an women, *are the girls pretty in Middlesbrough David asked, well said Wilf it all depends on wot kind of girl you like, d'you think Nell's pretty? Yeh, a mean no, a mean yeh, but not like that cause she reminds me of me dear old mam in er younger days like, so yeh she's pretty cause me mam was pretty.* That was a struggle of conscience for the poor lad, *hey lets play the slapping game again, no let's not were nearly there now any way,* pointing ahead, David snapped his head forward and let his eyes take in the big lights. As they reached the Dick Turpin Frank slowed the cart up and maneuverer it into the back yard were the landlord was changing a barrel. *Ello fellas weren't sure that I'd see you again, an ye've gone an brought a friend as well, an by gum he's a big un, you strong son? aye strong enough, well do me a favour and carry this barrel int'r bar for me will yeh me sciatica's, drivin me to distraction today.* So David did the gallant thing and jumped down from the wagon to give the man a hand, he picked it up and tucked it under his right arm, *thru ere is it mister, aye lad that it is. Good god Frank were the hell did you find im, oh it's a long story Tom, tell yer what pull us three flaggons of yer worst an I tell yeh all about it. Ok fellas I'll do that, you three stopin a while? yeh I guess but we've got some more business to attend to day after t'morra, but tonight were gunna party, I fear the worst* said Tom stroking his chin while, watching David.

After bedding the horses down for the night the three of them came through to the bar and were handed a tankered each, *only quiet today Tom, just cause its early that's all, a lot of normal folk avent even clocked off yet, you wait till later.* So they did and by nine o'clock the place was positively jumping, and crawling and clucking, they were three deep at the bar so the men shuffled down to one end so that new entries could get served. *Ere said one of the locals d'one of yer want to sit in* pointing at the dominoes on the table, *it's just that me mates gone home and we're one light, aye said Wilf I'll give it a bash,* and he wriggled onto the offered stool and was lost to the game. *Ere lad tek old of me beer ah need to go piss,* he handed him his leather tankard, *back in a bit since lad and off he wobbled.* David was never a lover of his own company and about seven seconds later he was bored so he started to look about and see if anyone wanted to play the slapping game, it was as he was looking he caught a swift glimpse of a young woman walk quickly passed an open doorway at his end of the bar. *Oye* the landlord shouted *don't you be goin getting any funny ideas my lad, sorry David replied I was just lookin….I could see exactly wot you was lookin at lad, now that's my daughter and she don't want the attentions of any fly be night bugger like you, sorry* he said again a little quieter this time his face all a flush. *It's alright big fella, tell you what go an get me another barrel and I might let her come through an say ello to yeh,* so he put down both tankers and sauntered off out the back, this time if he was going to impress anyone, he was going to do it right. He side stepped back behind the bar and asked Tom where he wanted them, *Bloody ell lad in all me years I've never seen that done before, ere Erin he shouted com'n look at this*, and a shy head just peeked around the door frame then vanished again quick as a flash. *Ere lad pop them buggers down ere an take that empty one out back for me,* which he dutifully did as Frank squeezed back to the bar he asked Tom *where did David go? oh im, he went an got imsell in love he did, wot? I've only bin gone five minutes how the ell did that appen then?* He stopped and thought for a second, *Oh bugger Jeffrey's gunna kill me.* As David was putting down the empty barrel at the back of the store room the shy young woman came and stood at the door to watch him, as he turned around she giggled and hid her face behind her long hair, David was always easy to embarrassment but as he stood in the darkening room his face felt like it was illuminating the whole of Middlesbrough and his tongue was trying to perform a half hitch all by its self, *I'm Erin* she said to him and giggled again when he didn't reply, she snuck away quietly. It was a good ten minutes before he managed to calm down enough and re-enter the bar and as he did he saw Wilf having a game of slap with the fella who asked him to play dominoes, *where the hell ave you been all this time, your ale will ave gone cold the amount of time you've bin gone, err sorry got lost, got lost there's only two rooms ow the ell did yeh get lost, oh it's easy when your smitten ain't it lad* came a comment from the landlord, David did it again so to take away the current discussion he picked up his tankered and drained the lot in one go, *by hek was tha thirsty lad, nuther ale please landlord d'you want another Frank? aye I'll drink with yeh lad,* he asked Wilf as well but he couldn't make out what he said due to the game of slap he was playing with his new friend. *There you go boys now what was it you was goin to tell me when you first arrived, ah well I was just thinkin like, if we could come up with some cheap barrels for yeh would you be interested in buyin some? wots wrong with it? nothing's wrong with it, is it nicked? no its not bloody nicked, ow soon can yeh get it? ow about day after tomorrow? I knew you's were up t'summat wantin me wagon an all, right it's a deal* and he offered his hand. *Ave the next on the house, on me, oh an yeh better tell yeh mate to watch that fella he's playin doms with he's known to cheat now and again,* they both turned to look and saw that the duo were now playing slap under the table.

After a while the landlord's daughter walked in behind the bar and stood by her father. *Gentlemen this is my daughter Erin, Erin this is Frank and David and that fella rolling about on the floor over there is Wilf, hello Frank, hello David it's such a pleasure to meet you…are you ok David you've gone a funny colour?* He was completely frozen with terror and the only reply that she got was a few illegible syllables and a few bubbles, Erin giggled at his discomfort then asked *where are you from David?* And after a little thought and a lot of confusion he managed to say…..nothing, so Frank using him as a glove puppet replied *Ull luv we're all from Ull, Ull? Well it's actually Hull unless you come from there, and where is Hull? As the crow flies about eighty miles south of ere or near as damn it. So why are you all here then, well amongst other things were doin a bit of business with your dad ere ain't that right Tom? It most certainly is mate, and I'd like to think we'll be seeing a lot more of each other in the future, is that right David will I be seeing a lot more of you in the future? …Bluub!.. Yeh luv you likely will.* So Tom commandeered Frank to talk business, which left the dumbstruck David to carry a one sided conversation with Erin. *So David have you got anyone special back in Hull?…Blubb!..I mean to say have you got a girl back home y'know like a girlfriend,* a shake of the head making her face positively shine. *Have you never had a girlfriend then David?* He immediately went straight passed red and directly to crimson…*Blubb!…your very quiet David, my mum always said stay away from the strong silent types…Blubb!… I hear that your all stopping upstairs is that right? Bluuu… y yeh that's right, oh so you do talk is there anything you would like to ask me? y..ye.. yer very pretty, oh thank you David, me mam always told me not to talk to girls specially the pretty ones she said that their only after one thing but I never found out what that was. But I'm sure she would luv you, you bein so bonny an all,* this time it was Erin's turn to blush, and all of a sudden they were the only two people left in the world. Erin walked from behind the bar took David by the hand and took him to a small two person table where they both sat lost in each other's company. Business complete Frank decided that Wilf had been playing slap for far too long and so broke up the game between him and his new friend. This time of night all the workers were starting to head for home and the place was thinning out, *howay lads lets have one for the road an then I reckon its bedtime.* Whether or not David heard was unclear but Frank and Wilf were back at the bar with Tom who were all yawning at each other, once their drinks were done the two excise men said goodnight to Tom and shouted over to David *don't you stop up all night, put her down and follow us up lad,* Tom smiled and added *in his own good time boys in his own good time.*

After the untimely death of his wife five years earlier Tom had been trying to find a suitable partner for his daughter, someone strong and innocent of heart so that he could take care of her and love her for always, but he must not be bright enough to be able to mess her about at the same time. It had always been his plan to leave her the Inn so that she would always have an income and he needed to see someone who would stand by her side behind the bar, he so wished that this could be the one, after he had kicked out the last of the drinkers he locked the door and blew out all but one of the lamps, he stopped and looked at the young couple for a few seconds, smiled and proceeded to walk upstairs to bed, and so to dream.

Two hours later the pair were still sat across the table together holding hands and telling each other there hopes and dreams they found that they both had room enough in their future for each other. As it started to get light outside David for the first time in his life called time, he stood took Erin by the hand and escorted her up the stairs as they reached her bedroom door she turned to face him, she raised her arms and clasped them behind his thick neck, he lowered his head and the two of them kissed full on the lips. They spent the next half hour innocently kissing each other with more and more passion, when they eventually came up for air Erin whispered to him *not here David not now, I want to save myself for you,* they managed to pull themselves apart and he gently took her head in his big hands and whispered to her *I luv you Erin, and if you'll have me I always will* a small tear fell from his eyes and she kissed it away and she knew deep down that this was true. She kissed him one last time turned and entered her room she fell with her back to the door and smiled a smile that only someone in love can. David stared at the door her face set in his mind. After a little while he crept along the corridor opened the door to their room and quietly went to bed. That night David, Erin, Tom, Frank and a very bruised Wilf fell asleep with smiles on their faces. It's a good night out in Middlesbrough.

After only a couple of hours sleep David was awoken by a friendly kick up the butt, *c'mon lover boy lets have you up an about, were going for breakfast are yer coming with us? Yeh, Yeh gimme a couple of minutes,* he rubbed his eyes, and took in a good old stretch and a yawn, as he sat up he looked towards Wilf who was examining his bruises in a tiny broken mirror that was rested on the back of a chair, *here'ya handsome chuck some water on yer face that'll wake yer up* some he said pushing the pale over with his foot, David rubbed his butt where Frank had kicked him got off the bed and bent down to retrieve a couple of hands full of water splashing it onto his face. *Wots the rush Frank I thought we had all day to ourselves today, change of plans luv, Oye pack that in right now both of yeh,* they both smiled, *we have to go back to Coatham to speak to Jeffrey about a spot of business, we are sittin on a gold mine ere an you my son look like you've hit the bloody jackpot. Wot do yer mean by that Frank, c'mon lets go get fed an I'll fill you in on the way.*

Howay Frank wots going on? well it would appear that the landlord likes you as much as his daughter does an she's well pleased at wot she sees, Oh god ere Wilf he's only gone an done it again so he as, you need to up your game a bit son, stop bein so shy all the time, I can't elp it Frank it's the way me mam brung us all up, ah well no harm done, look the long an short of it is were all rappin in the tax lark, were all going freelance, free wot? Freelance it means we won't be getting paid by the King no more, we'll be stealing from im instead. Stealin from the King? Does Jeffrey know about all this, Aye he does an so does Nell, oh well if Nell ses its ok then I'm appy with it as well, good lad I knew you'd see sense. Anyhow that's the reason that we ave to go see Jeffrey an see if he can up the order a bit, by ow much? by four times that's ow much, Tom sussed us out a while back an e's bin talking to his landlord buddies, an so it seems now they all want a slice of the pie, wot pie I'm starving, let's go for breakfast, righto lad let's get yer fed. Five minutes later they were on the street looking for a café, *here Frank I do feel a bit like y'know that I should've checked in on Erin just t'make sure she's alright n'that, now don't you go worrying about that son, you've got the rest of yer life to look after her, trust yer uncle Frank she's fine, yer sure? YES I'm sure for pities sake I didn't know it was gonna be this hard.* Within two hundred yards they had found a street vendor, *good morning gentlemen what can I get you this beautiful day, do yer do that posh toast pet,* Frank and Wilf looked at him then looked at each other and shrugged, *wot the ell are you talkin about David? Y'know toast with egg an drippin on it, Oh right,* as the penny dropped, *aye lads I can do that for yeh, with three teas? Aye sit yeh selves down and I'll crack on* she said chuckling at her own joke. Breakfast over and three burnt and blistered mouths later, the three of them started to walk back to the Dick Turpin stables, *does that stuff always burn yer gob like that?, aye it does, well if that's the case why on earth d'yeh keep eatin it? Well we're from Ull the big city, we after show em that were a bit farther up the ladder than these poor buggers. Oh is that right then so yeh buy toast that burns yer gob off so it sounds like yer've got a plum in yer mouth like the King is that right? Exactly that, God give me strength.* Presently they arrived at the stables and Frank knocked the posh way, *is there any bugger in ere, which brought the equally polite reply, piss off, oy yer little sod we've come for the landlords wagon, oh sorry gents I didn't know it was you I'll ave it ready for yeh in a jiff just finishing greasing the wheels like his nibs told me to, are the horses fed an watered an ready for a bit of exercise? aye they are that.* Twenty minutes later they were all packed up and ready to leave when the landlord arrived to see them off, *is Erin ok? David asked, she's fine lad still sleeping upstairs, listen I've done alright looking after her so far I'll give you a nod when I want you to take over. Tell her that we won't be away for too long will yeh, don't worry lad I'll be looking forward to your return as much as she is, an trust me she wants yeh back fast enough.* When all three were aboard Frank clicked his teeth and the horses obeyed and started to move off, they slowly pulled out of the yard gates ready for their next command, when Erin came running out of the Inn and shouted after David, 'stop' he yelled at Frank and the horses begrudgingly obeyed, she ran to the wagon and threw herself upwards where David caught her, once again she had her arms about his neck he lent forward and gave her a long kiss then she allowed herself to be lowered back down and whispered *hurry back* and David in reply said *I will luv I will.* At the nod Frank cracked the whip and the eager horses set off at a canter, in a matter of moments she was out of view and David's heart sank again. So intensely sad to the pit of his stomach was he that he thought nothing should hurt as much as this, all he could think of was getting back to her, he didn't want to talk and he didn't want to play any silly driving games either, which suited Wilf just fine, the few words he did speak were so pitiful that all conversation was put on hold lest the poor lad burst into tears. When they finally pulled in at Coatham the greeting they got was a mixed affair, *ello lads we wasn't expectin you till t'morra, hiya Nell is that fella o'yours about? Aye he's in the dunny I'll give im a shout an put the kettle on,* she looked at David and her smiling face filled with concern, *David are you alright honey,* he didn't answer her, he just slowly climbed down off the wagon and walked over to where she stood, put his big sad head on her shoulder and with tears in his eyes said *ah luv her Nell ah luv her. Orrr there there come into the kitchen an I'll boil the kettle,* she linked his strong arm and led him inside *c'mon luv sit yeh sell down and tell your aunty Nell all about it.*

Meanwhile Jeffrey had powdered his nose and was out front with the boys, you want how much? *like l said Jeffrey there's a big market over in Middlesbrough, word went round like wild fire as soon as we got one order we got a dozen yeh's ave done well boys, are yeh ok to head for Saltburn before yeh chuck it in for the day, aye why not all we're doin is sittin down, right let me fetch me coat an we'll go, I reckon we'll leave David ere with Nell, I don't know wots up with the lad but e's not im'sell not by half but Nell knows how to handle im. Nothing happened in Middlesbrough yeh say? No nothing Jeffrey we stayed in the lodgings all night, ah well Nell will get it out of im I'm sure* and so they set off for Saltburn. *I wish I could tell im that we're comin someone should invent som'thin that yeh talk to folk a long way's off wot y'mean like two empty barrels and a length o'string? yeh just like that, an where are you gunna come up with a ball of string eight miles long, you mark my words someone will invent one someday I hope yeh right all this drivin about is givin me a sore arse, just think of the money Frank just think of the money.*

John Andrew was pursuing one of his hobbies that afternoon by racing one of his neighbours on horseback along the beach between two markers in the sand, his neighbour was just ahead when they crossed the finish line and pulled to a stop. *Looks like we've got company John, trouble d'yeh think, no I reckon I know who these fellas are, an I think I might know why there here.* They cantered over towards the wagon and stopped short *hello Jeffrey, hello John wot brings you over to these parts this afternoon spoilin my game, sorry John didn't mean to spoil yeh fun but we've got a bit of a proposition for yeh, thought as much, follow us back to the Ship Inn an we'll talk more, last one gets the round in,* both horses reared and galloped back to Saltburn. Fifteen minutes later the wagon pulled up outside the mortuary and was tethered to the railings. In the dark of the Inn the fire was burning bright in the hearth. The five men crowded around a small table ale in hand and the talks began. *Right Jeffrey wots this all about? it's not Jeffrey's doin it's ours John, alright, Frank isn't it, aye, right tell me wots goin on, well we've made some contacts over in Middlesbrough who are wantin to deal with us, well I never did how did you manage to do that? Well it's a bit of a long story and a bit of a luv story as well.* When the tale was over Jeffrey said wot in love? *Aye*

So if its secrecy your lookin for you could say we're marrying into the family. Right I've one more question, wot appen'd to that guy from Hartlepool that was dealing over there a while back, he got sloppy an went and got imsell caught, Ok then let's go for it, so you've got Ull an Middlesbrough where next? How about Newcastle? bugger that they don't talk proper up there. Right then are yeh still up for tomorrow, oh aye wouldn't miss it for the world and tankards empty they shook and said their goodbyes. There was definitely a feeling of excitement on the return journey, *how much d'ya reckon we can make at this smuggling lark then? well a fair bit more than the King was payin us I know that an if we keep on getting more customers a whole lot more t'boot, we haven't even scratched the surface yet, we could try Scarborough, Beverley, Malton, Pickering, good god we could all end up millionaires.* As they pulled in at Coatham it was dark so Jeffrey held the two horses while Frank and Wilf removed all the tack and hung it up, a quick rub down and they were ready for feeding and ready for sleep, Jeffrey told the lads to pick a hammock each and he would go ask Nell for some supper. Nell? *In here luv* came the reply from the kitchen, as he walked through he had completely forgotten that David was still there, *well lad gone an got yer'sel in luv av yeh?* David smiled a pitiful smile and slowly nodded his head in reply, *now don't you go an tease the lad e's as empty as an unbaited lobsterpot e is, same as me an you when we first met, I reckon we'll hear weddin bells by the end of the year int that right luv, Hmm, by eck e as got it bad aint e, aye that's why I don't want yeh teasing im non, come on luv you make the lads a cuppa tea each an I'll rustle up some supper for them, will he be alright Nell?* He said in a whisper, *Oh aye course he will, this time tomorrow when he's tucked up with Erin he'll be fine, he's just got to get through tonight is all. Erin that's a strange name, Irish, Oh...Irish...Her mam was Irish or so he says, Ah... never thought for one minute he'd go an get imsell in luv, I only let im out for one night, you did didn't yeh, Oh aye but he's so young, an if he stops in Middlesbrough well I'll miss the silly bugger, all kids have to leave the nest at some time Jeffrey, anyhow wot's to stop us avin one? one wot? a baby, wot? Aye an why stop at one we could ave four or five...only if yeh want like.* He gave her a kiss and said *hurry up with that supper for the boys I've gone and gotten all tired all of a sudden* to which they both smiled, *Oh David do be careful with that teapot luv,* then Frank and Wilf appeared at the Kitchen door. *C'mon in boys an sit yer'selves down supper'll be ready in a few minutes, oh an David might need a hand pourin the tea*. The next morning David was still in the mopes, after his very late night the day before he slept better than everyone expected only sobbing a couple of times through the night.

After a breakfast of posh toast prepared by Nell that didn't burn your gob off and hot sweet tea the boys were ready for anything what they got was a game of questions and answers. *Right are the horses well rested? Aye! fed? Aye! rubbed down? Aye! Wheels greased? Next on the list, Hmm, Frank how much tea do you drink in a week? I don't bloody well know the same as every bugger else I s'pose why? Oh just a thought summit I might add to the shoppin list in future. Here Jeffrey isn't it a bit close to the knuckle us usin the tax payers money to finance this scam, well that's the best bit they'll never know an neither will Germain if we stick to the plan. So tomorrow we get your Middlesbrough buddies their lot, then take ours back down to Ull an stash it with the rest, you ok with that? Oh aye no bother, d'yeh still want us to ask for more money? Damn right if we're gunna do this then let's do it right, but this is the last time yeh? Yeh, we daren't push our luck too far but after that we're on our own. How are yeh gunna explain our disappearance, tell them we were killed in action? Let's get ourselves established and we'll work it out from there.* So the drop came that night same as usual, but this time the wagon wasn't large enough for it all, so it was loaded for Middlesbrough and the rest of the Hull consignment was hidden by John Andrew in Saltburn. By four in the morning Frank, Wilf and David were back at the Dick Turpin, Tom and Erin had stayed up to wait on them and when they heard the horses on the cobbles they came out to meet them. Erin couldn't hold in her excitement as soon as she saw David she ran into his arms and hugged, and kissed, and hugged him some more, David's heart didn't know whether to beat, jump or skip so it decided to do all three at the same time, he was so totally smitten he couldn't imagine a world without her. Tom grabbed the harness and led the beasts into the yard, he whistled when he saw how much they had brought with them, *right boys lets unload it into the spare stable for tonight an put it under lock and key.* They spent no time at all unloading the cargo they had given up on David they knew fine well that he was a lost cause. After unloading the last keg Tom said *c'mon boys let me get you a drink you've earned it* and the three of them walked into the bar. David and Erin on the other hand walked into their own little world, sitting at the same table as before holding hands and talking nonstop, *Christ said Wilf I think I preferred it when he was quiet, well at least he's happy again that's the main thing. Will we get an invite to the weddin d'spose, oh aye might even treat me'sell to a new cloth cap. Nice to see the two of them so happy though in'it, kind'a warms the heart, shut up yeh silly bugger an drink up im ready for another.*

The three of them were onto their sixth flagon when exhaustion cut in, they finished up their ale and said their good nights, as they were leaving frank said *we'll see you upstairs in a bit David, no you won't replied Tom, leave em be, I think you've just lost one of your own, d'yeh think so, trust me boys your lookin at the new landlord of the Dick Turpin,* and so they set off to bed, *goodnight you two, night dad, you's have a bit of a lie in in the morning, you've hurt long enough without each other, thanks dad sleep well, oh I will my luv I will* and with a smile on his face he wobbled off to bed.

Next morning Tom was up bright and early, *ello boys did yeh sleep well, oh aye fine Tom I think those last couple of ales saw to that. Listen before yeh go back to Hull can I be cheeky an ask to borrow me wagon to drop off the rest of the goods, well we can hardly say no it is your wagon after all, good stuff, we've got to do a quick detour to the coast but t,be honest ah don't suppose it matters if we don't get to ull till t'morra. That's great boys cheers Oh and by the way forget David he's ours now, yeh we kinda figured as much. Will the two of yeh give me a hand to do the drops that way ye'll know where they are for next time, aye course we will, great I'll fetch me coat.* Tom had written down the four establishment's names they were to visit and counted them off one by one. *Listen boys I don't know where this lot comes from and I don't want to know but word is getting round, y'know friend of a friend n such like, so I just wanted to ask is there a limit to the supply, in theory no, our supplier has been in the business for a few years now and has amassed a large stock pile on the coast so we should be good to go no matter how big the order, d'yeh know this just gets better an better.* The last drop was at the Middlesbrough working men's club. *I thought that clubs used their members funds to keep the beer cheap? Yeh they do but if you can buy it cheap in the first place then the prices drop like a stone, doesn't that have an impact on your place? No not really most drinkers are home birds, why walk a mile and a half home after you've had a skin full when for a ha'penny more you're on your own doorstep, aye that kinda makes sense I guess, anyway let's get this lot unloaded an then the wagons all yours, right'o let's put this t'bed.* As they pulled back outside the Dick Turpin Tom jumped down thanked the pair of them and wished them good luck, so Frank gave the shout and they moved off, heading back to the coast.

Are we going to head back to Ull t'day then Frank? Yeh I reckon so, wots the point in hanging about round ere doin bugger all, tell yeh wot let's just see ow long it takes to load up at Johns gaff an we'll see from there, that agreed Frank hurried the horses on. John already knowing what the boys required was hard at work in the underground tunnels and was lifting the merchandise up via the pulley system and into the morgue, which made him a little nervous truth be known because it left his enterprise wide open if anyone should enquire on his activities, the goods were still inside the morgue but the pulley made a loud squeal when in use no matter how much grease he applied and to his knowledge dead men don't make that sort of noise, well not very often anyway. As he lifted the last barrel above ground, he replaced the death stone and was stashing the pulley back into the wooden crate when there was a loud rap on the door, he went immediately rigid, had he been heard? He daren't move a muscle, but when he heard a familiar voice say *Oy John you in there?* With an exhale of breath he shouted back, aye Frank gi'me a minute, he opened the doors and was met by two smiling friendly faces, *hiya fellas good t'see yeh bring yeh wagon over an we'll get you loaded up.* As they walked the horses closer he looked around and questioned David's where about's. *Oh im in luv e'is, Eh, yeh like a kid with a new puppy, Oh hey,* women… *wot can yeh do? I know, I know, I'd rather be in jail than in luv again…* the two men took off their coats and started to load up. *Where's this lot going then Wilf back down to Hull, Yeh Ull, how long will that tek yeh then? Well if we get a clear run probably four or five hours maybe six if not, so you should be back before dark then? Yeh there or there abouts, well I wish you luck, it's when we get there when we'll need the luck, there's goin t'be one pissed off fella down there when we ask him for more money, Eh? don't ask our problem not yours.* The last barrel loaded and secured John patted them on the back, *I wish you all the luck in the world boys take care and I'll see you in a bit since.* As the wagon trundled off down the beach, John waved them off, turned and walked to the Ship for a couple of well-earned drinks.

The journey back to Hull started off well but after a couple of hours the weather changed and it started to rain, only lightly at first but as the sky darkened it came down like stair rods and bounced a foot in the air, and the more it came down the worse the road became turning to mud under their wheels. As they reached Filey it was a foot deep in places and in the ruts even deeper still which slowed their progress dramatically and on occasion stopped them altogether. *How much further frank, I've just about had enough of this carry on, you're not the only one mate, I should reckon on another couple of hours at this pace, well I'll tell you some'n see when we get rid of this lot I'm going get me'sell dried off and get drunk as a lord, don't yeh think that's a strange turn of phrase, wot? Well how many drunk lords do you know? I don't know any lords pissed or otherwise, that's wot I mean why don't folk say drunk as a drunk we know loads of them, aye that's true,* just then the wagon jumped heavily on the rear quarter and came to an abrupt halt. *Oh that's just fuckin great just wot we need pissed on an now pissed off as well. Wilf jumped down to investigate the problem and ended up knee deep in the mud, Oh this just keeps getting better an better don't it, stop moanin an see ow bad it is, Oh aye why don't I just go an do that then... no, no Frank you just stay there an don't move a muscle I insist.* As he slowly made his way to the rear of the wagon to assess the damage his left boot made a funny sucking noise and decided it didn't want to go any further and it was going to stay where it was without its usual resident. *Oh aye you just go an get yourself all lazy n stay there in the mud why don't yeh. Frank, wot? forget getting drunk as a drunk, the first thing I'm gunna do is find some foot friendly boots that don't roll over an play dead at the first spot o'rain.* Back stepping in his stocking foot he bent down to retrieve his treacherous boot from the mud. He pulled and wriggled it and tried to force into submission then with a great sshhhlup…it suddenly gave way and with Wilf throwing his arms about like a deranged windmill fell over backwards to great applause from the thunder. *Frank…* came a sad little voice, *Frank… wot? D'yeh like me Frank? depends why? Frank…wot? M'stuck, wot d'yeh mean stuck? Well like you have to get off yeh big fat idle arse an get me the fuck out'v the mud kinda stuck, oh for god's sake I don't see why we both af'ta get covered in crap try an wriggle about a bit. Fuckin wriggle, I'll give you fuckin wriggle when I get free'o this mud I'm gunna come up there an chuck you overboard an you can fuckin wriggle for the rest of the fuckin day how d'yeh fancy that then, ok, ok keep yeh boot on I'm commin.* Now Frank being a little sharper than Wilf climbed over the back of the wagon and stared down at his friend. Now it's a hard life being an excise man and you tend not to make a lot of friends and even fewer opportunities for laughter, but when he looked down at the pathetic looking form of Wilf stuck in the mud one boot on and the other one off, he started to chuckle and the chuckle became a laugh and the laughter became deeper and deeper so much so that he could'nt stand any longer and collapsed in a heap on the back of the wagon in hysterics. It was so infectious that Wilf started to smile and laugh himself. Frank gasping for air tried to get to his feet, stumbled on the wet timber and fell in the mud next to his friend, the pair of them tears rolling down their faces grabbed hold of each other and made it to their knees they hugged and slapped each other's backs. *C'mon you let's get you out of here and get to Ull for them beers.* They managed to free each other and with a bit of pulling and pushing managed to get the wagon free of the mud, they both climbed back on board and as miserable as they both looked they giggled all the way back to Hull. It was full dark when they reached their destination and because it had kept on raining throughout their journey the pair albeit soaked to the skin had been washed clean of the mud that had covered them both. As they squelched their way into the excise office they were confronted by Germain who was working a late shift, *hiya William is the kettle on? We're bloody freezing, what a journey that was,* and as they stood with their backs to the fire they both made a puddle on the floor. *Can you chuck us the keys for the lock up so as we can offload the evidence again, you can do that in a little while fill me in with wots hap'nin up in Saltburn? Well this is the result of the second deal with John Andrew and Jeffrey says he's startin to trust us more an more, so can we pull him then? well Jeffrey reckons not yet, he is getting into the fold but he still needs time to learn the names of everyone else who's involved he's got quite a racket going on up there, an so far we avent found out where he keeps his stash so Jeffrey says if we do one more deal with im we'll have enough evidence to close the whole operation down an give the hangman a bit of overtime, N'who knows maybe you'll get a medal on yeh chest.* That clinched it he opened a draw in his desk and threw them the keys, *it's still rainin out so yeh best unload that evidence of yours now before yeh get yeh selves dried out, ok boss will do* and the two of them squelched back out into the night to unload the wagon. Once done the pair put the horses in the stations stables gave them a feed, rubbed them down and put them to bed. As they walked back into station the rain finally decided to dry up. *Right boss are we ok to kip here tonight, aye not a problem stoke the fire a bit and hang your clobber in front of it it'll be dry as sticks by morning, oh an ere's yeh purse for when yeh get back up t'er Saltburn, I can honestly say to the magistrate that yeh not nickin it with all that contraband locked away out back. Right I'm off wot time will you be going in the morning? As soon as its light boss, ok well I'll still be in the scratchit at that time, so I'll say me good byes now and pass on me regards to Jeffrey an tell im from me he's doin a sterlin job up there. Oh an by the way tell him that I'll be coming over that way next week to be a part of the the next deal, see yeh's,* and the door slammed shut behind him. *Shit I didn't see that comin what'll we do? Well nothing right now but we'll tell Jeffrey when we get back t'morra, I thought you were goin out on the piss? nah can't be arsed now m'too tired n'besides all me clobber's still soakin wet.*

The boys woke to the sound of the cock crow and climbed into their warm dry clothes. *Will we have a quick cuppa before we start, aye why the devil not an if you can squeeze a bit of life out of that fire we can have a bit of toast to go with it* so Wilf made with the poker and Frank made with the kettle and the bread bin and as both started to warm up Frank walked over to the stables to feed the horses. *Wots it like out there today? well its overcast but it looks a lot better than it did yesterday.* So tea and dry toast later they went to work hitching up the wagon, once done they climbed aboard and set off for Saltburn. *Let's not go the coast road this time Frank eh, no worries on that score mate I don't want to have to go through all that shit again either.* So from Hull to Beverley and from there to Malton and Pickering and then over the moors to Coatham and when they arrived still dry and in fine spirits Nell was waiting with hot sweet tea. *So how did it go boys, well we'll forget about the journey down there, I wish I bloody well could, ok tell me how it went with Germain, well he was keen as mustard couldn't wait to throw money at us, said something about the magistrate couldn't say we was nickin the money due to all the evidence we was takin back with us. Is that it, no not by a mile he said that he was going to come up ere in time for the next deal next week, Oh shit! Yeh that's what we thought as well. ok let's not panic, we've got six more days to think something up, in the meantime you boys get yer selves back over to Middlesbrough an keep your heads down. Aye will do we'll call back in a couple of days an see ow your gettin on.* And as they were leaving Jeffrey shouted after them *and don't you's two go fallin in luv* and at that they left. Jeffrey asked Nell to give her two brothers a shout and when they arrived all four of them sat down to chat. *Bloody ell Jeffrey wot we gonna do about this fella Germain then, well as I said to the boys earlier we've got six days before the next drop so I reckon we should tek a trip over to Saltburn and see wot John Andrew thinks of it all.* So hats and coats donned the four of them set off, the two brothers like shit off a shovel and Nell and Jeffrey following on behind. It would have made a beautiful scene if it hadn't been so serious. *What do you think Jeffrey what's to be done about this fella, Oh Nell I've thought through every scenario luv and each time I do I just don't like the outcome.* They were quiet for the rest of the walk each lost in thought, so much so that the ship Inn came as a surprise when they looked up and saw it not fifty yards away. Nell took Jeffries hand and held it tight as they approached and once over the doorstep she still held it as Samson offered the two of them an ale each. As they removed their hats and coats they all sat around a small table at the back of the room Danniel said to the two of them *the barmaid has gone lookin for im and she said to ang'on ere till he arrives.* So that's exactly what they did, and after twenty minutes another tankered was thumped onto the table and John angrily said *right wots so bloody important that you at'ter get me out'er bed?. Please John sit down we've got some bad news te tell yeh,* and when seated Jeffery went through it all again. This time the anger left Johns face to be replaced with concern. *Are you sure a'mean really sure, no doubt what so ever John, es'commin in less than a week an we had all be ready for im when e does. Right first things first how many others is e likely the bring with'im, well there was only two more from our office, but it's feasible that e could enrole a few more from south of the Humber so maybe six or seven in all maybe a couple more, ok so the drop is on Friday as you all know, can we cancel it? No that won't do wot with your boys new contacts over in Middlesbrough we've tried that in the past an all it does is give folk cold feet an they don't want to deal with yeh no more, so the drop will have the go ahead no matter wot. Well what if we give'm some false information say its bein held someplace else or another day, no that's not gonna work either we've played the game so well with im e'll smell a rat for sure if we try that, an this way at least we'll know where he's at even if we don't want im there, Aye that's a very good point is that Jeffrey. So the way I see it rather than shy away from this, we'll throw everythin at it, I'll pull together any one that as got a vested interest in the operation and we'll teck the bugger on face teh face, agreed, aye agreed. Jeffrey you an the boys ere come over tomorrow, but not so bloody early this time and we'll draw up some battle plans, an see if you can get word to your lads over in the Boro cause they need to be informed as wots goin on as well, will do John,* and after all the pleasantries were done they all left for home.

The next morning Jeffrey yawned at the breakfast table, and Nell said, *you aright my luv you didn't arf toss an turn in yeh sleep last night, aye a'know I ope I didn't disturb yeh too much sweet'art, oh don't yeh go worrin about little old me I'll be fine,* and she placed a cup of tea in front of him. *So wots the plan for today then my luv? Well as you know the boys aint commin back ere for a couple'o days so im going teh go teh Middlesbrough an find them out then I'll tell em wots planned an see if we can drum up some support, Davids always good in a scrap, well you be careful an mek sure your back before dark I don't want to ave't be worryin about yeh. Ok my luv I'll mek sure I'm back, I promise.* After breakfast Jeffrey mounted up and after a kiss from Nell, rode off to Middlesbrough.

Wilf and Frank were just sobering up nicely and going for their morning ablutions when there was a loud thump on the front door, *bugger off we aint open yet* shouted Tom from downstairs this didn't have the desired effect as the knocking just got louder, *oh for pities sake, hang on, hang on I'm commin* as he unbolted the door he was almost knocked backwards with the force of the newcomer *here wot's the game then knockin a fella out of... Oh ello Jeffrey tis Jeffrey innit aye it is are my boys about I need to speak with them urgent like.* Tom turned and shouted up the stairs *Frank, Wilf you boys up yet yer've a visitor, Aye just comin, alf a mo,* and as they descended the stairs they heard a familiar voice in the passage way, *that you Jeffrey we wasn't expectin to see you till tomorra, Aye anno boys but I had to come an see yeh's, sumthin bigs appenin and I needed the two of yeh teh get it from the horses mouth so the speak. D'you fella's want me to bugger off so yeh can talk in private? No not at all this could affect you too so yeh might as well be apart of it from the beginin, ok sit yeh selves down an I'll get us all a hairy dog, now yeh talkin my language Tom.* So as the landlord pulled the ale the men sat down. Jeffrey waited till they were all sat and then started his tale. *Right there's no easy way the put this so ere we go, I had a meetin with John yesterday an I told him wot yeh said about Germain commin over here next week, an the outcome of that is that were goin the take im on, boys we're going t'war, wot? Yeh yer erd me right, we are goin up against Germain an anybugger daft enough to come with im, an when's this all gonna appen then Jeffrey, on Friday at the drop, isn't that a bit risky though wot if he comes heavy handed well that's wot were planning for were are gunna meet force with force. Your gunna do wot?* David inquired standing in the doorway *oh hiya son, come an sit with us a while an I'll tell wots app'nin, so as David sat Jeffrey said to him were goin for a scrap over at Saltburn, with who? with your ex boss that's who, great I luv a good scrap I do, an I never did like im much anyway. Hang on David wot about Erin? Oh she can't come she might get urt, but wot if*

she doesn't want you t'go, well the way I see it I want the very best for my
Erin an selling your cheep booze is goin to allow that to appen so if a scrap
is gonna save the business then I'm gunna fight for our future. Wot you bin
feeding im Tom, that's the longest I've ever erd im speak an with full stops
an everthin. Well that's David in, wot about you two, three, wot? Don't
you leave me out, if our David's goin then so am I as well, that's good t'er
hear Tom but I wouldn't blame yeh if yeh changed yeh mind, but if yeh are
up for it then yeh very welcome. D'yeh want me to bring a few of me mates
along as well? a few more? Where from? Oh there's a few locals that like
the low prices we've bin chargin of late, like your old domino playin friend
Wilf, oh aye ee's always up for a laugh and if ee's not up for a scrap he can
stand an chuck dom's at em. Right boys I've got teh get back teh the coast
for another meetin so lets have a quick head count then I'll be off. Right so,
David, Frank, Wilf, Tom, an me'self, wot about yeh locals then Tom, well
I would go with at least eight more. Blimey you wern't far off the mark
sayin this was a war, aye well if we're goin in then I want the odds stacked
in our favour.* He stood and shook hands, hugged David and said his
good byes, David walked with him into the stables to collect his horse
and as he mounted he asked *are yeh appy son? Like I said to Nell, I luv
her. Good I couldn't bear to lose yeh t'anyone less worthy, bye Jeffrey, see
yeh in a bit since son*, and he rode away and didn't look back. He arrived
back in Coatham mid-afternoon, and went straight in to see Nell who
grabbed him in a bear hug and only let him go when he started to
whimper. *Where's the boys Nell? Oh they set off about an hour since, right
I won't be long luv but I've got teh catch em up*, he leapt back onto the
horse and galloped off along the sands. *See that, that's your daddy that is*,
she whispered to herself. It took Jeffrey no more than fifteen minutes to
fly across the beach to Saltburn and caught the two brothers with two
hundred yards to go. As he dismounted he tethered the horse outside
the Ship and Samson shouted over to him, *the other fella's, are they on
board then? Oh more than you could imagine.* The three of them walked
into the gloomy bar and ordered ale. John was sitting in a corner at the
back of the room so tankards in hand they went to join him. *Hi John
mind if we sit down, aye on yeh go Jeffrey* and he pushed a stool towards
him with his foot, *wot news from Middlesbrough? Well I've just got back*

and I'll tell yeh summat I couldn't have got'n a better welcome, so are they in? Oh yes wouldn't miss it for the world, it seems that Middlesbrough is up in arms about it and yeh couldn't keep them away even if yeh wanted to. Ok so how many can we rely on from your side? Well a dozen or so from the Boro, me and the brothers from ere so at the very least fifteen maybe more, how about you? Well I've had a chat with a few of the locals and I reckon we'll amount to another dozen, so if me countins right that should make at the very least thirty seven. Right so wots the plan? Well we know they'll be hangin about in the background somewhere just watchin n wait'n so we can't have all of our lot on the beach in plain view cause they'll know that there's a rabbit away, so this is what I propose, we all meet in here just after dark, an go from the cellar out back down int're tunnel that will teck us all int're morgue I've spoke t'eh landlord already an he's game for it. The boat is goin to hit the beach right outside the morgue so when them buggers make a move we'll be right behind them. I like it John, that should work a dream. Right Jeffrey I've got to know, will they be armed? Not to my knowledge the budget would never stretch to that when we was on that caper but don't discount it altogether they could have their own weapons, mores to the point John will you be? Aye I will as an insurance policy, listen mate see these fella's, a lot of em are only trying to put food on the table an pay the rent, aye I get that Jeffrey but not Germain he's just a nasty bastard an I'm prepared to do anything I can to keep out've jail. Please don't let any of your lot get trigger happy, they won't I'll tell em to only fire if fired upon will that do yeh, aye it will, thanks mate... can I call you mate? Aye yeh can. Right I'm off home t'see Nell. The two men stood embraced and patted each other on the back then separated. What'r you's two doin? Oh we'll ave a couple more an catch yeh later on. Good luck Jeffrey an I'll see yeh Friday, oh aye yeh won't miss me I'll be the one with a big crowd around me. John laughed and said give my luv t'Nell, oh trust me mate I intend to, he walked outside, mounted up and rode home to his love.

The next morning there was a knock at their door and when answered Jeffrey saw the smiling figure of Tom, Dom as he was now known and a couple of others from the Dick Turpin *ello fellas wot brings you over these parts so soon? Well we was at a loose end an decided that a little oliday* might be in order so I've left the Dick in Davids safe hands an brought these dozy buggers with me. He drew us a map see, so we thought we'd pop in before we head off to Saltburn. Ok d'yeh want a cuppa the lot o'yeh? or'ey that'd be grand Jeffrey. As they made themselves comfortable Nell put the kettle on. Something I was meanin to ask yeh, is there any where that'll put us up for a few days? Yeh there's a few places in Redcar but if yeh's are wantin to stop in Saltburn then the landlord of the Ship Inn will let yeh kip by the fire for a few pennies, Oh now yeh talkin Jeffrey sounds perfect. Well if that's your intention I'd better come with yeh to introduce y'all, four strangers just walking in unannounced is likely the get yeh threw off the top of Huntcliff. Aye maybe it would be better if yeh came with us just t'be safe like, Jeffrey laughed aye no worries Tom.

Tea finished, mugs washed and weeds watered the five of them set off along the beach in the afternoon sunshine, I'll tell you wot Jeffrey you've got a luv'ly part of the country t'settle down in, aye when the weather's like this it is, but when that north wind blows up a storm it's enough to freeze hell over, aye that's when you need the luv of a good woman to keep yeh warm of an evening, aye an I've got one of them as well our Nell is a little darling, aye I can see how the two of yeh get on t'gether it fair warms ye'art, will yeh make an honest woman of her then Jeffrey? by you ask a lot of questions Tom...aye it's me curiosity its always getting me in t'bother, it's just that I can see our Erin an David getting wed an I just thought wouldn't it be a grand occasion if you an Nell got wed at the same time like, there wouldn't be a seat t'be ad in the church, well it might'n be a bad idea I spose, I'll have a word with our David after all this bother's over, we'll be in a better position to make plans when Germains out of the way. Oh about that, I was chattin to the landlord of the workin mens club last night tellin him about the bother yeh was avin an he said that he will be coming on Friday an that he would be bringin the committee with him, wont they be at work? Don't be daft it don't work like that, well how does it work then? Not like that! Oh ok then the more the merrier. As they approached the Ship they were all in high spirits, My round first, bugger off im on olliday I'll get the first ones in...Oy the lot of yeh, shut the fuck up a minute, don't go gobbin off in here, their always's dubious of townies, so let me get the *first round an I'll introduce you in good time, townies wot the hell is that? That is you lot, towns folk, an these are either cod heads or sheep shaggers dependin on their trade, I've never heard so much tosh in all me life there can't be ten mile between the lot of us, bloody cod shaggers, yeh I know but that's the lore down ere, you're all townies so get used to it, wot ever you say Jeffrey, lead on.* He led them into the gloomy bar in single file, *bloody ell its dark in ere... you could of heard a mouse fart it went so quiet, wot did I just tell yeh outside, well yeh but it is dark you've got to admit an why's the fire on its mad hot out there. Right turn around and get the fuck out right now.* As they gathered outside Jeffrey called a meeting. *Ok let's try this one more time, the lot of yeh shut the fuck up I want gobs shut for ten minutes when we go back inside yeh ok Jeffrey, right single file an me first.* As he approached the bar he spoke to the landlord in hushed tones, *yeh? Oh aye I spose if you vouch for them, trust me they might talk funny but their ere to elp us, aye well you've convinced me Jeffrey but im not sure about the regulars, ok let's put this t'bed right now.* And after the round was ordred he pulled up a wooden stool stepped onto it and asked for attention. *Right you lot know me an gave me a right ard time when I first came ere, but see these four idiots, thev'e come ere to elp us out an get rid of that bastard Germain, so yeh, their townies an yeh maybe they don't belong ere but be civil to em cause their on our side.* He stepped down, to a, *well if you do bugger all else t'day jeffrey that was a bloody good speech.* The five men sat a table in complete silence, after a while Tom whispered *by eck Jeffrey I know you said it would be a hard nut to crack but it's like bein a Geordie in ere, give em time boys, give em time. Ere ave any of yeh got any spare cash, aye a little, right go to the bar n'say nice an loud you want to buy everyone a drink,* so Tom stood and walked over, *landlord could I be so honoured as to buy everyone in here a drink.* That did the trick, within ten minutes they were everyone's best friends, Tom most of all, as it went...*landlord five of your worst if you please...aye landlord I would be very pleased to do that for you...thank you landlord I am most grateful...your very welcome landlord...*and so on and so forth. After an hour Jeffrey made his excuses and said his goodbyes knowing that the townies were in for a bloody good night. As the fresh air hit him he got a bit of a wobble on, and dragging his heavy feet he took an hour and a half to stagger home.

As the days went by more and more of them kept turning up, two here, three there until the only one missing was David until Thursday evening when he knocked on the door and shouted *Nell you home? Oh David come on in pet come an see yeh aunty Nell.* He walked into the kitchen and rather sheepishly announced, *Nell I've someone ere who wants to meet yeh,* and a very shy and very slim figure stepped from behind him, *Nell I'd like you to meet Erin, Erin this is my aunty Nell.* Well you could have heard the scream back in Middlesbrough, *Oh Erin me darling come on in,* she flung her arms about the terrified girl and almost hugged her to death, *now stand back an let me av a look at yeh…Oh aint you just the prettiest little thing I ever did see, Eee David you never said she was this bonny, c'mon darling you come and sit by me at the table while David puts the kettle on, Eee I can't get over how beautiful yeh are, Jeffrey, Jeffrey come ere an see who's turned up.* Erin was at a total loss for words she had never been so stage struck in her life. *Eee our David yeh little tinker, look at that gleam in you'r eye, no wonder yeh fell in luv with her I'll bet that every man in the Boro is jealous of yeh.* The two girls sat knee to knee with Nell holding her hands, and started on about…her family…her mam… wedding dress's…the price of fish…babies…strong husbands… our David this, our David that. Jeffrey stood in the door way and looked at David, smiled and shrugged his shoulders in a when the women folk get together, you've lost old son kind of way and David gave it his what the hell do I do now smile in return. *Pour the tea David, it's all your good for right now.* Tea served, Jeffrey grabbed hold of his protégé by the shoulder and led him outside, *yeh best let them talk a while son, Nell won't be happy till she's got her in a white dress an pushin a pram,* it was starting to make his head spin. *Jeffrey where will we kip tonight I've not organised owt? Oh that's no problem Samson and Daniel are stopping over at the Ship, best party they've ever been to apparently so the back bedrooms empty we'll push the two beds together and yeh's can kip up there. David… ere you is bein careful aint yeh lad? oh aye Jeffrey I brush me teeth every night an I'm ever so careful not to fart in bed…. Good… that's er good I knew yeh would be, so that's it settled then. Have any of the others turned up yet? Aye they've been coming all week and a damn site more than I first thought there would be, how many's that then, well at last count about forty or so, the Ship Inns never been as popular, will any of them be sober enough to be able to scrap d'yeh suppose? well I'd like to think so, now listen David I know how you like a good scrap n all, but there's more than a good chance that they might be bringin guns, so this is dead serious, if you see any one pull a weapon, or you hear a gun shot, get gone, I don't want you to look back just scarper we don't want no dead heroes, an I promised Nell that I would look out for yeh an I'm startin that right now. C'mon lets go back inside. An then they said to me Nell we need someone to keep the flys down….Oh ello boys wot'v yeh bin up to? Well our David's just bin tellin me wot a long day it's been an ow tired they both are, so I said that we'd put em a bed up, Eee wot must you think of me, rattlin on so, arf the night through, c'mon Jeffrey gi'me a hand with those beds, an finally David had a chance to speak with her, wot d'yeh think of our Nell then my luv? She is the most beautiful, kind and generous woman I have ever met, and she thinks the world of you ye'know…Hmm second best now I think, no c'mere you* and a kiss and a cuddle in the only home he'd really ever known and with the girl he loved, whispered *come on you lets go to bed.*

The morning of the drop still held the weather and as Jeffrey stoked the fire for the morning brew he found his mind wondering somewhat he wasn't nervous about tonight's plans but he would be a lot happier after they were done, *morning Jeffrey* brought him back to the here and now, *Mornin David hope yeh slept well, can't think of a time in life that I've ever felt happier, best I've ever slept in me life. Listen I was talkin to Erins dad tuther day and he mentioned you an Erin getting married in the future can you see that appn'in aye at some point Jeffrey I couldn't let our Nell down now could I, ah well its Nell why I'm askin see, Tom said why not mek it a double weddin like? hey Jeffrey what a great idea, but I'd ave to ask Erin first though, aye an I would af'ter ask Nell as well, tell yeh wot lets get tonight out of the way an then we'll talk some more, do us a favour grab that loaf and we'll put some toast on for the girls breakfasts. What we up to t'day then Jeffrey, well I'm goin to af'ter go to the Ship at some point an mek sure that every ones reasonably sober so why don't we tek the girls along an we could maybe ave a picknick on the beach it looks like its gonna be a luvly day, sounds good t'me, right im just poppin out back won't be long, ave one for me will yeh…will do.* Around ten thirty Nell had packed her basket with all manner of good things Cheese, homemade bread, cold ham, a rabbit pie, sausages and even a couple of bottles of wine *by eck our Nell I'm fair ravished can we not eat it now? Well see that's why they call it a picknick and not lunch or dinner cause yeh av't eat it outside in the fresh air c'mon it'll be fun,* and so the four of them set off two of them hungry and two having fun, *wot is it about men Erin why are they always moanin about summet, just their way I spose, they'll be fine once they've bin fed. Are we goin straight to the Ship then Jeffrey, aye I reckon so it'll be the perfect time to catch them, wot d'yeh mean? Well they will all ave had a skin full last night, maybe didn't crash out till the early hours so they will be just startin to come round about now, with a screaming hangover far too early to face a hairy dog they'll need a couple of hours to pull round an feel up for another session an so I would say we will be just about spot on time, I wish I'd gone to school when I was a nipper like you Jeffrey, trust me David there's no school can teach yeh stuff like that, its stuff yeh just kinda pick up along the way! Erin can I tell yeh summet as a secret like, just between me an you, of course yeh can Nell but wot can yeh tell me that yeh can't tell Jeffrey well it's a little too soon to tell im but if I don't tell someone I'm gunna burst, wot is it then…Erin I'm gunna ave a baby, Jeffrey's baby… Aaaaah honest, yeh honest… oh my d'yeh want to sit down, give me that basket, you should'nt be carryin that, yeh silly bugger, oh Nell wots it feel like? Well, it feels like everything is still goin on around yeh but it doesn't really matter anymore, does that make sense? Not in the slightest but I hope it does someday, oh darlin I'm pretty sure you'll find out soon enough.*

Jeffrey ave you decided where y'gunna settle when the business is up an runnin? I think you know the answer to that one yourself David, I'm stopping ere with my Nell, what about you? Well it looks like my future's set as the new landlord of the Dick Turpin, won't you miss Ull? Me? no, after our mam died us kids kind'a just drifted apart an none of them wanted me being the youngest an all in fact I'd still be at a loss now if you adn't pulled me out the gutter when yeh did, I want to spend the rest of my life with Erin in Middlesbrough, an with you an our Nell just ten miles away, who would have thought that life would turn out so well. we might still have to do the odd night shift here an there just to help out Frank an Wilf, aye if that's the cost of cheap booze in the Dick then that's the price I'll pay, wot about you? Well I've got no other income so I'll pull together with the other two, I reckon that if we invest in two more wagons then the business should take off big style it'll mean us trekking down to Ull now and again but that's what we wanted from the outset, so that's wot I'm gunna do.

As the four of them walked into the Ship it was more like midnight than midday it was mobbed and the whole crowed welcomed them like long lost friends, *Hi our Nell…I ope you two aven't bin causin any bother down ere our Samson an you our Sammy, no Nell we've bin complete angels… Ha that'll be the day, hiya Tom ave yeh settled in a'right, oh aye me an the boys reckon we might not bother going home after this we like the place that much, hiya sweetheart ow are you, I'm good dad, and ave you bin lookin after my daughter then young man? You know I'll always look after her Tom…call me dad, I reckon I will be soon enough,* as he offered his hand David knocked it to one side and nearly broke his ribs in a hug that made him smile and wince at the same time. Drinks in hand they sat at one of the few remaining tables. *I'm just gunna chat with John for a little while darlin I won't be long* and with a peck on the lips he walked over to where John was seated, *can I?* he asked pointing at a spare stool, *aye sit yoursell down,* and as he did John pointed to the room in general, *we've managed to build quite an army between us mate, aye we ave that. How d'yeh reckon we'll get on tonight? Well if Germain turns up with the expected half dozen law men or so I reckon we'll terrify them an send them packin, yeh don't think there'll be more than that do yeh? Well as I said before their really stretched at the moment, it is possible that he could rally some more from other areas I spose but why would he do that just to close one operation goin on way up ere, it's just that I don't want any of me mates getting caught up in any nasty business, don't worry John we'll send them off with their tails between their legs just you wait an see. Right it's time for you to make a speech…bugger that I get stage fright, you do it, well one of us is gunna ave to before this lot go an get themselves pissed again, ok I'll do it* and so Jeffrey stood and stepped onto his stool, banging his head on the low ceiling *shit that urt…Er…can I ave your attention a minute lads?… quiet gent's…*Oye shut the fuck up the lot o'yeh *right as ye'all know we've got a job to do tonight, that's why we're all here after all, I know that some of yeh ave bin ere a while and ave tret it like a bit of a ollyday but it as teh stop t'day by all means ave a couple o'dogs to pull yeh sells round but that's it, cause as of midnight tonight it gets real serious an people could ge'urt so I don't want any one getting ratted an getting knocked to the ground after one punch, we need teh be sober'n'eager to teach these buggers a lesson an when we've done that we can all mek a load 'o' money. So are yeh gunna buckle down or get knocked down?* There were a few disheartened yeh's and the odd mumble, *listen fella's I mean it if we don't do this right they'll be no more little ollidays down ere, the place will close an then where will yeh go?* As he stepped down, John shook him by the hand, *that should've done the trick mate, don't worry I'll keep an eye on them for yeh, thanks, right we're off I'll see yeh tonight. Come on you lot lets ave us a picknick,* which got David out of his seat in a flash. About a mile down the beach they found a nice little sheltered spot in the sand dunes that was out of the breeze and laid out their blanket on the sand. Nell started unpacking the food and uncorked the wine go on then you's two get stuck in I know you've waited long enough for it so the boys started to fill their empty bellies. Aint you gunna ave some of those sausages the pair of yeh? Jeffrey and David looked at each other aye you go first David I just want to finish up this bread an cheese first, go on the pair of yeh before they get warm, but they still weren't convinced. *Oh I get it did you by any chance bump into our Sammy in the kitchin the other day when e'was cleanin them rabbits ready for the pot, Err… we might ave done why? Because I don't put rabbit guts in sausages, that was a joke that Dan told Sammy when e was just a nipper, once it's all mashed up it goes onto the veg patch to feed the potatoes 'n' carrots mek's em all grow big 'n' fat* and she started to giggle and soon she fell on her back laughing at the two of them, *'E's ad you's two good an proper e'has* and so infectious was her laughter they all soon had tears rolling down their faces in the afternoon sun. After the food was eaten, including the sausages, they packed away and had a leisurely walk home paddling in the shallows and skipping stones to see who could manage the most bounces. Once at home Nell put the kettle on for tea, it was almost dark outside now and there was a definite chill in the air, *wot time are the two of you headin back out boys? oh I'dunno maybe about half past ten or some such, an wot time d'yeh reckon on bein back afterwards? well the drops at midnight about half an hour tops for the scrap, and an hours walk home, so if were not tucked up in bed by about half one I'll eat hay with the donkey's. Are yeh sure we can't come along as well, Nell we've been through this a thousand times sweetheart I don't want you an Erin mixed up with all of it an besides where would it end, the next run to Ull, the next run to Whitby? It's my job an it's my problem, once we've got shot of Germain we can all sleep a little bit easier. Well just so yeh know I won't get a wink till I know your home an safe, we'll be home before you know it, promise? aye I promise, right David you go an get an hours kip I'll wake yeh when its time, go on you as well if yeh must* and holding David's hand as they walked upstairs Erin smiled back at him. *They are such a good couple them two don't yeh think, better than us dy'mean? no, no one can better me an you, well? Well wot, well don't yeh think you need a lie down as well? Oh yeh never bin so knackered in all me life, c'mon you I'll tuck yeh in* and after a while the candle went out…*C'mon David I need yeh up an out in ten*, David really didn't want to move, wrapped in his strong arms was his only reason for living but he had a debt to return so he slowly pulled his arm to one side and let her head gently hit the pillow he quietly dressed and left her asleep as he walked down stairs, Nell appeared and quietly said *look after him David, I don't want im getting urt*, David hugged her as he would have his mam and wiped away her tear, *we'll be back soon our Nell don't you go worryin*. She kissed him on the cheek and said *be careful son* which broke his heart again. Fully dressed and ready for the task ahead the two men left and headed for the beach, *not quite as warm as it was earlier Jeffrey, you're not bloody kiddin son I should've worn me extra vest, I reckon, I should've worn yeh extra vest, get out, it wouldn't bloody touch yeh* and the pair laughed as they headed off to Saltburn helped by the full moon.

At the same time John Andrew was going through the final preparations with the men at the Ship, *so my men with the muskets will lead just in case, an then the rest of yeh come through an knock fuck out of the lot of em. But leave Germain alone E's mine.*

Unbeknown to both parties Germain and his men were already in position in the dense woodland behind Blue Mountain with one lookout hidden atop. He had already figured out that it would be the best vantage point to spot any incoming boats, so when the smuggler signalled the boat the excise collector would signal the opposite direction to ready his men. Germain had also been busy employing a couple of spies to keep an eye on Jeffrey and his companions. Up until now he didn't have any substantial proof, other than the illegal merchandise in the lock up back in Hull and a few rumours, but if his assumptions were correct he'd have all the proof he needed by the end of the night…four wayward excise men and his main prize John Andrew, the king of the smugglers. Germain checked his pocket watch, eleven o'clock only an hour to go, from his hiding place amongst the trees he could see a small section of beach and the only traffic he'd seen so far were a couple of locals heading for the Ship Inn, but other than them everything was quiet. At ten to midnight the light at the rear of the hill flashed three times, and from that signal he knew the boat had been spotted by the smuggler. He readied his men but kept them hidden to give the smuggler time to descend from his vantage point and onto the beach, to welcome the boat and start to unload its bounty. What no one could see was the mortuary double doors opening very slowly inwards and pale faces looking out over the shoreline. The smuggler from the hilltop had by now climbed down to the beach and as he passed the mortuary entrance whispered *all ready? Aye John everything is set.* As he helped his old friend Peter drag the boat onto the beach, they exchanged a few words, *how's things John? I'm ok Pete but I'm expecting some visitors this evening so pass me a few of them backy bales as cover and then keep your head down cause if I'm right things could turn very nasty very quickly.* As they were talking Germain was leading his men around the base of the hill and onto the beach, and as he did his prey came into view. So excited was he that all thoughts were forgotten of the four renegades, surely this had to be John Andrew in the flesh. He had been dreaming of this moment for the last four years and here it was his medal and promotion on a plate, he didn't even realise that he was shouting CHARRRGE…JOHN ANDREW I AM ARRESTING YOU IN THE NAME OF THE KING FOR EVADING TAXES AND SMUGGLING CRIMES THAT ARE OUTLAWED IN THIS COUNTRY looking towards the source of the shouting he put two fingers to his mouth and gave a shrieked whistle, this had a dual effect whereby the men in the morgue started to run out from their lair and shout their own battle cries, and Germain suddenly realized he'd been duped OPEN FIRE he yelled to his men and they turned to face their foe, the first volley was deafening as fifteen musket balls shot towards the smugglers, all around men were falling, dropped weapons were quickly gathered up and the second volley was fired back at the law men, it was carnage, blood was staining sand everywhere. David his fury rising ran ahead of Jeffrey as both attacker and shield to engage with Germain. He recognised David immediately and in a cool steady fashion reached into his tunic and pulled out a pistol, David was only twenty yards away when Germain aimed and fired the weapon, the projectile hit home and David was spun completely around before hitting the sand. Jeffrey, infuriated that his friend had been shot ran at Germain full pelt tackling him around the waist and throwing him backwards into the water, Jeffrey stumbled on top of him, grabbed him by the throat and pushed his head under the water, murder in his eyes. Germain was thrashing for all he was worth, knowing that he would surely drown but the more he thrashed the more Jeffrey held strong. Through the chaos he felt a hand on his shoulder *Jeffrey, let im go I'll not see you hang for that bastard, listen to me Jeffrey, David needs your help,* and at the mention of his friends name he let go and staggered back to his feet he spat turned and ran to where he lay. Germain coughing and spluttering sat upright and looked at his saviour, *I don't believe we've bin introduced, Germain…my name is Andrew, John Andrew and I know all about you,* with a look of confusion etched on his face, he coughed and asked *why then did you save me? I didn't* and in one swift fluid movement pulled his own pistol and shot him in the face, taking off the back of his head, he fell backwards and sank under water which immediately turned red like a halo, ironic John thought. Back on the beach, guns having all been discharged it turned into a bloody fist fight, both sides were picking up rocks and swinging muskets trying successfully as it was in cracking open their enemies skulls, but the sheer numbers of the smugglers finally overwhelmed the excise men and one by one they started to give up, a few weren't fast enough in surrendering and were drowned and a couple more bludgeoned to death, but it didn't all go their way and as they started to check on their comrades Erins dad, Tom had succumbed to a rock to the head and had died instantly as were three more from Middlesbrough. Jeffrey was kneeling over David, tears rolling down his face he had removed his shirt and held it to his shoulder in an attempt to stem the bleeding, but the wound was big and deep, as John ran over to them he could see immediately that it was a killing wound. *C'mon Jeffrey pull yeh'sell t'gether, we ave to get im to the Ship right now, if we don't he's gunna die.* So between them they stumbled and tripped to the safety of the Inn, he was laid by the hearth and in the firelight his face appeared ashen. GET ME A KNIFE John yelled A SHARP ONE at the same time he pulled a stick from the kindling pile and placed it between David's teeth, *we don't want him biting off his tongue now do we.* Once the knife had been handed to him he pushed it straight into the fire till it was mad hot. Hold him Jeffrey if yeh luv im hold im tight n'dont let go this is gonna hurt like hell but I can't ave im twichin else I'll do more damage than good. Once secured John picked up the knife and started to cut. Almost as if she could hear his screams Erin woke with a start, *Nell...Nell somethings wrong, we ave t'go right now.* The two of them were out of the house in three minutes flat, Nell grabbed the last pony from the stable and the two of them rode bareback into the night. David had stopped shaking but his pallor was deathly white, wot d'yeh think John? As he opened a bottle of brandy and poured it on the wound, David shook one more time and went still. I've done all I can Jeffrey, he's in the hands of God now mate, I've never bin a God fearin man as yeh well know, but please God don't take him, please don't.

As the fire was replenished Jeffrey had a strange feeling in his gut, and at that very moment Nell and Erin came crashing through the door, as Erin's eye's fell upon David's still frame she screamed and fell to his side, wot ave they done to you, wake up darling, please wake up, but as the fire rose his temperature dropped. Others started to enter the Inn, some injured, some bruised and most of them covered in blood and sand. Dom came across to speak with John, d'yeh want me to tell her about her dad, god no you'll push the poor girl over the edge, If yeh lookin for summat to do fetch a couple of men an go gather the dead an put them in the morgue, righto john I'll do that right now, we'll see how this pans out an go from there. The room went completely quiet as the enormity of the events washed over them the only sounds that could be heard was the crackling of the fire and the sobs emanating from the distraught girl. As the minutes past it was clear to all that the young man hadn't long left, his breathing became shallow and not a muscle in his body moved. Jeffrey held Nell as tight as he could his tear stained face imploring for someone to help, but the help wasn't going to come and his face screwed up in agony as David breathed his last. Don't you dare David, don't you dare leave me, the howl became a scream, as she beat him with her fists, don't you bloody well dare leave me you selfish bastard, she became more and more angry at her loss and the violence in which she kept hitting the lifeless body got stronger and stronger, Nell ran to her, *c'mon pet let im be he's gone now* 'No!!', and one more time she thumped his chest with all her might, and as she gave up and turned to Nell sobbing….he breathed….one long and slow breath. Erin's emotions were shot to ribbons she picked up his big hand in hers and gently stroked his face, by this time she was crying like a lost kitten, she whispered to him, stay with me David, your big an strong you can beat this. Jeffrey and Nell were also in tears, as were most of the men present, it seemed to many that if this young man pulled through the night was won, if he didn't then the whole ordeal was a waste of time and they had all failed. His breathing improved a little more, and he moved his lips trying to speak but to no avail, Erin put her ear to his lips and encouraged him to try again and he said in the tiniest of whispers that only she could hear *I luv you*…well if she hadn't cried enough already, her sobs of joy were now gigantean and through streaming eyes and a snotty nose she just about managed *don't you ever frighten me like that again, promise? I…promise…*she shouted for a blanket and pillow and they suddenly appeared, she carefully lay down next to him and covered the two of them. *C'mon fella's let's leave them be we'll go into the other room and drink to our lately departed* and they all fell in behind him. Jeffrey was pleased that it was all over and taking Nell's hand they left their two friends to get better together. In the back room john asked for Dom to fill him in on the casualties, *well the four we've lost are all tucked up in the morgue as you asked and the eleven excise men including Germain have been taken by the ebbing tide, good work, any news on the others, well I've spoke with everyone about that an we reckon that at least four of them did a runner, shit I could have done without that, they now have witness's to the whole nasty affair, what'll yeh do John if word gets back to the king he'll send an army to find yeh, an put a rope round yeh neck, dunno Dom aven't ad time to think it through, well your gunna ave to think quick cause as of now I reckon your Englands enemy number one, aye me an Napoleon Bonapart, maybe we should join forces wot d'yeh think, I think you've got to get the hell out of Saltburn as quick as you can, that's wot I think, your right Dom I'll leave when we've put our good friends in their graves an seen them off good, an proper, where will yeh go? Well I've got some friends over in Staithes I reckon I'll lay low down there for a while.* Four days later David still wasn't at his best but he could stand and walk a little helped by Erin, and It was time to bury her dad and his three mates so they laid them on four smuggling wagons and rode back to Middlesbrough accompanied by all manner of other transportation and just about the whole of Saltburns inhabitants. They were laid to rest in a fine spot in the local cemetery and Tom was reunited with his late wife, Erin cried her way through the whole ceremony but in the back of her mind was the fact that this could have been much worse had she not saved David and she was bolstered by the fact that her dad would be happy in that thought. The wake was back in the Dick Turpin and was a testament to the popularity of the landlord. When the last of the mourners left and had wished them both well for the future, Erin helped David up the stairs and unbuttoned his shirt ready for bed he said to her I was ready for death you know, and then I heard your voice calling my name and just knew I couldn't go anywhere without you, she kissed him and said come on you it's been a long day an you've got to open up in the morning. As promised John went into hiding the next day, and he told everyone with a vested interest that the operation was to be suspended for a while at least long enough for the dust to settle and so the whole of Saltburns residents went back to their day jobs and life got back to normal. Jeffrey Frank and Wilf still had a lot of contraband in the lock up back in Hull so for the near future they had plenty to occupy their minds. None of them could be certain that they hadn't been recognised from Saltburn but they reasoned that if they didn't recognise the excise men then in turn then they wouldn't recognise them either, so the three of them went into stealth mode which amounted to them wearing long scarves to hide their faces and when all the goods were moved to a safer location they set to work finding new buyers to pass on their ill-gotten gains.

1812 Gulf of Finland

As the battle was at its peak on Saltburn beach Les Contrebandiére had set sail and was at present heading due west towards Helsinki and then to the Baltic Sea. The first few days were cold but bright and on either side of the ship the men could see glimpses of both Finland and Estonia. Everyone on board were still in good spirits, except for Jean whose poor constitution was made all the worse for being constantly seasick. *How are you feeling this morning little brother, any better?* He was stood on deck with his head facing seaward and the slap on his back made him wretch even more, *sorry Jean I didn't mean to make it any worse for you.* The pale face turned to look at his brother and announced that he no longer was going to be a passenger on this god awful vessel and was going to jump overboard and swim the rest of the way home. *Come on Jean I know your suffering but I've spoken to the captain and he assures me that he's never known anyone be sick for more than a week, apparently your body just kind of gets used to it. I'll give a year's wages to the poor if anyone* can stop it now. *Well I've been told that you must try and drink plenty of water to keep you hydrated, just a few drops at a time till you get used to it and then try a few dry biscuit's so here's a flask try and take a few sip's and see how you feel.* He handed jean the flask, *I feel like I'm going to die is how I feel now leave me be Henri.* McCallister was up by the covered wheel conversing with the captain trying to up his language skills reciting nautical terms and committing them to memory. *So captain how long in your opinion will the journey take us? Oh I would say about two weeks if the wind and weather are kind to us, good at least poor Jean isn't going to suffer for ever, actually he will feel bad for a couple of days after we land, how does that work then, I have absolutely no idea I'm no doctor but that's what usually happens, oh great I can't wait to tell him the good news. Have you seen anything of that little mongrel that came aboard with us? I've not seen him since we sailed? Yes I saw him in the galley this morning teasing a couple of rats with a chicken leg, I think they're too quick for him and so he was trying to use it as a decoy so that he could ambush them, funny thing is I could have sworn blind that he had a smile on his face. So monsieur McCallister can I ask what it is that you and your men are transporting to France? I really don't think you need to ask that you know fine well what it is, yes I guess I do, have you thought about not taking it back? Day and night but no matter how you look at it, it's simply not worth the risk, Napoleon rules most of the known world so where would we take it? The other half of the known world is owned by the British, Portuguese, Russians or the Dutch who would kill us out right even without the gold, and I don't want to be looking over my shoulder for the rest of my life as for the new world well that's even more dangerous than being over here, no the best option is to stick to the plan, and deliver it to Paris intact and receive our just reward, money and medals and not to mention being heroes to boot. How about you? You could kill us all, throw us overboard and take the gold for yourself. See this ship you're traveling on? Yes, well how much do you think a ship like this is worth? I wouldn't have the first idea, a king's ransom that's how much, and what do you think the captain of a ship like this earns in a year? Well it would be rude to ask but I'm guessing not a king's ransom, I would have to sail a dozen life times to come even close, however see this ship you're traveling on? If I take you and your cargo back to France safe and sound…the ship is mine…so I won't be killing anyone tonight or any other night, beside I quite like your company.* And he slapped McCallister on the back, *everyone's a winner my friend everyone's a winner. Why don't you go get some breakfast I can smell the eggs frying from here, save some for me though, I don't like you that much.* As McCallister entered the galley all of his men, barring one were already seated and the cook was looking a little stressed. *Hiya Sarge have you come for some breakfast? Oy chef stick some more eggs on for our boss will you,* he wiped his brow and stoked the fire, it was going to be a long morning. *So Sarge how long are we going to be stuck on this tub then? Well I've just been talking to the captain and he reckons on about a fortnight give or take a day or two, that long I was hoping to be back by my birthday, well he says that he has to tack through the gulf of Finland and that will slow us up a while, tack what does that mean? I'm not completely sure but the way he described it was he has to sail against the wind, that's impossible surely? Oh I don't know it's a boat thing, if you've got any more silly questions then learn Finnish and go ask him yourself. Huh he'll tell us that people will fly next. Sarge? Yes, well I'm a little worried about my brother he's really unwell, he's never had a strong constitution but I've never seen him this bad before, I've tried to get him to drink some water to keep his blood nice and thin but he just says he can't keep it down, and when I asked him to try and eat something he just pushes it away, I'm afraid that if he doesn't eat or drink something in the next couple of days then he's going to be knocking on deaths door. So what is it you want me to do? Well I know this might sound a bit daft but he looks up to you for inspiration well we all do, so I was thinking what if you told him to eat, like an order so to speak, do you think that would work? Well it wouldn't hurt to try Sarge, aye maybe your right, let me finish my eggs and we'll give it a go, if it's all the same with you Sarge can you do it alone because if he sees me with you likelihood is he'll figure that I set you up for it, ok Henri leave it with me, and keep your fingers crossed, thanks Sarge I will* and just then a plate of eggs were unceremoniously dropped on the table in front of him along with some stale bread and a luke warm mug of tea, the cook thinking he couldn't be understood barked *stick that in your face you stupid French bastard,* to which he replied in perfect Finnish *yes I am French however unlike you I knew who my father was and he would have knocked you from arsehole to breakfast time and still have the energy to pick this crap out of his teeth, friend, now keep your opinions to yourself in future and that way I won't have to stove your ugly head in.* not one of his men knew what had just been said, but they knew the body language and as one they were on their feet, staring at the cook. *Let him go boys no harm done, what was all that about Sarge? Oh nothing much but I've a feeling that the food is going to be a lot better in future.* From below the deck was heard a growl and a loud squeak and McCallister smiled, but not as much as the little mongrel. Food eaten and tea drank he rose and walked over to Henri patted him on the back, right let's see what I can do about that brother of yours, and went up on deck. He found Jean in a foetal position in the middle of the coiled anchor rope, he had seen men on their death bed look better than Jean did just now and he realised just why Henri was so concerned, this was a lot more serious than he first imagined, so he took the task full on. *Rifleman Jean Verrel you are not ready for active service what do you have to say for yourself? Sorry Sergeant I can't I feel so ill, that is no excuse we all feel ill from time to time I order you to eat and drink and I want you on night watch duty at twenty two hundred hours, I'll do my best sir, best is not good enough, you will be on watch and no excuses, yes Sarge.* McCallister knew a lost cause when he saw one and this one was terminal, as he turned and walked away he berated himself...*shit!*

Mac having seen off one of the rats this morning was determined to get the rest of the smelly little bastards. The bait set he hunkered down behind a chair leg and waited, and sure enough the temptation of the chicken leg was too much and they closed in on the mangy tit bit. Stealth isn't in a rat's vocabulary and as soon as the coast seemed clear, they ran at it, Mac teeth bared launched himself at them, and if a dog could shout Geronimo he would have, he caught the first one by the throat and shook it dead, with a quick return he jumped at a second and caught it by the hind leg, he swung it against the chair leg and snapped its neck, the other's picked up on things real quick and buggered off. Mac sat and looked over at his little victory smiled to himself and then proceeded to eat the chicken leg.

Henri, a word if I could, yes Sarge how did it go? It didn't, shouting at him isn't going to make him eat, all it's done is make him feel worse about himself, how long has he been like this? Since we left the harbour, as soon as we got into the sea swell, he lasted about ten minutes then threw up and hasn't stopped since except now there's nothing left in him to throw up any more, he's just about turned himself inside out. There must be some way to cure him? Aye sit him on a nice sandy beach some place, no that won't work either for at least a couple of days, not according to the captain and besides there's nowhere to drop him we're still in enemy waters remember, to drop him anywhere round here would be to hand him a death sentence. Right, group meeting, gather everyone together in here, ten minutes, I need ideas and I need them quick. Right you are Sarge I'm on it. When everyone was gathered McCallister addressed them. *Right boys I suppose you know about the condition that Jean's in and its worse than any thing you've been told up to now, if something isn't done soon he'll be dead by the end of the week, I'm sorry to be so blunt Henri but it's the truth. Now as far as I can gather seasickness isn't a disease, it's an ailment due to the rocking movement of the ship. Most people get it for a day or two until they get their sea legs, Jean however seems to be an extreme case and he can't find any legs at all, so I'm throwing it out to the floor, we need ideas and we need them fast! So put your thinking caps on and fire away... could we put him in the row boat and tow him behind the ship Sarge? He'd still be bobbin about but not in the slow motion way we are on board. Alright I'll think on that one, anymore? Let's chuck him in a bath! What? hang on I know he's thrown up on himself a few times but I don't think there's any need for that. No you don't get my meaning, if it's the movement of the ship on the water that's making him bad then water could make him better, eh? well water in a tub or a bath will always stay level, right I grant you it will splash about a bit but it will still stay level, with him in it, do you know what, as daft as it sounds you might have a point there. No he hasn't, eh, the poor bugger hasn't slept for three days, we stick him in a bath tub and he'll drown sure as chucking him overboard. Shit, never thought of that. Hang on we don't have to use water, what so we throw him in a dry bath? No, listen you've all played conkers as kids yeh, yeh, well when you're waiting for the other kid to take his turn what's your conker doing? it's just sitting there, that's my point its sitting there dead still, if you move it doesn't it still stays straight up and down, so you want poor Jean to play conkers in his condition. Shut the fuck up the lot of you, he might just have a point, what does a ship carry loads of, Sailor's? no!, Rats? No!...rope ah, I've got your meaning we make Jean the conker, yes we run a rope between the masts and pull him up half way across on another rope and he'll just sit there like a conker, the ship can do whatever it bloody well likes and jean will be straight up and down, Hah... brilliant, well done I'll go and speak to the captain right now.*

After explaining their crazy idea to the captain he was only two happy to help the poor soul, he barked orders to the crew and they rigged up a large packing crate to use as the conker and scuttled up the masts like spiders to secure either end of the rope they threw a monkeys fist over the top of it and pulled over the conkers rope. Everything set Phillippé and Henri told Jean what they were doing and why, carried him over and sat him in the crate, and because he might be suspended for some duration put in half a dozen blankets, a flask of water, a bag of dry biscuits, another smaller rope to use as a hand line and a bucket, after all no one wanted puke raining down on them from above. Once ready half a dozen men hauled on the rope and lifted him sky wards, when he was about forty feet up they lashed the rope off and left him swaying gently in the breeze. When all was done Henri crossed himself and prayed for his little brother.

Mac pleased with this morning's result had now got a taste for the fight but without any more bait to offer he was struggling to entice them into the open again. He could hear them below the boards and behind the walls, scurrying this way and that and it was slowly driving him mad, it would seem that when there was nothing more to be had the rats would console themselves with eating the very wood that the ship was made of. It was as he was contemplating his next move lying on the floor in one corner of the captain's quarters that a darting movement caught his eye, too quiet to be a rat and a little bigger he thought. He rose from the floor and very cautiously crept over to where he thought it had gone, he stopped at the door way and sniffed the air, there it was, a definite new comer on the scene, he carefully started to peep around the door frame straight into a maelstrom of fur teeth and claws a hissing screech emanating from this horror fairly made his hair stand on end, trying to retreat from this creature had absolutely no effect whatsoever all it managed to do was move the onslaught back in to the captain's cabin with no let-up in the fury, but this gave the creature more room to manoeuvre now and it proceeded to stand upright and box with its claws out until he feared he might lose an eye, he finally had the wherewithal to turn about and run for dear life. He leapt up onto the captain's table scattering charts and all manner of other unimportant articles as he struggled to stop himself from going over the far edge. He took a breath when he finally stopped, and turned to look at what kind of creature had attacked him with such voracity, there prowling around the bottom of the table was the most battle scarred thing he had ever seen. With ears gone no tail to talk of and only one eye it was epitome of evil...a cat. Once Mac had got his composure back he laid on the edge of the table and stared at it, and with its one good eye it stared back with so much venom that it made his eyes water. This was ridicules a feline and a female one to boot out staring him, this was not going to happen not in his lifetime...so he closed his eyes. After an age the cat got bored and with a superior swagger and a flick of the head it left the room. After twenty minutes he figured the coast was clear and it was now safe to climb down. It was only then that he realised something, the whole time that the cat was in the room the scratching noises had stopped and only now that it had gone were they back again, this gave him pause for thought, if the rats were that frightened of it, maybe they should join forces, then he shook his head, and thought don't be so bloody ridicules. He walked, very gingerly, back to the kitchens and as he entered the room to his horror there it was on top of the counter being fed bacon scraps by the cook he instinctively took two step back which didn't go unnoticed by his feline nemesis, who grinned a superior grin and turned her head away, Oh like that is it, right I'll show you, just you wait and see if I don't! And he turned about and left the room.

After four or five hours of swinging about in the rafters looking down upon the activities on board the decks Jean was actually feeling a little better he'd just about finished the flask of water and now with renewed confidence was even trying a nibble on the biscuits. When Henri shouted up to him to enquire on his health he even managed a half-hearted joke with his brother, *aye I'll be better than you in a fort-night.* McCallister could not believe the transformation in the lad, *he was on deaths door this morning. Well it's a funny thing sea sickness you can have it for an hour or a week but when you've found your sea legs then you'll be right as rain again in no time, so your saying that he would have got better by himself? Likely, all you've done is speed it up a little bit, I was talking to a ships surgeon years back and he told me of a cure that wasn't a cure, I don't follow? Well what he said was if you give someone a leech and tell him it will help, in his mind he's already convinced himself that it will even though it's a complete lie, he used a fancy word for it, a placebo or some such but then he said a better way of explaining it was headoligy, tell the head it's going to work, and if you sell it the right way it will. Well I never did, so how much longer do you think he will have to stay up there then, oh I would say leave him there overnight and by morning he'll be begging to be let down. And to be honest it might be just as well, I don't like the way the wind is picking up, and it's coming from the wrong direction. What direction should it be coming from? Well at this longitude it should be blowing from East to West and we should be tacking all the way but it's now blowing direct North like a full winter storm, maybe winter has come early this year, won't be the first time. Right captain I'm going to hit the hay, you do right, and to be honest I won't be far behind you, as soon as the first mate turns too I'm off myself, I'll bid you good night then, aye good night Sergeant* and with a shake of the hand they parted company.

The wind increased through the night so much so that the ship was going at a fair old lick by morning and when the captain relieved the first mate the log stated that the wind had increased by another fifteen knots from the previous day which far from alarming the captain, put him in good stead, at this speed he thought it would likely take another day off their journey, no longer did they need to tack, they simply had to hold against the North wind. When he was joined again by McCallister bringing with him a hot mug of tea he told him the good news, *can't you make it another five days Phillippé would love to be home for his birthday. I'm afraid not Sergeant but if it gets any stronger I might be able to get him there in time to see all the revellers away home, oh I'm sure that will cheer him up no end.*

Mac had been sulking all night, how could a bloody silly cat make him so miserable. It wasn't as if he had anything to prove, good god he was a dog, bred from wolves, and she was only a dumb cat with evidently no breeding whatsoever. So why couldn't he get her out of his head, the only way to do that was to prove that he was a better ratter than she was. So he needed a plan, and unfortunately that was a problem because he didn't make plans, he normally took life head on and went where ever it took him. He sat and thought it through it took him all of twelve seconds and went something like this: 1, go down to the bottom of the boat. 2, bark and get cat's attention 3, run to other end of the boat. 4, cat frightens rats and they run away. 5, catch rats. He was most pleased with himself, he'd never planned anything as intricate as this before, the last time he had to think something through it went 1, bark at master to throw ball. 2, catch ball and bring back to master. So for this latest plan he deserved a qualification at least and letters after his name, Mac Bsc (Beat Stupid Cats). Right plan reviewed and found to be perfect, it was time to put it into action. He went down into the bilges at the rear of the craft and started to bark for all he was worth, and sure enough as planned the cat's curiosity got the better of it and it leapt down off the counter and ran to the source of the noise. He waited for a couple of heartbeats then ran like buggery to the pointy end, crouched down and waited and as the cat got to the point where the barks emanated the rats pulled up there skirts and did one. As they ran passed him it was like a kid in a candy shop and in no time at all he had dispatched a dozen of the smelly beggars. So unbelievably happy with the outcome of his plan was he, that he shouted YAP! Now dragging rats down stairs by the tail isn't usually a problem so I'm told but dragging rats upstairs by the tail is a completely different kettle of fish, and try as he might it wasn't going to happen not all at once anyway, so he had to reduce the weight and take them three at a time, which kind of pissed on his bonfire a little, he wanting to make the grand entrance but thankfully the cat came back to the kitchen the same way as she left therefore not interrupting his venture. When he had gathered them all together and lined them up outside the kitchen door he put every last tail in his mouth and with one almighty heave entered the arena. He dragged them all in full view of the cook and the damned cat, whereby they both stopped and stared in astonishment. The cook who was always plagued by the rats had a huge smile on his face and started to clap his hands shouting bravo he then started to rummaged around in the larder to find a suitable treat for such an act, the cat just sat there completely gob smacked. Mac however barked to her '*YAP*' *let's see you do better than that then, cat!*

Jean having spent a rather draughty night under the stars was shivering when they lowered him back down onto the deck. Phillipé and Henri were there to welcome him back. *How are you feeling now little brother you look a lot better that you did when you went aloft yesterday, I feel much better than I did but I'll tell you something I'm bloody ravenous is there any breakfast on the go do you think? That's more like the Jean we know and love, come on we'll all go and eat together.* And they left the deck hands to tidy up and stow the gear, with a thumbs up and a smile and headed towards the galley.

McCallister was at his usual morning haunt at the wheel with the captain and two mugs of tea. *Has the wind picked up again from last night do you think? Aye it certainly has Sergeant another eight knots from last night, not a problem is it? No not at the moment in fact it's in our favour just now but it could turn out to be a problem on the next leg of our journey, how so? Grab that chart and I'll show you,* as McCallister smoothed it out in front of them the captain started to explain. *Right see this point here, well that's where we are now at the bottom end of the Baltic Sea so as we stand the wind is at our back, pushing us along nicely however when we get to the Southern tip of Sweden we have to swing around to the North which means that the wind will be in our face which in its self wouldn't be a problem if we were out at sea with plenty of room, but we aren't we are heading for the Denmark straits which is a narrow channel if you need to tack which we will, so it could be a little bit hairy trying to manoeuvre a big tub like this through a small channel like that. Are you worried? No provided that it doesn't blow any harder then we'll be fine, and once we get through the straits were only a kick in the arse away from the North Sea and its all plain sailing from there. I'm very pleased to hear it, would you like a top up? Aye go on this one's gone cold, right you are give me your mug and I'll be back straight after breakfast.* As he walked into the galley the Verrel brothers and Phillippé where knee deep in food, *everything alright boys, aye Sarge the foods never been better since you had a word with the cook, good I'm pleased I'm good for something, how are you now Jean, got your sea legs at last? Aye Sarge I could take the world on now, just let me finish up here first. Stand down soldier we don't need to take anyone on now, we'll be home and dry in no time. Cook can I ask, what the hell are all these dead rats doing in here? Ah sergeant see that little dog of yours he has to be the best ratter I've ever known, killed the lot of them so he did, well I wish he would clean up after himself as well their fair putting me off eating, don't worry Sarge I'll get them tossed overboard right now, sit yourself down and I'll knock you up a full plate. After he had eaten and got the captain his fresh mug of tea he walked back up to the wheel and handed it over. Jeans looking a lot better this morning, I've just seen him in the galley asking the cook for a third helping, good I'm very pleased to hear it, nobody likes a happy ship quite as much as I do.*

After finishing his reward of a plate of sausages Mac was ready for a bit of a lie down to sleep them off, but the trouble was now he had proven his worth he couldn't shake that damned cat, everywhere he turned she was there with a pathetic lovelorn grin on her face, well he'd had enough it was time to ditch her so as he passed one of the stools he cocked his leg to relieve himself and of course she being a lady turn her head away averting her eye and as soon as she did, he ran for all he was worth, he had no idea where he was going but then a thought entered his head, the captain's table had saved him once maybe it could do it again, so he ran like the wind, found the cabin and at full pelt launched himself at the desk, but this time he was moving too fast, caught his leg in one of the charts, rolled and went straight off the other side landing quite conveniently on the leather chair which gave an angry squeak as he landed. Heart pounding he watched silently as the cat glimpsed into the doorway and then moved on, satisfied that he had finally ditched her he curled into a ball farted and quickly fell asleep.

I think there's a bit of rain in the air captain, aye you could well be right I don't like the look of that sky over there black as midnight, fare chance of a clap of thunder in it as well I don't doubt. Have you ever thought of covering the wheel, not just a roof but a full all around cabin to keep the elements at bay, trust me Sergeant, if the weather gets so bad that I need a cabin to sit in, you'll be stood here by yourself. In due course the weather did indeed take a turn for the worse, it started with big slow drops and very soon became a windblown tempest. Sergeant take the wheel if you would I feel a need to visit my cabin and fetch my oilskins, *You have got to be joking I don't know the first thing about sailing a ship, you don't need to just keep a hold of the wheel and keep it going in the same direction, what could be simpler, I'll be back in two minutes flat.* McCallister stood at the wheel and held it still till his knuckles went white, terrified that if it turned it just a fraction the craft would break up on rocks and all souls lost, it didn't matter to him that the nearest land fall was a good hundred miles away. On land he wasn't afraid of anyone or anything, but this had him terrified, he was well out of his comfort zone. So when he saw the captain walking back up the staircase fully dressed for all the elements he could have hugged him. Here have the damn thing back and don't ever do that to me again, not ready for a change of employment then Sarge? Ready for a change of underwear more likely, it's terrifying how can you do this on a daily basis, well I guess some people get used it after a while but see me when I first took control of a ship even as briefly though it was I knew there and then that this was what I wanted to do for the rest of my life, well rather you than me, give me an open field and an enemy any day of the week, if we were all the same my friend then the world would be a very boring place, aye I suppose your right but all the same don't do it again. Oh by the way I've just had to chase that dog of yours out of my chair in the cabin, snoring* *away he was, made himself right at home and making the place smell like a badly swept kennel, and I don't know what's gotton into the cooks cat but it was sat looking up at him like a love sick teenager. Talking of the cook go and pop down stairs and get us both a fresh brew I'm fairly parched, and as McCallister started down to the galley, the captain looked up and frowned at the sky, I reckon this next leg isn't going to be as easy as I first envisaged.*

Mac was at the end of his tether, try as he might to get rid of the cat she just wouldn't take the hint, he'd tried running away and hiding but the trouble with a ship was that it just isn't big enough, so after a little deliberation he decided if you can't beat them then join them, which was a bold move on his behalf. So the next bit, because he didn't speak cat and as far as he was aware she couldn't speak dog was going to be a bit tricky, so he walked to where he had finished off a couple of rats a day or so back and started to explain. He crouched down in front of one of the dead rats and growled, after she got that bit he leapt up and grabbed the poor creature by the throat and shook it to death a second time. He put the carcase down and looked at her, once he was sat she went through the same performance she crept cat like…hmm let's say a cat, up to the rat and then after a pause leapt at the still creature and knocked buggery out of it. Once they understood each other the rats never stood a chance and one by one they started to clear the decks of the horrible critters. Each morning the two of them would haul their victims into the galley to show their success's to the cook and each morning the cook would give them a reward for their hard work and once fed they would curl up together, fall asleep and dream the dreams of heroes with the odd twitch here and the odd fart there. Some might say that love between species can't happen but try and tell that to a six year old and a new born kitten, and if ever there was love between species these two felt it about each other, no matter how hard you tried you could not find a stronger bond.

By mid-afternoon the ship had passed Bornholm Island and was starting to turn into the north wind. *Sergeant remember when I said when we came to the southern tip of Sweden we would have to turn into the wind and start to tack through the straits, aye, well guess what we're here, however there is absolutely no chance in hell that I'm going to attempt to do that in the dark, so I'm going to make a tactical decision and head for port in Ystad we will overnight there and set sail again at first light. Well that should please the men to get their feet on solid ground for a change, maybe for my men however I must insist that your men stay aboard ship, one too many drinks and it will be plain to all that they are French soldiers at best they could run to try and save themselves, at worst they will all be killed and if that should happen and you can't get the gold to Paris, then I lose my ship and I'm not prepared to let that happen. Ok I see your point, well we will just have to make the best of the situation that we can. Will there be prostitutes around the harbour? You show me one that hasn't, ok that's how I'll sell it to them, they are to stay aboard but I will gather women together and bring them aboard to enjoy the superb rum and the even better company. A fine idea Sergeant that way everyone stays safe and have a good time and I get to keep my ship.* That evening went as well as anyone could have expected the ship's crew did indeed go into town to sample a few bars, but because of the dreadful weather found that most of the hostelries were either empty or closed, people simply didn't want to venture out just to get piss wet through. So they mostly did what the French were doing, linking an arm here and an arm there and escorting the ladies to the row boat and deliver them to enjoy the party on board ship. The festivities went on till dawn but come daylight the captain had everyone that wasn't part of the venture escorted back to the harbour, a little happier and a little richer than the night before.

Right Sergeant here comes the tricky bit. As they sailed between the harbours walls, *this is where we test our resolve into the face of the storm.* The captain chose his words carefully for albeit no one on board had really noticed, but the wind had picked up again through the night bringing squally showers with it. The crew were ready and willing to do their duties, however had they been a little more sober perhaps they wouldn't have been quite so keen. *What should we expect today captain? Well when we get away from the lee of the land and turn fully into the wind, expect a rough ride, there's not much fetch between here and Norway so the swell shouldn't be too high but the wind blowing this strong will still push a lot of chop our way, it's as I told you before it's a very narrow channel that we have to negotiate whilst tacking, I reckon the crew are going to have to sober up damn quick because if they don't their very likely to go overboard or run us aground, if I had the choice of the two I'd rather lose a couple of drunk crew members than the ship, as they are always easy to find anew.* McCallister puzzled at the captain's remark looked questioningly at him, seeing his face he said, *I'm kidding mate, I'm just trying to make light of the situation, besides have you any idea how much it costs me to pay the family if I lose a man over board?* This put a devilment smile on his face. *Will you need a hand from any of my men? No I appreciate the offer but they will be better off below deck out of the way you might want to tell them to strap themselves in for a while though, and maybe not order the soup.*

Mac and the cat were on their usual recon essence of the ship looking for rats when they saw quite an amazing sight, without any encouragement whatsoever the rats were running to the upper decks and one at a time they were leaping overboard, the pair where completely perplexed, had the word gotten round that the two of them were bad ass rat killers? And it was a better chance to swim for it than face these two head on. Well whatever it was they were going to be very soon out of business, no rats equalled no food so they thought as one and decided to cut them off at the pass, as they chucked themselves over board they would grab them mid-flight and cash them in tomorrow, this worked pretty well at first but after a while the foe simply stopped coming and so ended their profitable enterprise. The cat looked at Mac with a questioning eye and all he could do was shrug his shoulders, he needed to think this through and he couldn't do that on an empty stomach so the pair dragged a couple of rats each over to the galley and showed them to the cook. As was the deal he rewarded the pair with a bowl of sausages and they ate them like it was their last meal. Contract met they found a quite cabin curled up together and fell asleep. When they awoke the whole world seemed to be rocking and rolling, first it would tilt this way then it would pitch that, curious to a fault they scampered upon deck to see what was happening, and immediately regretted it, anything and everything that wasn't fastened down was skittering across the deck, and the captain howling at the wind and laughing like a mad man seemed to be causing it all, he would wait until everything had rattled starboard and then he would turn the wheel and everything would do the return journey and skittle to port. A pale collided with the two of them and sent the cat tumbling along with it. Bruised and dazed when the wheel was turned again she came tumbling back in front of him and Mac hardly keeping his own paws planted grabbed at her and brought her to a sudden stop. Well enough was enough and the pair of them turned before the wheel did, and scampered back below decks. The galley was in disarray there were plates and tables all over the place, the French soldiers had strapped themselves to the main beams so that they didn't get swept up with the pitching ship however they were now sitting ducks for the rest of the flotsam and jetsam that was getting flung around the room, the stools were the worst because they knew how to pack a punch but a stray knife was equally as dangerous even more so as Phillipe found out having to extract one from his shoulder. How long are we to endure this hell he said through clenched teeth, captain said anywhere between four and eight hours, Oh that's just fine and dandy, I wouldn't have missed this for the world. The captain was wrong the torture lasted for ten hours, however the last hour was a lot easier and as the ship approached Anholt Island the captain instructed the crew that he was going to pull to the lee side of the Island and to lower the anchor. He chanced getting as close as he dare to the islands south side before he gave the order to drop, but as he did he was the most popular man on the ship, thank the lord for that, was the general consensus. The crew happy as most to be out of the wind tied up the sails and after a hearty meal settled in for the night, pleased to be over the worst of it. *Well captain it was shear hell for me and my men, but what did you make of the day's work? Well sergeant I wouldn't want to do it again in a hurry trust me on that, but as such I lost no crew and it appears that we live to fight another day, crack that bottle of rum and we'll toast our good fortune, amen to that cap'n.* The rest of the men on board after living on adrenalin all day were absolutely exhausted and after a quick shot of rum they were all ready for their hammocks so by half past ten the only ones left awake were Mac and the cat, after finding one of the pantry doors swinging open, they ate their fill and decided to turn in themselves. By eleven o'clock not a soul stirred on les Contrebandiére apart from the very bravest of rats.

Overnight the temperature plummeted and the wind brought with it snow straight from the arctic which covered the deck a foot and a half deep in places as the first one out the captain pondered over the foolishness of sailing out in this storm. As the crew started to join him on deck he ordered all of them back down to the galley he made sure that if they had to work in these conditions they would at least something warm in their bellies the cook was pushed to his limits as they all walked in as one. Once fed he returned to the wheel and McCallister joined him as he had every morning throughout their journey. *Well captain what are your thoughts on the weather conditions? I'm none too pleased about it truth be known sergeant this wind has to be gale force by now and if we can feel it here at the lee side of the island, then god only knows what we will sail into when we leave its shelter, surely you have sailed through worse weather than this in the past? Well there's only one way to find out my friend, and that is to up anchor and drive straight into it.* With that said he instructed the crew to break the ice off the sails and rigging while McCallisters men cleared the snow from the deck, once done he gave the order to raise the anchor and lower the sails. *Right monsieur McCallister this would be a good time for you to pray to your god and hope like hell he's listening.* As the ship caught the wind and filled her sails the captain slowly pulled away from the safe shelter of the island and into the full fury of the elements, he was taken aback at the strength of the storm before him he still had to tack north until they reached the northern most tip of Demark, only then would the wind be behind them and could put it to good use, however for the next couple of hours the crew would have to work harder than they ever had, it wouldn't be quite so violent as yesterday because he had more room to manoeuvre and with the wind being so strong he had to run on less sail, but it was still dicey he had never seen swell so large in such a small fetch, it must have built to twenty five foot at least, which meant that it was all or nothing, he couldn't turn around to try and run for shelter because if he was caught by a wave whilst broadside the ship would be sunk for sure, so this was it…do or die. As the hours went by the ship took more and more punishment, until at last at the southern tip of Norway he could finally turn the craft towards the North Sea, and gently ease it around to head south. He was happy enough to manoeuvre into that position but wasn't ready for the outcome, he thought that once heading south the wind would aid them but he wasn't counting on the swell, it was now travelling the full length of the north sea and was truly mountainous. The ship wasn't sailing anymore it was sliding down the waves one after another at an horrendous rate and for the first time in his maritime career he was truly terrified. As the ship fell into the troughs the prow would disappear under water throwing spray thirty foot into the air which immediately froze on the sails and rigging, making the craft top heavy. He ordered the crew to climb the masts to try and clear the ice however it was a perilous task, that no sane man would ever attempt, and for a brief moment he was hugely proud of his crew, as he focussed back onto the job in hand there was a scream from above as one of his men slipped on an ice covered beam and lost his grip he fell like a stone, cracking his skull on one of the lower beams and was dead before he finally hit the deck. The ship was now in disarray, the comrades of the fallen sailor tried to contain his body as it slipped across the icy deck so as not to lose him to the depths, but try as they might they couldn't contain him, till one of the crew fetched a hammer, laid across his lifeless body and nailed his hand to the boards. As if adding insult to injury it started snowing again and this time it meant it. The captain couldn't see his compass anymore not that it really mattered the ship was under complete control of the storm all he could do was try and fight the wind and keep it from turning the ship broadside. As he was thinking that things couldn't get worse…they did, with a sickening crack as loud as a gunshot the mainsails masts fell under the weight of the snow and ice and came crashing down onto the deck killing another two crew members and breaking the legs of a third. They were now running on the fore-and-aft rig and the captain was fighting with the wheel to keep the ship true, he ordered water barrels to be secured with rope at the stern and thrown overboard to create drag, which helped. The next task was to remove the mainsails off the deck and get the wounded sailor down to the infirmary. Every able hand was put to the task armed with axes, hammers and any other tool that was available. After an hour of working in horrendous conditions the sails were cut free and the beams were in two half's, as the ship lurched to port the end of one mast dipped into the water and in a flash was dragged overboard quickly followed by another, two of the deck crew who weren't fast enough to avoid them were dragged away with the timbers their screams largely unheard lost in the howling gale, the masts now gone freed the injured man, who was carried below screaming and crying at the pain in his shattered legs. By mid-afternoon fatigue was starting to show on the captain's face, he had been fighting the elements for hours and he was physically drained. McCallister struggling against the wind, approached him and shouting above the gale asked if he needed to take a break offering his own services whilst he rested. The captain declined his kind offer knowing that if he with thirty years behind him was struggling then a mere novice wouldn't stand a chance, in recompense he asked if he would fetch the bottle of rum that they opened last night to take a little Dutch courage. He asked that under the circumstance was that such a good idea, the reply was lost in the gale, but he knew exactly what he had said, and thought maybe he would take a nip as well. As he struggled below deck he could hear the screams of the injured deck hand. Even after he was given opium and generous amounts of rum he was still sobbing like a child, he knew as every sailor did that if he didn't die before surgery chances were that he would die on the table, and so he was confronted with only two options, either die slowly and in excruciating pain, losing both of his legs in the process or ask for a pistol, he chose the latter. And out of eyesight in a lonely cabin in the middle of the North Sea a shot rang out and the screaming stopped. McCallister keeping a tight hold on his prize slipped and staggered his way back to the wheel and a grateful captain, pulled out the cork with his teeth and spat it away, took three or four large gulps, enough to put a wild bear on its arse, and passed the bottle back to McCallister who declined, it was time to ask, and after a few heartbeats he plucked up the courage, *captain will we get out of this?* He didn't get an answer just a shrug, but then the captain became more vocal and shouting at the top of his voice declared, *I don't know, we're in the middle of the North Sea I've got very little control, the ship is basically being pushed along by the storm and where we will end up, if indeed we get that far, who knows? Our fates right now are in the hands of the almighty.*

THE KREMLIN 1812

Napoleon was pacing up and down again with his hands behind his back, frustration and anger on his face every now and then he would slam his fist upon the table as he passed by, and every hour he asked the same question, why the hell hasn't Alexander contacted him with terms and conditions of his surrender? Every morning he would gather his council around him, and ask *what news?* And every morning he would get the same answer, *no news Emperor.* And so he decided that he would give the Tsar two more weeks, and if by then there was still no sign of surrender, he would gather up his remaining troops and head for home.

In the city his troops were getting more and more desperate, they had searched every building several times over in the hope that they may have missed something on the previous attempts, but it was clear to all that there was no longer anything to eat, and the starvation was putting them in a murderous mood, fighting one another for a stale piece of cheese. As Claude came back from a fruitless search of the neighbourhood, his brother sank into another depressed state of lethargy. '*What's going to happen to us Claude, if we stay here much longer we will all die for sure, I lost another two teeth this morning and swallowed them just to have something in my belly, I know it's tough Adrien but we mustn't lose all hope I heard two of the kremlin guards talking, and they were saying that if he hasn't heard from the Tzar by the fortnight then we'll all be heading home, oh how nice that'll be marching all the way back to France with nothing to eat, well it's got to be better than sitting here doing nothing but feeling sorry for ourselves, how do you keep so positive all the time Claude? trust me brother it's all bravado inside I'm just as hungry and scared as you are,*

119

I just choose not to show it, well I wish I had that talent, but I don't, I'm still hungry and I'm still pissed off. The next day the weather turned for the worse, at first it was just a cold wind heading out of the north, but in due course it started to snow as well. While the troops were still in the city it was nothing more than an inconvenience and an opportunity to melt fresh drinking water, however over the next few days it didn't let up. As Napoleon was looking skywards one morning he turned to his council and announced, *gather the troops we are to march home! In this emperor? Yes in this, would you rather stay here and freeze to death.* So word went out, to gather belongings and fall in at the southern gate. Napoleon and his generals rode their starved horses to the front of the amassed men and gave the order to move out, and so the remnants of the largest army ever assembled for war set out for home, beaten, starved and totally down hearted. *Well Adrien it's going to be a hard slog, I know but if we just put our heads down and march it'll fly over, there you go again, it's going to be hell on earth, we have to march fifteen hundred miles in this weather, on empty stomachs, we'll all be dead before we get anywhere near France,* and for the optimistic Claude he finally had to admit that his little brother was right, this was not going to be a walk in the park.

In the first few hours everyone was finding their pace with the stronger of the troops heading out first following their emperor and lagging way behind were the ill and weak. Claude and Adrien Deveraux found their pace about mid field, with Claude trying to encourage his younger brother with each step. After a climb upon a small hill, they had the opportunity to assess the troop's numbers being able to look forward at the leaders and to the rear the stragglers. *How many are we would you say Claude? Well if you look at that crowd just ahead and say that is one hundred souls, then count similar groups ahead and behind I would estimate just short of twenty thousand. Good heavens is that all that is left of us? We were half a million strong when we started this god forsaking campaign, Aye that's one hell of a loss of life, and how many of us will be left to finish the journey do you think? Well I reckon that those up front may stand a decent chance, and I'm not leaving you in this hell hole of a country even if I have to carry you, you and I are to be buried in the family grave back in France, and that I promise you dear brother.*

The rear of the party were already starting to depart, slipping in the snow and mud and not strong enough to get back on their feet, they were simply left to die in the freezing conditions, everyone too malnourished and exhausted to care. That first night, fires were lit to try and coax the chill from their bones but this had an adverse effect insofar as they were beacons for the Cossacks to track them down, and track them down they did. Charging night time raids to pick off the already weak and vulnerable. As the two brothers went to crowd around a fire Claude came up with a revelation under the circumstances. *Adrien, I was just taking a leak and was talking to one of the riflemen when he noticed my belt, he asked me why I hadn't eaten it yet? And in a flash I ran back into the crowd. What do you mean eaten it, don't you see, its leather an animals skin, if we can eat the meat then what's to stop us eating its skin. Take off your belt and bash it as thin as you can, then we can cut it up and soak it in boiling water, it'll be as tough as hell but it will fill our stomachs, Oh and what's going to keep my breaches up then, your bloated belly that's what. Listen Adrien, we've got to do whatever we can to survive this ordeal, we both have belts, and if needs must we also have our boots, but we must be very careful not to lose either, and if I have to I will walk back over to see what I can retrieve from the already dead, as they'll not need them anymore.*

After days of snow storms the weather worsened even more, with the night time temperature dropping to minus thirty they were now trudging through four feet of snow and ice, even the night time raids had stopped, the Cossacks leaving their enemy to the mercy of the elements. After they had literally eaten their boots they were forced to walk in stocking feet which froze until they were black with frostbite with toes ready to snap, which many did. After another week of torture Claude went missing for an hour or two and on his return, Adrian asked where his brother had been, In reply he put his hand into his tunic pocket and pronounced that he had found a dead horse and had liberated much of its hind leg. Adrien could have danced for joy, at last after weeks of starvation they could finally have a decent meal. They daren't cook the meat on one of the fires as to do so would have got them both killed so they feasted on it raw, and after a sleepless night they had the strength to rise and march again. The next night the Cossacks were back and in true form they murdered more of the sick and ill. The two brothers feeling sustained by their meal of horse meat had almost caught up to the front of the party and saw Napoleon not more than half a mile ahead still sitting astride his starved white stallion. As the pitiful army marched on, mile on mile Adrien asked of his brother, *I wonder how the Verrels and Phillippé Oubre are getting along? Probably dead I would think, why would you say that? they were well supplied by all accounts, and had the healthiest horses that could be found, that's all well and good, but they were heading up to St Petersburg, further into enemy territory, wearing Russian uniforms and none of them speaking a single word of the Russian language, any way you look at it they would be shot before they got fifty kilometres up the road, I suppose your right, shame though, I got on really well with Jean and we've all been through so much together over the years, yeh Jean and Henri were good sorts, but I couldn't get away with Phillippé treating us all like kids, well I suppose to him we are, he must have a good ten years on the rest of us, well I'd go to his funeral I suppose but I wouldn't want him as a school teacher, never mind their all dead so there's no point concerning ourselves with them, come on were slacking, lets catch those fella's up again and try to keep pace this time.* As they walked on there was no chance of getting lost as they were using the same route as they did getting to Moscow, and everywhere the corpses of the fallen were guiding their way back home. As they approached the battle field of Borodino the fields were covered in the fallen, countless thousands of bodies covered every inch of ground so that as the procession progressed they were forced to step over and around them but as everyone was so weakened with hunger many stumbled and fell lying amongst the dead, and if god gave them grace and allowed them to make the journey home they would carry this nightmarish scene with them for the rest of their lives.

LES CONTREBANDIÉRE 1812

The Verrels and Pillippé Oubre were having their own nightmare aboard ship, by now the temperature had dropped to minus twenty and the wind getting ever stronger was pushing the craft to its limits. The captain wanted to throw another couple of water barrels over board for drag but without putting any more lives at risk to lessen the sails he didn't dare put the extra strain on the remaining masts. The snow was now a constant blanket, which made navigation totally impossible. The captain seemingly unconcerned about the conditions was an inspiration to the men on board, little did they know he had finished one bottle of rum and was halfway down a second, his reasoning being if he was going to die anyway at least he'd die with a smile on his face. McCallister pointing to below decks with his gloved hand expressed his intentions of going to check on his men, he was given thumbs up in reply. As he held the hatchway against the gale and started to climb down he was confronted by utter chaos anything and everything that wasn't tied down was making its own bid for freedom. Albeit a little quieter out of the wind he still had to shout to be heard over the creaks and groans that the timbers were making. *Phillippé have you had chance to check on the cargo? No Sarge not today I haven't, when was the last time you did checked it? About three days ago Sarge. Right come with me and we'll check it together,* and as they steadied themselves against the violent motions of the ship they made their way aft into the horse enclosure, were they found the animals dead, no doubt from fright. The rats were busying themselves on the poor creature's remains and in the cramped conditions the smell was incredible. Holding their sleeves against their noses to try and lessen the smell they moved onwards to the cargo hold. When Phillipé entered he was knocked off his feet by one of the wagons which had broken free of its restraints and was charging from aft to bow and back again with tremendous force due to the chests of gold it was still carrying, so much so that it had cracked a couple of hull timbers which were now letting in water. *Go and fetch some more help Phillippé and hurry about it.* As he set off McCallister rummaged about for something that would stop the cart freewheeling out of control, and there up against the bulkhead was a length of four by four that might just do the trick. He waited for the wagon to reach its zenith and let fly with the timber under the rear wheels this had just the effect he was hoping for, as the ship lurched again the wagon stayed put, however this was just a temporary fix, he had to find a more permanent solution to the problem. By this time Phillippé had returned with the Verrel brothers and nearly fell into the cargo hold as the ship lurched again, this time however the timber wasn't sufficient and the wagon jumped its bond and came crashing into the newcomers Henri and Jean managed to jump aside but Phillippe wasn't quick enough and was hit in the chest and crushed against the bulkhead, the huge force crushed most of his ribs, a couple of which punctured his lungs and his heart, as the wagon started its return journey again, Phillippe slumped to the deck already dead. *Stop staring and stop that bloody wagon from hitting anyone else,* Move that last word broke the spell and Henri lifted the timber and this time pushed it between the spokes and stalled it completely, they then made with the bindings and fastened it more securely, as they were finishing up McCallister went to his fallen comrade and felt for a pulse, finding none he gently closed his eyelids and said a quiet prayer for his friend. Once the wagon was secured he staggered back up to the wheel to inform the captain of the breach below. *How bad is it sergeant? Well it still holds but for how long is anyone's guess,* the captain then reached into his oilskin jacket and produced the second bottle of rum, offered it to the sergeant who declined and took a huge slug himself and then he started to sing, with the whole world coming crashing down on him he sang, and laughed. Realizing madness when he saw it he left the captain alone in his stupor and went bellow to try and still the rising panic. By this time the Verrels had told the rest of the party of Phillippe's demise, and the bulkhead breach which was met with a dower response. In one corner of the room was a cat and a dog huddled together for comfort and if anyone choose to look closely they would have seen that the dog had tears in his eyes.

BORODINO 1812

Back in the fields of Borodino the troops had to slow to a crawling pace there was very little open ground left to walk upon without standing on the bodies of their fallen comrades. As the Deverauxs picked their way through the horrific scene, Claude remarked, if he, looking towards Napoleon hadn't held us back when he did, then we could be here amongst the fallen, it was while he was looking towards their leader that he noticed a curious thing, not once did he look at the devastation around him instead he choose to look directly ahead and be guided by his trusted steed.

LES CONTREBANDIÉRE 1812

McCallister staggered back in to see his men, carefully avoiding any conversation that involved the captain he reasoned that it wouldn't do anyone any favours explaining that they were now in the hands of a raving lunatic. Instead he put them to work. *Come on you lot lets have you over to the cargo hold, we need to try and seal that breach and we can't leave Phillippés body to the mercy of them rats. We'll see to our friend Sarge* the Verrels offered, and staggered off to the aft of the ship. As they entered the hold one of the rats was already having a go at the fresh meat, Henri infuriated ran at it and kicked the creature straight into the bulkhead killing it outright, *help me pick him up Jean let's take him somewhere those horrible little bastards can't get at him.* When at first he didn't move he turned to look at his younger brother only to see him silently sobbing, with tears rolling down his face, Henri gathered his brother up and held him tight, *I know little brother I'm going to miss him as well but we must stay strong until we get off this god forsaken boat.* While the Verrels were taking care of their dead friend, wrapping his body in sheeting and placing him atop the very wagon that crushed him, McCallister had four of the team gathering up hemp rope ends, once amassed they dipped them in hot candle wax and with hammers they were forcing it into the gaps of the cracked timbers which on the face of things was more pro-active than the Captain was being. As they stood back to examine their efforts, they had to admit for a bunch of land lubbers they had actually done a half decent job. Before he left McCallister gave the whole area a good coating of looking at and reasonably happy with what he saw started to stagger back with his men, thinking all the time, what the hell was he to do with that nutter in charge of the wheel? As he stumbled back through the galley he thanked his men for all their efforts, and decided he must speak with the captain, for if anyone was going to get them all safely through this ordeal it was going to have to be him, and he couldn't let him be overwhelmed by the fear of it all. As the hatch door slammed open caught by the wind the conditions fare took his breath away, the deck was awash with snow and spray, all of which stung his bare skin, as he managed to get to the wheel without falling, he turned to the captain and at the top of his voice shouted for the bottle of rum, thinking he had a drinking partner he reached into his oilskin and offered it to McCallister, who took hold of the neck, took one look at it and deftly threw it overboard. The captains eyes went wide with horror and without the aid of sober speech just looked at him as if he was mad. *Now listen here you, you might think your frightened by all this with all your time at sea, well let me tell you something, my men are fucking terrified but they have still got the fight in them and have just been down in the bilges and stopped your precious ship from sinking beneath your bloody feet while you have been up here feeling sorry for yourself now pull yourself together and get us all home, because we can't do it without you, you selfish bastard.* Then a strange thing happened, I've only ever seen it happen the once, but the captain had actually drank himself sober, all it needed was the trigger which was delivered by McCallister. *Please accept my apologies sergeant, these are the worst conditions I've ever witnessed and it got me down just now, but trust me, I will to the best of my abilities get us all out of this, thank you captain, now if I can get the cook to start a fire without burning the ship down would you like a mug of tea? That sergeant is a fine idea but if he is going to all that trouble, make it half a dozen.* And with a smile and a wink he staggered off below deck again. As he entered the galley and looked around the cook was nowhere to be seen, so out of instinct alone he shouted, *Phillippé get a fire started we need a brew for the captain right now…* just as the last syllables left his mouth he realised his mistake, Henri filled the silence, *I'll do it Sarge, thanks Henri it could be a matter of life or death for us all.* Henri wiped the cold damp ash off the fire stone with his sleeve and started to erect the kindling into a small pyramid with some unravelled hemp rope at its centre but no matter how many matches he struck he couldn't get it to light. Hang on here he said I'll be back in a minute and he staggered of to the hold. In the semi darkness he fumbled about till he got to the wagon where his old friend was laid. *I wish it was you doing this mate, you're going to be sorely missed, let's just pretend that you're down here to guard the gold, and I'm here to offer you a drop of rum to stave off the cold, no, no please don't get up on my account, you stay we're you are I've just come to fetch some powder to light the galley fire,* and as he rummaged around Phillippés cold body his hand touched the pouch which was still tied to his belt, as he untied the knot he took the pouch and tied it to his own belt, he tucked the sheet back under his friend, and softly whispered, *keep watch my friend, and no matter what the foe, you just have to call,* he wiped away a tear, and left. Once back in the galley he poured some of the powder over the kindling lit a match and stood back, he tossed the match onto the stone, and in a flash he lost his eyebrows. Eventually the pan boiled and he managed to keep most of the tea in the mugs. *Here you go Sergeant take this up top for our saviour,* McCallister took the offered mugs and thought if only they knew. For the second time that afternoon the wind and snow took his breath away, the sudden drop in temperature could have almost have frozen the tea but all that aside it was gratefully received by the captain. Speech between the two was nigh on impossible and so they were reduced to improvised sign language again. *Where are we?* with a shrug of the shoulders, the captain pointed his finger and drew a basic map in the snow, he recognised most of Europe and Britton, and when he pointed to where he thought they were, McCallister couldn't believe how far they had travelled in the last couple of days. He raised his voice once more and asked *how soon to Le Havre,* thinking on his feet he shouted two days.

BORODINO 1812

Thankfully they were just about out of the killing fields as darkness drew, the poor souls at the rear of the precession would have to walk through the dead at night and live their worst nightmares. As fires were lit camps were occupied for warmth and company, it was the latter that was more sought as everyone that had marched through the fields, were haunted by the memory of what they had seen. It had been two days now since the devarauxs had eaten and their stomachs were growling again. Claude can we see if there are any other horses to be had I can't walk another step unless I eat something, anything, wait here Adrien and I'll see what I can do, and he walked off into the darkness away from the living and into the realms of the dead. An hour passed until his shadow once again touched the living, and as Adrien smiled up at his brother Claude produced more horse meat that was greedily consumed by the younger, until he got to one end of a bone and found the remnants of some ones thumb. He recoiled from the thing throwing it to the ground *this isn't from a horse,* thinking that his brother had made a mistake. As he started to retch he said in gulps *that's some ones arm, was he killed? crushed by the horse as it fell? No brother there was no horse he said between mouth fulls and it wasn't a horse the last time we ate, there is nothing here but the dead, deep frozen and as fresh as the day they died. We should have died that day Adrien but we didn't and I'm not going to make their sacrifice stop us from living…Ever.*

Adrien, wrestled with his conscience all that night while others slept, and dreamed of better times. He couldn't get away from the awful truth, that no matter how you looked at it to eat another's flesh was morally wrong, but then if it stopped him from dying, was it the right thing to do? to choose not to eat was indeed a kind of suicide, which the scriptures stated was a mortal sin that would condemn you to an eternity of hell and damnation, so if that was the case was it better to eat the flesh and live? Towards dawn his head was spinning and was no further forward in a conclusion to the problem. Soon the order was given to move out, and so he and everyone else that had lived through the night brushed the snow from themselves gathered their possessions stood and started to march. *Here Adrien I've another coat for you to stave off the cold. Keep it* he said to his brother maybe a little too harshly. *Listen Adrien I never meant to compromise your morals, all I wanted to do was look after you, so I can get you home safe. And what happens after that, brother? I don't get your meaning Adrien, why are you talking in riddles? It's no riddle brother, how will God judge us come the day, what will we answer when he asks us, why did you eat the flesh of another, why didn't you trust me to look after you and get you home safely, why did you commit that sin, what the fuck are we supposed to say to him Claude, we are both damned, better we had died in the first instance at least our souls would have been saved. You're talking bollocks brother we've neither of us been church going men, why have you all of a sudden gone and got yourself all religious? Because brother until now I have never had the occasion to eat another human being, now piss off and leave me be.* Claude's shoulders dropped and his head sank with the enormity of what his little brother had said.

LES CONTREBANDIÉRE 1812

The captain was at a total loss as to where they were, all he had to go on were the bare facts, which were compass bearings, speed and time travelled, so when he worked it out he figured that he wasn't far out on his estimation of a couple of days from France, which in itself filled him with dread. It was a total white out, so unless the conditions improved dramatically he wouldn't be able to see land for bearings, and worse still what if the land decided to make an appearance too soon, he certainly didn't fancy a swim in these seas. All he could do was pray and hope for the best. When McCallister told his men that the likelihood was that they would be on dry land in a couple of days, and likely at their own firesides in a week. It was like him handing out tickets for the party. Almost all the hell they had been through was swept away, apart from poor Phillippé whose loss would take a lot longer to heal. *Can we open a bottle of rum to celebrate Sarge? Aye why not I can't see the harm boys, just don't overdo it, trying to walk in these conditions is difficult enough without you losing complete control of your legs, and I most certainly don't want any more accidents.*

I've heard it said that cats not only nine lives but also a sixth sense, this maybe the case, I guess we'll never know for sure, however there was no consoling Mac's friend, she was beside herself with worry. Mac himself didn't particularly like how the boat was rocking and rolling but this was his first cruise so as far as he knew this was perfectly normal. In he's experience if someone was feeling down in the mouth what they needed was a good lick on the face to make things better, so that's what he did, well the look she gave him could of melted snow, she had a stare that said what the hell did you do that for you stupid animal, don't you know we're in peril. With his tongue hanging out and a daft grin on his face that said...what? She didn't know how or why but she knew she'd never been thrown about on-board like this before and so she led him out of the relative warmth of the galley outside onto the deck, whereby he stared at her with a look that said are you bloody mad woman, what the hell are we doing out here in all this...this...cold stuff? She led him to the bow and into a coil of anchor rope, it wasn't as warm as the galley but once inside it was sheltered enough and the two of them settled in for the night...oh and by the way, don't you ever do that to me again!

THE OUTSKIRTS OF BORODINO 1812

The weather was getting worse, if they hadn't had the snow covered bodies of the dead to lead the way they would have surely been lost in the wilderness. As it were they had to steel from the dead just to try and keep warm, Adrien wished he had taken up the offer of the overcoat from Claude, but he was still mad with him, even if his intentions were noble enough. He had promised himself that he would not entertain the idea of a cheap meal again unless he could see for himself were it came from. He had also convinced himself that because he wasn't aware about what he was eating at the time, god would say that he was innocent of the crime, and so he was now on even ground, so long as he didn't do it again. And with that resolve he was starting to forgive his brother, but he would still keep it up for the rest of the day just to prove the point. In between snow storms Bonaparte was struggling to keep his horse against the wind, it looked from afar as if he was doing dressage. Then the snow returned and he was gone from view, the foot soldiers had to lean against the wind and the snow and try to press on. The further they marched away from Borodino the less bodies were apparent and the forerunners started to lose direction, as the road and the fields moulded into one blanket of snow. In the end they had to admit defeat they could no longer ensure the correct directions. As napoleon was told this news he flew into a rage, he descended from his steed and called his council around him. *What is this nonsense about halting the troops, it is perfectly obvious the direction we need to follow,* pointing at a compass he had in his hand. *We follow this and we head straight home, we do not need any other directions, just this!* And so they remounted and set off again, even his council doubting the decision.

SALTBURN 1812

Life got a little too slow in Staithes for John Andrew, the small fishing community didn't hold as much adventure as it did back home, so he bade his friends good bye and walked back over hunt cliff to Saltburn, and received a hero's welcome in the ship inn. He went straight to the fire and brushed himself down *by it's a rare old storm out there this evening, boys.* Dom who had decided that Middlesbrough was no longer for him had moved to the village on a permanent basis and welcomed his friend back. *Do you not think it might be a bit soon to return John? Possibly my friend but I was going stir crazy over there, I know where I belong and that is here, I have every intension of starting the business again, I have a supply chain to cater for and it starts again as of now.* Once he had warmed through he asked if anyone had been in Blue Mountain while he'd been away. *Only Jeffrey* he was told to take a wagon load over to Middlesbrough for David, he had apparently taken to the trade like a duck to water and was making a small fortune, packed out every night, since he had dropped the prices to the lowest in the town. *I'm very happy for the two of them, is David fully recovered now? Aye pretty much, and the two of them are still head over heels with each other, wouldn't be surprised if we didn't get an invitation to a christening in the near future, it fare melts yer art don't it. Right I'm going to do a quick stock check, d'yeh want to come and keep me company Dom? Aye why not, can we use the passage from the cellar though I don't want to chance going out there, a man could die from hyperthermia within minutes in weather like that. C'mon then let's get it over with then we can settle in and knock a few back in front of that fire.* They disappeared behind the bar and walked down the back stairs into the cellar, moved the side board that covered the passage and with a lighted candle walked the eighty yards to the underside of the morgue, once under Blue Mountain John reached for the urn he used to keep the ledgers dry and while sucking the end of a pencil tallied up his stock. *By hell David is doing well aint'e, told yeh e's a natural, I reckon if we ad another three of him we could retire in a couple of years. Wot an miss all the fun, hmm point.*

Right I reckon I'm about done down ere, good c'mon it's my round, let's get back round that fire, I'm bloody freezing, you go ahead Dom and get em' in I'm going to go back through the morgue, I'll see you back at the bar, suite yeh sell John, rather you than me, don't be long now, I'll not and at that he ascended the ladder put his back against the death stone and pushed with his legs, the stone moved a couple of feet sideways, just enough to squeeze through, the cold hit him like a sledge hammer, *bugger maybe I should have listened to Dom after all.* He landed with a thump onto the floor, he looked around and decided everything is as it should be. He pondered for a second, should he climb back down and return through the tunnel? but he remembered trying that once before and try as he might, the death stone was too heavy to replace from below, so he pushed it back into position and decided to make a dash for it. He opened the door just a peep to see just how bad the snow was just now, and immediately shut it again, ok he thought I'll give it five minutes and try it again. In the darkness he started to get the first signs of the creeps which was unusual, because he knew the place inside out, he built the damn thing for pities sake but for whatever the reason it just didn't feel right. After a few more minutes he checked again and this time the snow had stopped. He pushed the door open against the wind and stepped out into the night. It was far too icy under foot to take a decent run so he hunkered into his overcoat pulled the collar up and set off towards the ship inn. He was about to enter the front door when something caught his attention, out to sea there were a couple of lights offshore he only noticed them briefly before the snow came down again, but it held his attention, surely no one was daft enough to have sailed on a night like this. He stood under the shelter of the ships doorway and squinted his eyes, but couldn't see anything, thinking it was a figment of his imagination he was about to turn away and enter the inn when he saw it again. Shit some ones out there. He rushed into the bar and pronounced *fellas there's a ship out there, give over yer silly bugger, no one's daft enough to sail in these conditions, aye that's what I thought too but it's there and their in deep shit, its gunna ground any minute.*

The captain only saw it briefly a split second between the snow showers, no it can't be? Surely to god there can't be land over the starboard side that's impossible any land mass had to be on the port side, it didn't make any sense, and so he put it down to all the hours he'd been working and started to go over his calculations again in his mind. No it can't be it can't be there, as the snow came in again good and thick, he decided it was completely foolish and so dismissed it out of hand.

NAPOLEONS HOMEWARD MARCH 1812

The decision to march to the compass, in the generals eyes maybe wasn't the best idea he'd ever had, they couldn't see a hand in front of their face, and to press on made no sense whatsoever however he was there leader and his decision was final, so they marched. For the first few miles everything went fine until the snow started to fill in the footprints of the advanced party, after that the whole parade was in disarray. *Claude where the hell are we? I can't see my hand in front of my face. Listen Adrien, do you hear that? I can't hear a damned… there did you hear it that time?* In the distance came the unmistakable sound of the bugler. He had been told to walk back until he was just in earshot of the forward parties bugle and to lead the column through the snow drifts by sound alone, as he fell in two of the drummers walked passed him to go even farther down the column to add their drums to the blind march. As the column moved forwards the weakest at the rear kept dropping back and collapsing in the snow, wanting sleep but receiving death as they froze where they lay, nature laying a cold blanket over their rigid bodies. *Claude shall we not rest? I am so tired, fighting this wind all the while. Look ahead of you Adrien, do you see any of them resting? If they can do it then so can we, as long as the bugles and the drums sound we can press on and get out of this bloody country, never to return.*

SALTBURN 1812

As the patrons looked out sheltering their eyes from the maelstrom, every now and again there was a distant faded light to be seen, fighting in the huge seas. *What do you think John? What do I think, I think there's going be a lot of dead sailor's on this beach, very soon depend on it is what I think.* It would be high tide in an hours' time and the forty foot waves were already thundering into the base of hunt cliff, rattling the rocks and bringing them down to crash into the sea. *Right boys we either help them poor buggers or we leave them to die and mop up the mess tomorrow, now I don't know about you lot but I've seen enough death on this beach to last a life time, so I'm going to fetch my ropes and my cork vest, and try as hell to save them all, now your all welcome to join me but I will fully under-stand if you think it's too dangerous especially those of you that have family. Well I came to Saltburn for a bit of adventure, and to date it hasn't let me down so count me in John, thanks Dom, I've a spare cork vest in the back room, let's go get ready and see if we can't save them poor buggers out there.*

LES CONTREBANDIÉRE, SALTBURN 1812

As McCallister held on for dear life climbing up onto the deck he slipped and stumbled and almost fell onto the captain as the ship fell into another trough, How are we doing captain? I think my eyes are playing tricks on me Sergeant, I've maybe been at the wheel to long, wait till the next lull and look over there, tell me if you see anything. As the ship was carried over the top of another monstrous wave McCallister was given a view that he would never forget. There's a bloody cliff, we're in the middle of the North Sea, why are we heading for a cliff? He had just gotten the words out of his mouth when the ship dived into another trough this time however, it hit rock and as soon as that happened chaos ensued the prow was now momentarily stationary which gave the rear of the craft time to catch up and the whole ship turned side on. Everyone on board we're thrown to the floor, as the next wave hit them it lifted the vessel and smashed it into the cliff face, snapping the masts and throwing debris everywhere. The captain holding tightly to the wheel stayed where he was, McCallister however was thrown overboard, and remarkably, landed in about six foot of water as the last wave drained back to sea, he clawed at the rocks and kelp so as not to be dragged along with it cutting the flesh from his numb hands and removing fingernails. With the towering craft now above him Instinct told him to get away from the ship lest it crush him bellow the waves. He had never been a good swimmer and to be honest this wasn't the place to improve. As look would have it he was thrust into the way of a loose crate carrying several dead chickens, which he made a lunge for and held onto with all his might. As the next wave lifted him and the crate they hit the cliff hard at about thirty foot up and as it fell to either side, he was washed away with the white water.

Seawater, any water has to find its own level so when its topped out at forty foot, a wave will collapse and try to flow back to level, which creates an internal current to flow back to sea by the easiest route, and the easiest route on this occasion was along the beach through Pennies hole and deposited on Saltburns doorstep. He coughed and gagged to get the seawater out of his lungs, and finally found his feet.

Frozen to the core he stood shivering, pulled his sodden coat tight around his shoulders and looked around, the snow had started to fall again and as he turned to walk up the beach he bumped into two maniacs running towards the wreck. *Wow mate did you just come off that monster, 'aye'* was all he could manage through chattering teeth, *how many souls aboard mate? About two dozen. Right we're going to see if we can save a few, get yourself up to the Inn and warm up* He nodded his head in reply and slowly made his way towards the dim light appearing through the snow flurries.

Back on board it was chaos, no one stood as the ship was being battered, smashed again and again into the cliff. John and Dom, roped together inched their way deeper and deeper into the huge swell, the ship was acting like a barrier against the waves and allowing them to get ever closer. They were within forty yards when another huge wave lifted the craft and threw it once again into the cliff. The two rescuers were getting equally beaten by the unforgiving sea sheltering as best they could between waves in crevasses at the bottom of the cliff. Shouting against the elements for any survivors, a sudden bark was let out and two very small shapes jumped over board to splash into the cold sea, the cat being a cat didn't care to much for water and started to drown immediately as she mewed in panic Mac plunged his head under and gripped her by the scruff of her neck and with all his strength started to swim to shore. Below deck the passengers and crew were fighting for their lives in the dark, water was flooding the ship fast and anyone caught by it were immediately swept off their feet and drowned thankfully the French were only one deck down and started to climb up into the open, Jean, here to me, his younger brother, never keen on water even at the best of times, was absolutely petrified, trying as best he could to follow his voice and keep up with Henri, he was caught in an eddy and was being pulled backwards, the cold was unbearable and in seconds he lost all feeling in his legs, finally reaching his brother he tried to grab for him but missed several times which exhausted him further, getting pulled under again he managed a gargled shout to Henri, who leapt back in to grab at his brothers coat he pulled him to his side and pleaded to him to wake up and swim but by this time he was lost, once the realisation hit him he sobbed and hugged the limp body the salt from his tears mixing with the salt of the water, as he drifted away. Back in the here and now self-preservation kicked in and Henri started to save himself, he managed to locate the stairway and started to climb, with the water tugging at his legs, he finally made it onto the upper deck, just as a tiny dog and his feline friend jumped overboard into the horrendous conditions. After the loss of his brother, Henri was passed caring, and so after he saw the two animals jump, he decided to do the same. As he hit the water his breath was taken from him, and he knew that he was soon to join his little brother. He sank into the embrace of the cold sea and was about gone when an arm reached down and dragged him back into the land of the living. John pulled at the mariner and between him and Dom, managed to fight him to relative safety. I'm going back to find more John shouted above the roar of the sea, don't be bloody stupid you can't do that again, it was crazy to go in the first place, anyone left on board now will die for sure it's starting to break up already, all we can do is gather up the dead in the morning, c'mon let's get this one back to safety, you've nothing to be ashamed of John, you did your best and that's enough, see reason, if we both go back out there again we'll both die as well you know, lets come back in daylight tomorrow, and see what's left. John had to agree his friend was right, to go back out was madness, so the three staggered back onto the sands and back to the Inn, followed by a small dog and a moth eaten cat.

The few patrons were relieved to see John and Dom walking into the inn and a space was cleared by the fire to let them warm their frozen bodies. When McCallister saw Henri enter he stood and embraced his friend and questioned him about Jean, he just shook his head in reply and McCallister held him closer.

Several logs and whiskey's later, John asked of the two sailors, *why on earth were they out in seas like that?* The Sergeant decided that once again honesty would be the best policy, and so the tale was relived for all them. *'French?' yes gentlemen French and as you can see we don't have two heads and a pumpkin for a nose, but how is it you speak English, it's a long story I'm afraid and at some time I will tell you everything, however for now can we just grieve our lost comrades and leave things till morning?* the general consensus was to let them sleep by the fire and reconvene at first light. So as they got as close to the fire as they could, to steal every last bit of warmth from it the cat and dog nudged their way in to curl up with Henri and fell straight to sleep, steam emanating from their wet fur.

After four hours of restless sleep, John woke the two Frenchmen to ask them one burning question that had been playing on his mind, why were you in such a hurry to get back to France during the worst storm he could remember in ten years, what are you not telling me? *I'm going back out there just now to see what if anything is left. So tell me now, what should I be looking for? If it's what I think it might be, and I don't get your help I'll come back here and shoot you both as spies.* McCallister translated the conversation to Henri, and watched as the reality sank in...*he's going to find the gold, it's the only thing heavy enough not to float back out to sea, at worst there'll be coins scattered all across the rocks, or at best there will be four big chests sitting there waiting to be gathered up. Ask him what assurance he will give us if we help him?* McCallister translated again and was told that their lives would be spared and that they would be put into hiding until such time as they felt they could travel back to France unaided. Dom arrived and caught the latter part of the conversation... *wots up John? Their hiding summet and I'm bartering with their lives to find out what.* As the two Frenchmen whispered between themselves, they both came to the same conclusion; if they escaped and managed to get back to France alive they would spend the rest of their days in jail for losing the gold, or worse shot as thieves. McCallister gave them the only answer left to them. *Do you promise as a gentleman to keep your word?* He offered his hand and repeated, *I promise and as the two men shook, McCallister came straight out with it. Gold, there are four chests full of it, about eighty thousand pounds worth if my mathematics are correct,* the two Englishmen looked at one another, and Dom came to his senses first…*fetch your coat… we're going beach combing.* After speaking to Henri again he asked a request, *can we come with you? Henri here lost his brother in the wreck and would like the chance to retrieve his body if at all possible, yeh why the hell not, and you can give us a hand with the gold, it's not as if you're going anywhere at present, we'll help if we can.* And so five hours after high tide, the four rode a wagon in freezing temperatures down to the wreck site, to see what they could find.

What they found was total devastation the bulk of the ship was no longer there, but the whole area was covered in detritus, pieces of rigging, scraps of sail, large beams, the carcass of a horse that had gotten wedged between the rocks, even a random wagon wheel that had lodged its self about thirty foot up on a small ledge in the cliff face, as they looked about, Dom let out a slow whistle and it being the first wreck he had ever witnessed said that it looked as if the devil himself had come from hades with a big hammer and smashed the ship to pieces during the night. Henri was desperate to find the body of his sibling and hurried to every undistinguishing shape on the rocks. Albeit low tide the seas were still massive, and John estimated that they only had a couple of hours before the waves would be perilously close again ready to inflict even more damage. As they started to rummage through the debris, Dom stated more to himself than anyone else, so *golds heavy right? So a big box of gold is very heavy, which means that if the box broke free of the ship it wouldn't travel very far, in fact,* as he started to walk slowly towards the cliff, *a big box of gold wouldn't move at all,* he bent down to move a large section of torn sail fabric and whispered *bingo. John over here I think we've hit the jackpot.* After a second glance, he shouted over to McCallister, *sergeant you best give Henri a shout as well.* As the men folded back the sail one edge was tangled around a victim's body and as Dom started to untangle it Henri let out a cry, he had found Jean. Henri bent down and lifted his brother free from the rocks, carried him over to the wagon and placed him very gently onto its boards, he pulled some sheeting over his body as if tucking him in at bed time, something he used to do when they were children, he took one last look at his peaceful features and covered his face. After he shook himself down and regained his composure he walked back over to where the others had exposed the chests, and said to McCallister *right let's get this done.* Three of the chests were still in tacked however the fourth had sustained some damage and had spilled some of its contents onto the bedrock, in the gloomy morning light, the coins glittered and shone like the stars in the heavens. *Dom bring the wagon as close as you dare, we don't want to strain our backs if we can help it.* Once the wagon was close enough, John gathered up some of the rigging ropes, he uncoupled the pony and told the men to gather rocks and place them under the wheels to act as breaks he then tethered the ponies yolk and drew the rope back over the wagon, being careful not to disturb Henri's brother in the process, he then asked the men to search for some timber to fashion a ramp up to the rear of the bed. Once done, he tied the rope to the first of the chests and slapped the pony on its rump, as it took the strain he guided it forward and inch by inch the chest was dragged up onto the back of the wagon and across its boards into position. They repeated this three times over and secured them all on board. The last of the chests was a little bit more complicated, because of the damage it wouldn't hold the weight of the remaining gold, so with the tide now on the push the decision was made to man handle it onto the wagon, which was laborious and time con-suming however with them all keeping an eye on the threatening waves they didn't stop till the last coin was pocketed. With only moments to spare they removed the rocks, jumped aboard and pulled away from the cliffs. Once back onto the sands the pony struggled to pull the laden wagon and so everyone jumped down to walk and tease more strength from the poor animal. At last they approached the morgue and pulled right up to the doors to the pony's relief. With the day pressing on and the chance of being spotted the gold was unceremoniously dumped onto the door step and dragged into the building. Once all trace of the treasure was hidden, the four men out of respect picked up the body of Henri's brother and reverently placed it upon the cold stone, where it was covered again and left to rest. Shaking each other's hands the deal was confirmed and the four men returned to the Ship Inn. As they warmed their aching limbs by the fire, McCallister asked *where are we to be hidden? On the other side of the cliffs at a small fishing village by the name of Staithes.* The two Frenchmen totally at the mercy of this man, hoped more than believed him to be genuine.

HOUSES OF COMMONS, LONDON 1812

He killed how many? Well m 'lord details are a little sketchy at present but I am well informed at the very least a dozen excise men. Well if this be the case we must bring this Smuggler to justice and make him dance for his crimes. As Prime Minister, Robert Banks Jenkinson was relatively new to the post after the assassination of his predecessor in May of that year, and was against capital punishment on the whole, however a crime of this nature, in his eyes had to be punished in the severest manner. *Summon Sir Harry Calvert, I will speak with him in my private quarters and instruct him to deal with this fellow in the North.* Sir Calvert had recently been honoured with the position of Knight Grand Cross, and had a long and illustrious career in the armed forces, so to call on his expertise seemed a logical decision by all concerned.

When the two men met it was with a warm hand and a fine scotch, *please Sir Calvert do sit down.* Once the pleasantries were out of the way the Prime Minister came to the matter in hand, *I don't know if you are aware Sir, but we have a Smuggler in the North Country who is quite frankly running amok, the countries excise officials have been aware of his illegal activities for some years, however they have had up until recently no evidence to bring him to justice. It would seem that they finally got the evidence they had been looking for and so put together a band of officers to arrest the fellow and catch him in the act so to speak. Unfortunately it seems that he had been tipped off and gathered his own men to fight our brave officers and between them a fracas ensued on the sands and they killed a dozen of our excise men. So Minister what roll am I to play in this plot? Well Sir Calvert, three of the party managed to escape this Smugglers trap and are resided in London willing to testify against him, so what I am proposing is that if you are willing, to put a team of soldiers together to flush this fellow out and bring him to justice. Well Minister as you are fully aware our troops are spread a little thin at the moment what with the troubles in the America's and so forth, however if it will stop you from losing face then I will put a small band of men together and we shall bring this upstart of yours to justice.*

THE SHIP INN SALTBURN 1812

As the four sat at a table at the back of the Inn, McCallister was starting to flag a little, they had all had next to no sleep and with the exertion of the morning they were all feeling the effects, it was only the thought of the treasure now hidden away that kept them pepped up. Henri was in his own world idly stroking mac who was sat in his lap, making strange smells every now and then, and being scrutinised by the cat. *So let me get this right your father was Irish, you were born in France to your French mother and you speak six different languages, well six fluently I can get by with a few more, what a remarkable man you are Sergeant, and it was your talent for languages that got you on this mission, and almost killed, I might add yep a remarkable man. May I ask what you intend to do with the gold now you possess it, well I most certainly won't be giving back to Bonaparte that's for sure, maybe we will share it between the four of us! Who knows? For now it will stay where it is until we can be certain that no one is going to come looking for it, and that being the case we four must promise not to breathe a word to anyone about it, well we're hardly going to say anything, we only know you two, and if I'm very much mistaken I don't believe anyone else in this establishment* speaks *French, true but are we all agreed* and once translated to Henri, they put their hands over the table one on top one another's, and this was their bond, four wanted men in league together.

LONDON 1812

The chosen men were all assembled and Sir Calvert cured their curiosity and explained the mission and the reason why they were chosen. *Gentlemen apart from one or two new faces I know most of you and I know you are all familiar with myself, so I will trifle with you no more and explain why you have all been chosen for this mission. It would appear our Prime Minister is in a predicament insofar as there is some upstart up in the North country that is embarrassing him, and now that the fellow is a multiple murderer of the kings men, we have got to the point whereby he must be brought to justice, now the regular Jonnies have tried and failed and so we rely on you to bring him back for the hangman. You must understand that he has to be brought back alive, you may injure him if you must, but the villain must go on trial and must hang. The Prime Minister has offered you funds from the treasury for your inconvenience, a kind of finder's fee I suppose, so what say you? Are you all up for the task?* And without hesitation they replied, *Aye Sir.*

NAPOLEONS RETREAT NOVEMBER 1812

As the troops marched relentlessly on in the terrible conditions, the Russians started to attack them with renewed vigour, knowing the French were weak with hunger and disabled by the cold the Cossacks especially, turned the one sided fight into a game picking them off with their lances one after another. As the advance party neared the Berezina River in late November they found their route blocked by the Russians, and were brought to a halt. Eventually Napoleon forced a way through and built makeshift bridges so that they could cross. After the bulk of the army had crossed three days later, he ordered the bridges burnt, stranding ten thousand stragglers on the other side. *What's he doing Claude does he not know we still need to cross? Why is he leaving us to the mercy of the Cossacks, The bastard's running away that's what he's doing leaving us here to die, after all we've been through, well I'm not going to give him that satisfaction, quickly Adrien follow me to the river bank.* They pushed their way through the astonished and crest fallen crowd, and down to the water's edge. *Right throw away your musket and sabre and follow me into the water, are you bloody mad we'll freeze to death, no we won't, if we get too cold we'll swim closer to the fires, and if we get too hot then we'll swim further away, now come on and stop moaning.* As they both entered the river, the cold took their breath away, and they both started to shiver immediately, but then Claude's plan started to work, they kept hold of the burning bridge, working hand over hand, and with their legs floating near to the surface the radiated head was keeping them reasonably warm. As they neared the middle of the river the bridge broke in two, and the pair had to swim to catch the far side as it was taken slowly by the flow. Thankfully it was still tied to the far bank and so the free end carried them over to the other side. As they bumped into the river bank the pair scrambled up onto dry land, putting the flames between them and the far bank. *Quickly Adrien get undressed and throw your clothes onto the fire, are you mad, we'll freeze, you will if you don't do as I say, now get those wet clothes off right now.* It was quite surreal with the pair of them sitting naked on a river bank in Russia, in the middle of winter watching the Cossacks slaughtering their countrymen on the other side. After ten minutes they dragged their clothes back from the fire, and all though they weren't completely dry they weren't far from. *Claude, you might be the craziest man in the whole of France but for the first time in two months I'm actually warm. Come on you, we'll have to move on we're not out of trouble yet, and I've got a debt to pay, what debts that? I'm going to catch up with that cowardly bastard and rip his heart out with my bare hands.* As the two brothers set off they picked up their pace to try and catch up with what was left of Le Grande Armée. The more they advanced the more bodies started to pile up in front of them, and after a few hours they could hear the sounds of fighting in the distance. Travelling alone, the enemy didn't take a lot of notice of the pair, even so they gathered weapons from the fallen as they advanced. In time they caught up to the rear of the main troop and from here they worked their way forward until there in the distance, they could see the Emperor still riding his white stallion, surrounded by his generals. It was December the eighth, when Claude and Adrien finally got close enough to be able to take a shot at Bonaparte. It was starting to get dark when the horses slowed and then stopped, the riders dismounted and gathered themselves together to talk, as Claude watched, he decided this was his chance, he slowly walked into a cluster of trees, not more than twenty five yards away. He loaded the musket he had gathered, and put the barrel to rest between the fork of a branch. As he watched there was a lot of waving arms and pointing back to the main bulk of men. It appeared to Claude that whatever the discussion was about, it had reached a conclusion and the men were ready to mount up again, he aimed the weapon approximately were he thought Napoleon would mount and felt the trigger with his cold finger. Napoleon mounted not five foot from where he was aiming, he adjusted the aim to hit centre of his body mass, squeezed a little harder, breathed out and took the shot…just as a general leapt up to his mount and the lead ball hit him in the back of his head taking off his face which exploded all over the Emperors riding cape. Claude dropped to the ground and peered from behind the tree, to see Napoleon Bonaparte complete with the rest of his Generals and advisors, gallop from view, never to look back. Adrien heard the shot and ran to his brother, *did you hit him Claude? No I missed,* inside he was cursing himself thinking he had frightened them away. But as he told his brother later while eating the general's horse, *there'll be other opportunities Adrien, other chances* and six days later what was left of Le Grand Armée finally crossed the border and marched out of Russia.

LONDON 1812

As the soldiers readied themselves for the ride north, their Major gave one last inspection, checked the inventory and gave the order to move out. He had always loved the sound of shod hooves on cobbles it gave the mounted men a natural drum roll as they left for their foe. Dressed in all their finery the green jacketed riflemen demanded respect from whosoever laid eyes upon them and it gave the whole party an air of superiority that that they loved. They expected the journey to take just short of a week at a steady pace. They also expected the job to take only a couple of days, and so the whole venture should be completed well within three weeks, and they would be back in London by the end of the month all that much richer, so the whole party as they rode away were all in fine spirits and full of expectation.

SALTBURN 1812

The next day, John had to broach the subject of the burial of Henri's brother. *Sergeant I've been thinking on our resident over in the morgue, and where to put him to rest, do you think you could have a word with Henri about it cause if we don't do something soon he'll start to smell worse than Henri does,* liking his dry humour he smiled, *he's over there now, Henri's been sitting with him most of the morning, it's sad to see someone grieve so much, they were very close you know and he was the only family that he had left. Well he will have to sort himself out and make himself some new family, he'll have to have a bath first though, and get rid of that stinkin dog. Hang on here I'll walk over and see if I can persuade him to come and talk to us about it.* He rapped on the door and walked in, *how are you doing Henri? He wasn't coping very well you know, I think all the battles got too much for him, one of the last conversations we had was about leaving all the fighting behind, and starting anew, this mission was to be our big break, and now without him I've no one to share it with, I can't go home, not that it matters cause there's no one left there anyway, to be honest with you Sarge I feel absolutely lost, I don't have the first idea of what to do! Well I've just been talking to John, and he reckons you should start a family of your own, oh aye that's a great idea and how many French girls do you know around these parts? Come on let's leave Jean be and get back to the land of the living.* The two of them walked back over to the Inn and ordered four flagons. *Here you go boys one for each of us, oh by the way, John when is that barman going to ask for payment? Oh don't worry about that it's all on my tab, you can eat and drink as much as you like, I've told him that I'll pick up the bill, oh, well that's very kind thanks, you don't have to thank me, you two have made us very rich men. Right to business, tell him I'm very sorry for his loss but things have to be decided upon, there's a small fishing village just up the beach by the name of Marske and on the cliff top there is a church and grave yard that overlooks the sea where I've had to bury some of my friends over the years, and you'll have heard of Captain Cook I suppose, Aye, well his dads buried there as well, now what I'm thinking is that Jean will be in good company, so wot do yeh think?* When McCallister finished translating he could see the transformation in Henri's face, *Captain Cook? Aye, Mon dieu, Oui Oui Jean aimerait que.* McCallister looked at John and in a sober voice quietly whispered…*Thanks,* John just smiled in reply. That afternoon John and McCallister took Henri with them across the cliff tops to Marske, the winds were starting to settle down a little and for the first time in weeks the sun made an appearance. It was only a short walk and to pass the time they chatted about the Napoleonic wars and the part that the two Frenchmen played in them, and John opened up a little about his dealings with the excise men that were out to get him, and all in all it made for a very pleasant afternoon. When the three of them reached the church with its low sandstone walled grave yard, John took them over to one very substantial white marble grave stone and pointed to the inscription on the front, *there you go Captain Cooks dads final resting place,* it was only then that McCallister had to admit that he couldn't read or write and asked if John could read it out for him to translate to Henri. *Six languages…*John started to say, when McCallister cut him short, *Yes I am perfectly aware how many languages I can speak and I am also aware how many languages I can't read or right in, so just read the damned thing and I will translate because unfortunately you can't!* John smiled, and started to read it to the pair. *To commemorate James Cook Snr father of Captain James Cook founder of the new world born 1694 died April first 1779 aged 85. Well Henri what do you think of that? fine company for Jean to rest with,* he was about to answer when John gestured to a couple more stones, and this time no one had to translate, they were very plain and made from sandstone, and there was no inscription at all, carved into the stone was a very simple skull and bones. *These two were very good friends of mine, but I couldn't carve their names, because to do so would have brought the authorities down upon their families, so to* *mark their profession I had the skull carved. So now you have seen the place do you still want Jean to rest here?* When McCallister had translated for Henri, and he looked about the place, he couldn't think of a finer spot for his little brother to be put to rest, then Henri did a strange thing, he walked over to John as if to shake his hand, stood for a second and drew him into an embrace, *Je vous remercie mon ami. Right let me walk over to the vicarage and speak with the parson and I'll ask if he can do the service tomorrow? Oui…sorry, yes.* After the meeting John called the pair to walk with him to another Ship Inn this one much smaller in Marske. *Come on you two I'll treat you to an ale, but please try not to speak French in here, you'll be ok with me but they are very suspicious of any outsiders and if they hear a foreign language they'll hang the pair of you.* As they settled in to the small dark building John told them a tale which didn't alleviate their fears. *See on the other side of the Tees, North of here, a ship came to ground much the same as yours did at a town by the name of Hartlepool and the ships mascot a small monkey survived and got swept up onto the beach, well the locals had never seen the likes of it and took it as a French spy. They dragged the poor animal into the town square and hung the bugger, so when I say keep quiet, keep quiet.* The next day was Jeans funeral and as arranged the four brought his body wrapped in a shroud on the back of the wagon for midmorning. The parson was a little curious, that the deceased brother did not speak a single word throughout the service but was informed that he was very close to his sibling and was distraught at his loss, which he said was understandable under the circumstances, as the last prayers were said and the customary earth was thrown, the parson closed his bible and nodded to the grave diggers as he left, but before they had a chance to walk across John jumped into the grave and uncovered Jeans face from the shroud he reached onto his pocket and pulled out two gold coins, he lent forwards and placed the coins onto Jeans closed eyes, once done he covered him once more looked up into the faces of his friends and said *for the ferryman,* and Henri shed one last tear for his little brother. The return journey to Saltburn was very sedate and it wasn't until they reached the Ship Inn that John turned to them and said *right you go get the beer in, I'll put the wagon away and then we are all going to get completely ratted,* which is exactly what they did. I'm sure it was mentioned at some point through the evening that they were to travel to Staithes the next day, but perhaps it got lost in translation because when the cock crowed no one seemed very keen in traveling anywhere, so at the crack of dawn…about half past ten they set off over the cliff tops and walked the ten miles or so to meet with their future landlord. McCallister as they approached Cowbar had to ask, *are you sure we will be safe here John? As safe as any of us can be mate, and hey who knows you might even like it here, they are a friendly bunch,* and as they crossed the footbridge into Staithes they were met not by a landlord but a landlady, *Gentlemen may I introduce you to my sister Sarah. I thought you had no family left John? Aye well Staithes holds a lot of secrets Sergeant and we happen to be the newest.* Sarah hurried them down one of the narrow streets and into a small door, which led into a scullery and then into the living room that was occupied by four young women all seated repairing fishing nets and lobster pots, McCallister turned to John with a questioning expression, and once again he replied with nothing more than a smile, *I think you might enjoy hiding out in Staithes gents, I think I already am.* As they were seated John did the introductions, *gentlemen this is my sister Sarah as you know, and these are our cousins Ann, Mary, Maureen and Kathleen, ladies may I introduce you to two friends of mine from Belgium, this is Henri Verrel and this is Sergeant McCallister both of them on the run from the French for stealing one of their ships,* as he was explaining this, McCallister looked at him and raised an eyebrow, which brought an even bigger smile to Johns face, and he winked back at him. *Sarah, will you please show these two their new accommodation in the priest hole, it's a little cramped but no more so than that ship you managed to sink.* As the introductions were being made Maureen seemed to like what she saw and as john was telling them about the stolen ship her face positively lit up, it would seem all girls like a rogue, especially a mysterious handsome one.

HULL 1812

As the riflemen were carrying out the Prime Ministers orders, helping the excise office to continue its duties, and bring a known felon to justice it was, in their eyes only right and proper to bed their horses in the excise office stables when they decided to overnight in Hull. Once the horses were fed and watered the men sought an Inn where they could find some supper, and something to wash it down with. Once found and judged by all to be sufficient for their needs, they settled in for the evening. The conversation eventually turned to the business in hand and the following days plans. *Will we reach Saltburn tomorrow Major? Well it's a full day's ride from here, so if we get an early enough start, we should be settled in as we are now.* As the night drew on one or two of the riflemen would no doubts regret drinking as much as they were at present, however that was hours away and they were enjoying the good company. The curious locals inquired after their foe and a loose word here and a speculation there soon had them fully aware of what they were up to. One of the regulars, who happened to know, a friend of a friend, managed to get word of the newcomers to Frank and Wilf, who in turn happened to know a rider that might be heading to Saltburn before daybreak. And so long before the soldiers were even pulling on their boots, even in Staithes John was aware of what was happening. *What do you think John? Well I for one would like to see these people who the Right Honourable Robert Banks Jenkinson thinks will capture me and send me to the gallows, and once I have I'll decide then what is to be done. So are you thinking of going back to Saltburn then? Not thinking I'm going back in the morning, is that wise John? Maybe not but forewarned is forearmed, so I'll be back in a day or two and I'll let you know exactly what's happening.*

SALTBURN PRESENT DAY

Now what are you staring at? Nothing really, it's something you said before about the tales of smugglers tunnels that you were told about as a kid, yes but as I've said already, I searched high and low and I never came up with so much as a penny, well maybe you were looking in the wrong place. How do you mean the wrong place? Where else would you find a tunnel but under your feet? Well you know when you said that the original Saltburn, got its name from the amount of sea water that was deposited into the stream after a particularly high tide, yes, ok come with me onto the beach, she took Ryans hand and followed him down to the high water mark and the pair turned to look landward again. *Ok Sherlock what am I looking at? So look at the water level in the stream and then cast a glance to the Inn, right and this proves what exactly? Well as a rough guide I reckon that your home is about ten to maybe fifteen feet higher than the stream, and well that's it don't you see, there's not enough height to dig down, the tunnel would flood at every high tide. So what does that tell us, that they dug up? Have you gone completely gaga no one can dig up, it's impossible. Not if you start at the high tide level it isn't. You've lost me completely now. Is there a cellar in the ship? Yes a great big bugger there's a hatch behind the bar that takes you down to it, that's got to be it! Got to be what, stop talking in riddles, I'm not, look I'll bet that your cellar floor is about level with or just above the high tide mark and couldn't go any lower than that because it would flood all the time, so if we say that your cellar floor is maybe fifteen foot down then there would be about seven foot of earth above your head if you decided to dig a tunnel down there, more than enough to keep a roof over your head. So you're saying that there is a tunnel under the ship. Yes why not, I mean the measurements are only rough but I bet you there not that far off the mark, will your dad let us have a look do you think? Yeh provided he doesn't see us going down there with a sledge hammer and a shovel. Come on you lets go and have an adventure.* She took his hand again and the two of them walked briskly back to the Inn.

Hull 1812

As the troops were rallied, there were the inevitable hang overs, and so once the horses had been fed, the head sore soldiers mounted up and set off around ten o'clock at the Majors annoyance. *Sir where is our route to take this morning? We will set for Beverley, and then onto Malton and Pickering, then it's across the moors and on to Saltburn. Will we still make it before dark sir? I believe it will be touch and go after our delayed departure however if we up the pace we may just manage it in time* and so with the order given their trot became a gallop.

SALTBURN 1812

When John arrived in Saltburn it was midmorning, and as he walked into the back room of ship Inn he was confronted with not just Frank and Wilf which was a shock in its self but the word had got out and Jeffrey with his two future brother in-laws Samson and Daniel, David and Dom were sat there too. *Well I'll be who invited you reprobates to the party? Hi John, just thought you might need a helping hand mate, we'll not let the buggers get their hands on you, not if we have anything to do with it! Hang on boys let's just reel it in a bit we nearly lost you last time round David I'll not put Erin through that again. Don't worry John none of us want a repeat of that, all were saying is if you do need us then were here for you after all if a bloke doesn't have mates then he's got bugger all. Ok let's agree now, there is to be no confrontation this time no one gets hurt, but that doesn't stop us tying them in knots, not physically with rope, but verbally we will fill their heads so full of rubbish that they won't know their arse from their elbow, false information can throw any one especially if its corroborated by a third party, so we'll have them running up and down the beach until they bump into one another other, and when they brush themselves down we'll do it all over again.*

SALTBURN 1812 EARLY EVENING

As the saddle soar Soldiers canted onto the beach and up to the front door of the Ship, the Major dismounted, handed the reigns to his second in command and went to enter the Inn, as the door was opened it spilt light and warmth into the cold evening air. The barman who was a party to the conversation of earlier wasn't surprised as the room went quiet and he looked up into the ruddy features of the Major. *Young man, I am come here to inquire on lodgings, oh aye for how many? There are twelve of us in all, so we will be looking for six rooms, and we will pay handsomely for them, how handsomely is that then? Well if you will accommodate us for a week, I might say one Guinea per room per night, so what say you? We don't rent rooms Sergeant. Well what the devil was all that bartering about just now? Curiosity Sergeant, bloody rude I would call it and refrain from calling me Sergeant, my title is Major. You could get some digs over in Redcar I reckon, there's a couple of boardin houses in the town centre, and how far is that man, my troops and I have been riding all day and we are in want of rest. Oh it's about six mile just keep ridin till you run out of sand then look for the lights, obliged my man, I will bid you farewell,* and just as he opened the door to leave, the barman shouted after him *goodnight Sergeant,* which sent the customers in to fits of laughter. *Ride till you run out of sand is what the man said, and then look for the lights, now as far as I can see they are the only lights around, go and rap on the door and ask for lodgings.* Obeying his order the soldier dismounted and walked over to the homestead as the rest of the troop dismounted to stretch their legs. As the door was opened, Jeffrey asked *what can I do for you soldier. We are in search of lodgings and require some directions could you possibly help? Well youv'e passed the finishing post by a couple of miles mate this ere's Coatham, Redcars back that ways a while. Ok are there any lodgings to be had there? Oh aye if you go through the centre to the back of the town you'll come to a big wooden building in want of a lick of paint, knock on the door there and I'm sure they'll put you up. Many thanks sir.* He turned on his heel and spoke with his comrades. *It's back that way boys, a couple of miles he said, right lets mount up and try and find the retched place before daybreak shall we?* As the soldiers rode into the town everything was as the house holder had described, there in front of them was the building in question, so the tired troops all dismounted and walked over to the door. *What do you find so amusing Jeffrey? Oh not much my luv, come on somethings tickled you, wots doin? Well see those soldiers wot are huntin John? Yeh, well it was them at the door just now lookin for beds for the night, oh aye, well I've just sent the bloody lot of em to the abattoir.* It started as a giggle but ended in hysterics for the both of them. *Oh I can't wait to get my turn, this is going to be the most fun we've had in years.* It was barely daybreak when the soldiers decided enough was enough, if it wasn't the god awful smell it was the bloody flies that kept them awake all night, but after all the refusals for accommodation, they got last night this was the only other option, and as one said *well at least it's a roof over our heads.* Not only did the troops not sleep but neither did the horses, as they entered the building they got all skittish, instinctively knowing what the smell meant and wondering which one of them would be next. By morning every one of them were wild eyed and itching to get out, hoofing the ground in near panic. The now ratty soldiers decided to leave the building and find some decent accommodation whilst it was daylight, rather than last minute like yesterday, so they gathered up their bed rolls mounted up and made a dash for the fresh air. As they gathered outside a trades-man happened by and the Major stopped him and a little less brusquely asked, *kind sir please could you direct us to some accommodation, for us to rest this evening. Wasting your time round ere mate, you want to ride over to Middlesbrough, got much more chance over there. And how far is this Middlesbrough sir? It's about ten miles in that direction, no time at all on them fiery beasts I'll bet. Thank you sir we will follow your advice and try our luck, good day to you.* As they set off in the direction shown every one of the horses wanted to gallop as fast as they could to get away from the smell, but try as they might they couldn't escape the odour that clung to them and the soldiers garments and so the ride was not one without problems, many a soldier was un saddled on route and sat while the others tried to catch the terrified creatures. Eventually they found Middlesbrough and entered the streets looking for an Inn with stables. *There sir down that street.* The troop all stopped and turned to where the soldier was pointing. *The Dick Turpin, well let us go and see if there is room at the Inn.* As the exhausted men sat outside the major walked inside the establishment, and was met by a very burley young man who questioned there intensions. *Sir my men and I haven't slept in two days and our horses are in need of attention also, would you have room to spare for twelve men and the same of beasts? Well I reckon I can put you all up but at a cost, Sir I will gladly pay what is your charge? Well let me think, how about a Guinee a night per person and a Guinee a night per horse, WHAT! That's daylight robbery, maybe so but that's the price, ok, ok we will pay the sum, in advance!* For once the Major was lost for words but nodded all the same. The arrangements and payment met, the Major asked if there were any where they might breakfast and was directed to the stall holder down the street, and with earnest gratitude said *thank you. Oh and ask for the gypsy toast it's especially good* so the whole company went to eat. As they were waiting for their order the Major was asked of his plans for the day, the men secretly hoping for a day off but it was not to be. *Once we have breakfasted we will ride to Saltburn and see if we can find this John Andrew character, for the sooner we apprehend him the sooner we get out of this god forbidden place.* As they were finishing up four of the soldiers had their thumbs in their mouths, as did the Major, trying to burst their blisters. Right mount up and lets ride and with the order given twelve men rode back to Saltburn. As David was standing watching them go Erin came up behind him and put her hand in his. *Is something the matter darlin? No not as such, but I think we might hold a party tonight, what's the occasion? Does there need to be one? No I spose, then a party it is in honour of our engagement, what engagement you avent asked me.* On that he turned dropped to one knee, and took her hand in his. *Erin my love, will you do me the honour of becoming my wife, I can't offer you much but if you will have me I will look after and take care of you for all of my life.* Erin simply burst into tears, and in between sobs she just managed to say yes. After the couple got back out of bed David asked if she would like a trip to the coast in the wagon, to go and visit their friends and tell them the good news. *Oh what a wonderful idea David I'd love that, I can't wait to tell Nell, and see the surprise on her face, right you are, let's get dressed and set off right away.*

The soldiers had already arrived at Saltburn and were trying to get information from the locals. Going from door to door, threatening eviction unless they were told of John Andrew's whereabouts. When they reconvened the Major gathered all that they had been told, and wrote it in his ledger. *Right we have two accounts of him living in a cabin in the woods, one that says he went back to his birth place in Scotland. Two that states he drowned at sea. And two more that he is buried in an unmarked grave in the grounds of the church on the cliff top at Marske, oh and one that he lives in a tunnel network underground, that I for one think is highly fanciful. Right let's put these falsehoods aside as best we can, starting with this cabin in the woods. We shall leave the horses here and fan out in the woods, then cover the entire distance between here and Brotton, it should take no more than a few hours, and if we find nothing then at least we can tick it off our list.* As they started out it was fairly easy going however as they advanced the valley walls got steeper and the scrub became more dense so the soldiers had to hack at it with their sabres to enable progress, after two hours of nonstop fighting the men were absolutely exhausted and they weren't even half way through, the Major especially was finding the pace hard going and with very little sleep, he had to admit defeat he spotted an old fallen log and sat down heavily onto it, *Major, are you alright* came a voice from somewhere up the track *yes I'm fine keep going till you reach Brotton then cut back over the clifftops on your return, I'll see you back in Saltburn presently.* As he listened to the chopping and the grunts of labour getting more and more distant, he reached into his tunic and retrieved his hip flask. As he felt the burn of the first swallow run down deep he had to admit it was always good company. Word in the barracks was that maybe he drank a little too much, but in his eyes, no more than anyone else, anyway what's it to them it's my liver after all. While fighting this argument once again in his head, he hardly noticed that he had emptied the thing. Oh bother I was just getting a taste for that. He recorked the flask and returned it to his pocket, and on shaky legs stood and turned about determined to retrace his tracks and was certain to be back in Saltburn in half the time it took him to get to this point. As he set off he noticed just how quiet the woods were this time of year, in fact the only noise he could hear was the sound of his own laboured breath and the twigs snapping under his boots. As he travelled further through the undergrowth he found himself using his sabre more and more, *this can't be right where is the path I cleared on the way in?* there was now no sign of any sliced briar to be found, he decided the best policy would be to walk downhill until he reached the stream and then follow it back to the coast, he may get his boots wet but at least he would be out of these damned woods, as he stumbled and tripped on his descent he found himself at a large land fall, almost a cliff in itself that the stream having delusions of grandeur had gouged out of the rock and swept away. As the Major descended further still he reached out to slow himself on a clifftop sapling, which he found had no more strength than he did and clutching it still fell over the precipice and dropped forty foot onto the streams embankment. When he gained consciousness he was half in and half out of the water. His sabre had cut a slice out of his leg which was bleeding profusely. As the major assessed the damage, he was enough of a realist to know he was done for and decided not to fight it, he'd had a good life, had some fine friends and a good reputation. In fact he had nothing to be embarrassed about when he met his maker, and so he relaxed breathed out and said bugger as a log caught in the current hit him on the shoulder, if dying in the wilderness all alone isn't enough you have to go and pour salt on the wound. He then passed out. When he came too he was on his feet, well almost he was being carried towards, what looked like a building he should know, but was too groggy to figure it out. *Does this fella belong to you? I found him half drowned in the woods. Major are you ok?* He obviously wasn't and as they took charge of him they asked his saviours name so that the Major could thank him himself when he was a little better, *oh don't bother the Major with little things like that, I'm not looking for any medals, now you get that cut seen to, that could turn nasty that could,* and as they watched the stranger walk away they loaded the Major onto a horse and set off for Middlesbrough.

When David and Erin pulled in to Coatham Jeffrey was stood outside their house having a quiet smoke. *Hello you's two this is a nice surprise. As they jumped down she said you'll have to give that up when the baby comes,* pointing at his pipe, *it'll hurt the little ones lungs, wot little one? Has she still not told yeh? Told me wot?* As the penny started to drop he yelled out for Nell. As she appeared at the doorway Erin said *sorry Nell I didn't mean to let the secret out, I just thought you'd ave told im by now! Told me wot Nell, Oh Jeffrey I'm sorry luv I would have told you sooner but*

I was afraid summat might happen, we are going to have a baby my luv, wot? When? Summer, next year. When it finally sank in he ran to her and hugged her, then stopped and started fussing, *e'yah luv sit yeh sell down lass, can I get you anything, aye, you can get my fella back I'm not too keen on this new one who fuss's all the time.* So it was congratulations all round Nell had never had so much fuss made of her, and was secretly enjoying the attention. *Right well we've got a surprise as well, oh yes!! stop it Jeffrey it's not that, not yet anyway, no it's that well were going to get wed. Eeh pet when did he propose, just this morning and to celebrate were havin a party at the Dick Turpin tonight an we want everyone to come. Well wot do yeh think Nell? Wot do I think, I wouldn't miss it for the world, come ere lass an give us a hug.* As the girls sat gossiping, David suggested he and Jeffrey ride over to Saltburn and invite John and the boys. *Aye on yeh go we've got far too much to talk about.* So the two of them jumped aboard and set off down the beach. *Are Frank an Wilf still about? Aye I reckon they said they were going to stick around awhile, until john decides wot to do with them soldiers, oh the ones that are stopping in the Dick Turpin, them soldiers! Get out when did this appen, just, they knocked on the door this morning and said they wanted to rent the rooms upstairs, so I said ok and its costin them a small fortune, yeh but their the enemy, I know but remember the old phrase Jeffrey keep your friends close, but keep your enemies even closer, you never know john might get some info out of them if their guards are down, hmm not a bad plan even if I do say so me'self.* As the two of them pulled up outside the Ship they tied up the horse, and walked inside. *Hello fellas hows tricks, hiya John, things are good and we have news, well get yeh'selves an ale an come an sit with us. Right give it up, well, I'm gunna be a daddy! congratulations Jeffrey I'm chuffed to bits for you both, how's Nell, oh head in the clouds, as ever, don't think I'm getting soft or out but I didn't think that I could luv her any more, but I was wrong, I luv her so much I'm ready to burst, aye soft, oh definitely soft, pack it in the lot of yeh. And we have more news! But this time it's down to David, go on then lad, wots up, well me an Erin are gunna get wed, an were avin a party tonight at the Dick Turpin to celebrate an we'd luv it if you could all come. Sounds good to me, wouldn't miss it for the world, count us in, great Erin will be so pleased. I've got some news now, see them soldiers wot are after me, aye, well I only went an pulled there Major out of the river this morning, ad to carry im all the way back ere, alive? Only just I reckon if I hadn't appened by he'd be dead by now, wot appened then, well he reeked of whisky I think he got a bit tipsy an fell in, is he ok then? Oh aye I handed him over to his mates an they took im away to patch im up, aye to the Dick Turpin. Wot? I've got the lot of them stopping upstairs, ave yeh now? Yup an if their Major is laid up I reckon the soldiers will be at the party tonight. Hey life doesn't get much better than this. Drink up boy's it's my round.* When the two of them finally arrived back in Coatham, the girls were waiting for them, *oh we was wondering when you two were going to grace us with your presence look at all these sandwiches we've made, likely they'll be all stale by now. We've only been gone an hour or two, they can't go stale in that time, oh give over Jeffrey, she's only pullin yeh leg, aye yeh daft bugger, come ere an give us a luv,* she said with her arms out wide. *Wots with all these sandwich's then girls wot are they for? For tonights party we can't ave folk coming from far an wide, an not feed em, wot a good idea, never even thought about that. Men were would they be without us eh? Well we'd all starve for one. Right wots the plan? Are you two coming back with us or d'you want to make your own way over? Nah we'll jump in with you if that's ok? Aye of course it is, great, let me go an make myself presentable I won't be long, an keep your hands off them sarnies.*

Back at the Dick Turpin the company surgeon, who was a butcher by trade finished sewing up the gash in the Majors leg, *you'll have to keep your weight off it for a few days Major, not a problem it hurts like hell, can you fetch me something for the pain, a stiff whiskey should do the trick, you'd be better off pouring it onto the wound than drinking it Major, listen your very good with cat gut and needles but I'll be the one to decide on the medication, so go and fetch a bottle and be quick about it.* As the land lord was out on business the soldier helped himself to a bottle of the finest from behind the bar and left a note telling him to add it to their bill. As the Major settled in, the soldiers decided they would go to the stables and rub down their horses, they were half way through the task when a wagon rolled up driven by the landlord. *Hows the Major doin boys, oh he'll live just be a bit sore for a little while, awe that's a shame, we're havin a party tonight and we was going to ask you all if you wanted to come along. Well the Major is bed bound for at least a couple of days but were not I think that I speak for all of us in accepting your kind offer. That's settled then, what time are we talking? Oh about seven'ish I should think, right count us in.*

As the guests started to arrive, they were all offered a whiskey to celebrate the engagement, and stood in queue to be served at the bar. The local skiffel band turned too and asked David where they could set up? David shouted to the barman to pull five ales and sent them to the corner table. When they thought that they couldn't fit any more folk in the saltburn crowd turned up closely followed by the soldiers, and when the band decided that they had finished drinking for now they tuned up and went for it. The Major who had drank himself into a stuppour upstairs, was awoken when the band had started their second tune of the evening, and the whole crowd started to sing along. The noise was absolutely deafening, as John shook the hands of several soldiers and joined their company at the back of the Inn. What do you think of the Northern hospitality then boys? He didn't need to hear the answer back, the look on their faces was enough to know that it had been a long time since they had been to a party like this one, if indeed ever. So gentlemen wot brings you to these parts? Well it's a secret so we can't tell you that were after John Andrew, why? Wots he done wrong, this Andrew? Oh he's a known felon killed the kings men, and robbing him of his tax's. The bugger! How are you going to find him? Well we had a go today but there was no sign and our Major got injured to boot, got rescued by one of the locals, had a look of you as it happens, you weren't down that way earlier were you? No not me I was off in one of the fishing boats, only got back two hours since. So do yeh know what Andrew looks like? No not as yet, but we'll get him, I don't suppose you know of him do you? No I don't but there's a friend of mine in here tonight wot does, john stood and whistled to Dom, knowing that this was his queue he pushed through the crowed and found a seat at the table. Dom, these fellas are lookin for John Andrew, apparently he's a bit of a wrong'un and they mean to arrest him for his crimes. I've told them that you know im in passing like and they would like a description to make sure they have the right man. By now the soldiers were mesmerised and all ears. You've met im yeh sell mate, no I haven't oh but you have, do you remember last summer when we had a spot of business on the coast and me an you rode over to Saltburn. Aye, well do you remember that Geordie fella wot met us in the Ship Inn? Aye, well that were him. No, oh yes that was the very fellow, him with the broke nose an the missing leg? Aye the very one, but he told me not to say anything cause he keeps himsell to himsell and don't like folk looking into his business so to speak. Every one of the soldiers was gripped by the conversation going on in front of them, and one even started to take notes. So Dom how tall would you say he was? Oh, well he's not a big fella by any means, maybe five foot two, maybe three I reckon that wooded leg of his makes him look smaller than he really is see'in as he keeps wearin it out n that. But I'll tell you summat, if he was to walk in here now, you couldn't mistake im. Is he likely to walk in do you think? Well corpral he does tend to stick around Saltburn barely ever coming round these ways, but you'd know im if he did. By this time it had gone midnight and the Major had just about had enough of the infernal row that was coming from down stairs, so very gingerly he pulled on his breaches and a loose shirt and hobbled to the door, he reached for the handle and missed completely, falling against it and it fell open leaving the Major in a heap on the floor. After the pain had subsided a little, he climbed up the wall and stood at the top of the stairs, swaying as if in a stiff breeze he went to take the first step determined to silence the crowd, unfortunately he picked the wrong leg and as he went to put his weight upon it, it collapsed beneath him and he fell head long down the stairs hitting every other one on the way down. When the pain finally got too much for him he passed out on the bottom stair. What the hell was that? As the music and conversation died, the soldier nearest the door made to look for the source of the noise and as he popped his head back into the room to speak with his comrades, announced *he's done it again lads, call muster.* As they carried the Major back upstairs with a leg and an arm a piece, the music and conversation started again even louder than before. The order was given amongst the soldiers to bed down, as they would be an early start in the morning, but try as they might, because of the noise from the party not one found that relief and as the last of the revellers left and the door closed and locked the cock crowed and the Major shouted for his second in command.

John and the rest of the Saltburn residents had all climbed upon two wagons and left the horses to find their own way home, some still held onto an ale or a bottle and sang to keep the animals spirits up, the rest collapsed into sweet dreams and as John fell asleep he smiled at the events of the night and took comfort in all of the good friends that he had around him.

David and Erin, Jeffrey and Nell took to the two beds in the landlords room, the two men fell asleep before they hit the pillows but the two girls talked about their evening and how it went so well, then all of a sudden Erin said *why don't we have a double wedding, wot, yeh it makes a lot of sense, why don't you an Jeffrey an me an David get wed on the same day, ah but pet e asnt asked me, only cause he asnt thought of it that's all, I'll mention it to David t'morra an then we can really start makin plans,* and no matter that it was now daylight the two of them talked till mid morning.

The Major woke in a bad mood and with a thumping head, he was determined to let everyone else share his pain. *Acting Major Jones, get the men ready for work, right now, we need to catch our foe and get the devil out of this den of iniquity and back to civilization.* The tired soldiers stood at the bottom of their Majors bed and came to attention. *Right let me know what you found out about our Mr Andrew and how you mean to capture him. Well sir we have indeed used our time well and now have his description and where he might be found, excellent work gentlemen, go forth and capture this vagrant and allow us to go home never to return.* The soldiers saddled up, and even with the lack of sleep, found the ride over to the coast, quite refreshing. As a matter of course they pulled up at the church on the cliff top at Marske, they tied up their mounts and split up, four of them calling on the parson at the Vicarage and the rest, investigating, any new graves in the church yard. It was nothing more than a paper exercise, he knew however acting Major Jones was determined to do his job to the best of his ability, so albeit he could not confirm or deny the fact that Andrew was lost at sea, he could at least get a written account from the parson that he had not buried any corpse in an unmarked grave in the last six months, the other accounts of him going to Scotland was obviously a fabrication as he had first hand witness information that the man in question was indeed from the Newcastle area, which with all the best will in the word could not be substantiated So after this detour the only port of call would be the fanciful tale of the tunnels in Saltburn. And so once that was proven to be another dead end they would have no other course of action but to lie low and hope he would make a mistake, or leave for home, with all the boxes ticked. The parson with four soldiers at his door was only too willing to agree to anything just to get rid of them, even though he had at times hidden some of Johns ill-gotten goods in his bell tower from time to time, for he had to admit himself that he was partial to the odd sherry now and again. So with the signature in place the soldiers bade him farewell and headed back to Saltburn. As they dismounted and tied their steeds, acting Major Jones started to assess the village as he and his soldiers walked the full length of all the properties and something became immediately apparent, the tide was almost full and so as they stood upon the beach with the waves lapping around their boots and looked. *This is preposterous no one can dig tunnels here, they would be up to their knees in water in no time,* and so they took a different stance, if you can't dig down maybe you could dig across. *Look gentlemen there is simply not enough earth to dig below our feet but see how the properties at the south end of the village are all backed up to the cliff, what's to stop someone digging through their rear walls and into the cliff itself if that was the case then someone could walk from house to house unseen,* and the more they looked the more they were convinced that this could actually be the case. *So what are your orders Sir? I want you to enter each and every property at this end of the village forcibly if need be and search for any sign of hidden tunnels.* It was about this time that the villagers were stirring themselves, and the locals were non too pleased at being disturbed in their own houses. The screaming and shouting attracted some curious on lookers one in particular being John Andrew and as he stood back and watched the commotion, he realised what the soldiers were looking for. They have obviously found out about the tunnels and were now actively searching for them, thankfully in the wrong place, non the less this had him worried, for if they kept this strategy up sooner or later they would find his treasures. He had to come to a decision and fast, so he walked into the Ship Inn to consult with Dom. *So what do you think we should do? Well as I've already said they are a mile off just now but sooner or later they'll sus us out. Best case next year worse case next week either way I'm going to have to reel it all in, till they bugger off for good.*

COATHAM SIX MILE NORTH

Jeffrey can I have a little chat with you while the others are sleeping, of course poppet what's up well I've been thinking what with you an Nell avin a baby an everything why don't you make an honest woman of her? How do you mean? Well ive bin thinkin an if you was up for it we could ave a double weddin, me an David an you an Nell. What a great idea, ah but d'you think Nell would like that? Trust me Jeffrey she'll think it's a great idea, right I'll ask her as soon as she wakes.

SALTBURN SIX MILE SOUTH

It looks like they've given up for the day, did they find anything? No the two gin houses ave there tunnels startin below the floor boards which are well concealed and they reckon that all the houses this end of the village and the ship are too far away from the cliff to be able to have any tunnels, thank heavens for that. Listen mate can you spread the word down to Hull and across to Middlesbrough that we are going to have to close down for a bit. Yeh leave that with me I'll sort it, but what are you going to do? Me I'm going to start and remove the evidence, and with a shake of the hands they went their separate ways.

Staithes eight miles South

Sarah what on earth are you girls up to? Every time we walk into the room everyone starts giggling and you all speak so fast I can't keep up, oh don't you go a worry'in its just that Maureen ere was wonderin if Henri's got a girl back ome? No he does't have anyone I'm afraid, I think he's kind of missed the boat so to speak! Oh I wouldn't say that, how do you like the accommodation? Oh we like it…very much indeed, ah that's nice. Would it be alright if Henri and I took a walk down to the harbour for a bit of exercise? Aye I don't see why not most of our neighbours know what's going on, you might get a few strange looks but that's just folk being nosey, nosey? What does that mean? Their just interested that's all, oh that's alright then. He bowed and slowly turned to fetch his friend. As the two of them walked through the narrow streets, a door would open slightly here and a curtain twitch there, which made them feel like the stars of the show with a bad case of stage fright. The sun was catching their eyes as it flickered through the roof tops, and as they appeared from the village and stood overlooking the beach they had a sense of wonder at such a beautiful place nestled between the cliffs. The two sat on the harbour wall and each lit their pipes, the smoke illuminated in the morning sunlight. *Well Henri what do you think of our new home? I don't think I could be happier anywhere else in the world Sarge, I just wish that Jean was here to enjoy it with us, aye I know mate I'll tell you something else as well, and what would that be? Well I think that Maureen is a bit sweet on me, aye I think you might be right there Henri…I think you might be right.*

Saltburn

After the disappointing search the soldiers decided to call it a day and ride back over to Middlesbrough to report back to the Major, at the slow pace they were going it would take them a good couple of hours however no one complained. When they finally pulled into the stables and dismounted it was late afternoon, so they fed and watered the horses, while acting Major Jones went upstairs to give his report to his superior. *Ah Jones come in and give me your report. Well sir I followed your orders and went to see the parson in Marske and got his signature to swear that he had not buried anyone in an unmarked grave within the last six months, good, good what next, well sir next we rode over to Saltburn to try and investigate these so called tunnels, and alas non could be found, where a bout's did you look? So Jones explained the lay of the land and the reason why they searched were they did. Excellent work Jones, well done. So sir what is to be done? Well as you can see I am still bed bound for a little while longer, so I would like you to take the troops back to Saltburn and hide out in the woods, keep a look out day and night and log any comings and goings and if he still be alive we will hopefully catch him in the act. Yes sir and for how long would you like us to keep vigil? Two weeks from now, within the fortnight I will be able to ride again, and with the information we have already and two weeks observations to back it up we can go home with heads held high. Yes sir I will inform the troops immediately, good man Jones, and in two weeks' time we will remove ourselves from this god awful place, never to return. Amen to that sir.* As acting Major Jones walked into the stables, the soldiers were just finishing up and then he explained the orders to a crestfallen team, *what now sir? Yes right away saddle up your mounts and we will return to Saltburn.* The troops had now been awake for the best part of three days, and were not in any state to start a twenty four hour vigil, however they would never disobey an order so reluctantly they mounted up and made to return to Saltburn.

STAITHES

As the two Frenchmen were finishing their smoke and were ready to return to the safe house a small shape appeared out of the shadowed village and came to talk with them *bonjour madam,* which made her smile, *d'yer mind if I sit, but of course please do, so giggling she sat between them. Mr McCallister does Henri here not speak any English? Yes I do but only a little, I've been teaching him for a while but he is a terrible student, maybe you should take over and see if you have more luck than I have.* So Maureen took his hand in hers and went off on a tangent explaining everything from a cloud to a duck, which had them both in tears of laughter within minutes. McCallister bade their leave and took a stroll onto the sands and turned to admire their hideaway village. As they all sat down to their evening meal, Sarah smiled at the way that Maureen had sat next to Henri and how they held hands throughout the meal.

SALTBURN

John Andrew disappeared under ground and started the arduous task of taking his stock up into the back of the tunnels, he toiled all night long in the candle light, but realised that it would take him many more nights until the task would be completed to his satisfaction, so as daylight turned he snuck out of the Ship inn to go to his bed. *What's that bugger doing sneaking about at this ungodly hour do you suppose? Oh probably fell asleep in front of the fire last night full of ale, lucky beggar I wish we could.*

MIDDLESBROUGH

Hello my luv, did you sleep well? like a baby, I just wish I could have another couple of hours, well maybe you can sleep on the trip back to Coatham ere'ya pet I've med yer a nice mug of tea, that'll perk you up a bit. He handed her the mug and sat at the table opposite her. *Listen luv I've been talkin to Erin this morning and she's put an idea in me head, Oh I and wot idea would that be then? Well yeh know how them two is getting wed an all? Aye well what would yer say if me an you got wed an all…on the same day… at the same time like…with them. Well I don't know this is all quite sudden Jeffrey, oh I'll understand if you don't want to like cause I ere that some women like it to be their special day…so…well… I'd love to Jeffrey, stop frettin Erin asked me the same thing earlier this morning an I think it's a wonderful idea.* And as they stood to embraced across the table, the tea spilt everywhere.

The journey back to Coatham, didn't turn out to be a restful one at all as the four of them were much too busy making plans. *So when do think we should have it then, well I reckon the sooner the better, wot like t'morrow, don't be daft, we need to let folk know first, especially the parson, ok well why don't we go straight to Marske an see wot he as the say about the matter, an we'll go for his earliest date, aye that's a grand idea, an then we'll head on to Saltburn an tell everyone there.* When Jeffrey knocked on the Vicarage door the housemaid informed him that he was over in the grave yard *doing a spot of weedin. Let's leave the wagon here and take a stroll to the church, it's turned out to be a half decent day,* and sure enough when they all entered the grounds they found the parson on his knees pulling at some troublesome thistles. *Are they getting the better of yeh James, they'll be the death of me is wot they'll be, no matter how many I pull out of the ground, there's two or three that takes its place, anyway I'm sure you haven't come over to gain my gardening tips, wot can I do for you all? Well we was just wondering if you have any time next Saturday out of your busy schedule to marry us, who, I mean which two of you are wanting to be married? All of us, eh, put that one by me again? Right me an my Nell ere are wantin to be wed, an David and Erin are wantin to be wed at the same time, would that be a problem? Oh no not a problem, just a little unusual that's all, are yeh all god fearin folk, oh aye that's us alright, every last one of us, well I can't see that it should be a problem but surely you would want to be married at the Sacred Heart in Redcar it would be a lot closer for you, beggin your pardin yeh parsonship but we can't think of a more beautiful place in the world to be wed than ere, n besides we intend to celebrate at the ship in Saltburn afterwards, and of course you would be more than welcome, in fact invite your housemaid too, it looks like she hasn't had a good laugh for years.* As the five of them walked back to the vicarage the sun appeared through the clouds and illuminated the church tower in a golden hue, *there you go James blest by the almighty himself,* and they all made the sign of the cross, just to be safe side. Once loaded back on the wagon, they said their goodbye's and set off for Saltburn.

As they pulled over and jumped down John was there to greet them, *hello fella's, ladies, how are you all? Never better John isn't it a beautiful day, John looked about and suggested aye it's alright, wot game are you lot up to then? We want to invite you to a weddin John.* And suddenly an idea came to Jeffrey, he grabbed a hold of David and pulled him to one side and whispered *Bugger. Wot? Bugger I never gave it a thought, how bloody stupid, wot're you going on about Jeffrey? A best man, we haven't picked a best man, and the best, best man is stood in front of us, that's alright* David said in his innocent way, *ere john me and Erin, an Jeffrey an Nell are all getting wed next Saturday an we wondered if you would be our best man. Why thank you David I would be honoured,* and as David turned back to Jeffrey with a big smile on his face, Jeffrey gave him a hug. *Is Dom about John? Aye he's inside, proppin up the bar,* and with a skip in her stride Erin disappeared into the Ship. *Dom, where are yeh? Oh ello pet this is a nice surprise* and he kissed her on her cheek, *where's that fella of yours? I've left im outside talking to John, but I wanted to catch you alone for a second, why's that then luv? Well you know that me an David are goin teh get wed, aye well its goin to be next Saturday in Marske, we've been to see the parson and everything's set but I've got one more problem, well tell me wot it is and if I can help in anyway then you know that I will, well it's to do with the weddin, I've got no one to give me away.* She started to get teary eyed as she carried on. *An seein as you are me dads oldest friend an I've known you since I was a nipper I wondered whether you would do it on me dads behalf.* As he wiped away her tears with his thumbs he looked straight into her sad eyes and said, *my dear girl I would be honoured.* She gave out a choked thank you, buried her head into his chest and gave him the biggest hug he'd ever had. When she finally let him go, he turned to the opening door and wiped his nose on his sleeve. *Ello Dom, wots up with yeh eyes you look like you've had a sneezing fit, aye that's wot I've had a sneezin fit, that's wot. Oh David I've asked Dom if he will give me away when we get wed an he's said yes.* David reached out and they shook. *Well Dom you're a better man than me, there's no way in hell that I could ever give her away, thank you. Nell, who's going to give you away at the weddin? Oh I'll let our Samson an Danniel fight over the honour, good god I wouldn't want to get caught up in that, they'll kill each other, they had better not or I'll murder the pair of em.*

Right gents I'm goin to steal your young ladies away from yeh for the rest of the day, wot for? Never you mind wot for, you's just stop ere an keep Dom comp'ny an we'll be back about tea time, c'mon you two lets go grab us a horse each an off we go.

STAITHES

I wish you'd tell us wot this is all about John I'm not right good at all this cloak'n'dagger stuff, not much longer now ladies, just across the bridge, lets tie the horse here an walk over, Staithes? Aye Staithes, wot on earth are we doin ere? You'll see now follow me, and he led them down the narrow streets an politely knocked on a door, which was flung open and a strange woman threw herself at him and gave him a hug. Ladies I would like you to meet Sarah my sister. Won't be long you said, be back soon you said, I've been worried sick now come on in an tell me where you've been. As they entered the cottage John introduce the bemused Nell and Erin, and those three sat over there are our cousins Mary, Ann an Kathleen, where's the other one at Sarah, oh she'll be down the beach with Henri, smitten she is with that there pirate you brought over here. Anyhow where have you been I ad you down for bein arrested or worse, Sarah I'm a grown man I can take care of myself, your my little brother and I'll always worry over you. Well see these two ladies, their goin to get wed next Saturday and I was wondering if you still have that bail of silk wot I brought over for yeh, aye it's up in the dead space at the back of the cottage safe an sound, good cause I was thinkin that you an the girls could make them both a dress each as a weddin present from us, when the two brides realised wot he had just said they screamed and threw themselves at him covering him in kiss's, *e're steady on there's no need for any of that carry on. Oh thank you John, we was wonderin what to wear, cause we've nowt presentable. Well, well, you don't ave to worry about that now do yeh, Sarah I'll just pop down to the beach an see if I can catch up with McCallister, can I leave these two ladies in your capable hands, aye on you go, get out an leave us to it.*

Saltburn woods

Who goes there? Stand down soldier, Major Jones reporting, come friend. I must commend you on your vigilance however you must be a little less enthusiastic in future soldier we are after all supposed to be in hiding, we can't have the whole area knowing our whereabouts. So what news? Everything noted in the log Sir, ok take me through it, entry by entry, well Sir for such a small Village there appears to be a lot going on, and all of it seems to revolve around the Inn, and I've been thinking, about when we first came here, we were told that they didn't rent rooms, that is correct, well sir the amount of time they stay in there beggars belief look at this fellow here he came in yesterday evening and didn't leave again until sunrise, and today there were two couples went in but only the women folk came back out, with what looked like the fellow who found the Major in the stream the other day, and off they rode into the distance not to be seen since. Hmm, strange behaviour to be sure, but apart from the locals coming and going, nothing incriminating? They haven't been seen carrying barrels of brandy into the place? No sir not as yet, come to think about it, we haven't seen a dray either, well gentlemen it is early doors, and so we must be ready, if and when we do see anything suspicious, good work men, keep it up.

Staithes

As John walked out of the narrow streets, into the sunlight, he spotted McCallister sat with his legs dangling over the sea wall. *Hello Sarge what're up to? Just watching the waves an the seagulls an having a quiet smoke John, do you need a hand to do that then? Please do, he went to sit and reached for his own pipe. What news from Saltburn? Aye I have news, well? Well those bloody stupid soldiers are hid in the woods at the back of the Ship, keepin an eye on all our comins an goins. Every time that one of them lifts a spy glass to his eye and we see it glint in the sunlight the boys go into fits of hysterics, their now bettin on how many time a day they give themselves away. So you've nothing to worry from them? No not really, I reckon there just biding their time till the Major gets well enough to travel again, so we'll be rid of them soon enough. Anyway wot's with Henri and our Maureen then? Well their both like love sick puppies can't keep their hands off each other, but after what Henri's been through losing his brother and all, I wish the two of them well, aye me too I just wish that there was someone for all our cousins, don't you be looking at me when you say that, as pleasing to the eye as they all are, I don't want to be settling down just yet, I'd go mad being in this place for the rest of my life. I'm not explaining this very well am I, it's as pleasant a village as I have ever seen and some day if god pleases I would love nothing more than to return and settle here, but John there's a want in me, and until I find it I can't settle anywhere, don't you worry no offence taken, I know what you mean though, I know it's not the other side of the word, but that's why I've stayed in Saltburn, and kept tradin, I reckon it's that little bit of danger that keeps me alive, so how long will you stick around? Oh I don't know, I might stay till spring when the weather improves a little, and where will you head for? I think that I'll stay in Europe at first, knowing all the languages is always a big help, yeh I bet it is, but then I might head onto the silk road, they say there's language's over to the East that no man can learn, and as you know I've always liked a challenge. Well all I can say is you'll be sadly missed my friend, now c'mon back to the house, and I'll get our Sarah to put the kettle on. As the two men entered the cottage it was in absolute* chaos, both Nell and Erin were standing on stools while the girls hurried about them, pining and stitching, in fact the only ones that weren't getting involved were Henri and Maureen they were in their own little world. *Is it safe to come in our Sarah? Not if your feared for your lives it's not now bugger off before I stick a pin in yeh. C'mon Sergeant, I'll buy you an ale down the cod.* And the two of them turned about sharpish and left the girls to it. It was about an hour later when all the girls came into the cod and lobster, looking for them, *ah ladies are you all done then? Aye that we are, and is everyone happy?* He didn't really need a reply to that one as Nell and Erin were positively glowing. *Come on then I'll stand you all a round but then we must be getting back the boys will be wondering where we are.* So twenty minutes later with brown paper parcels under their arms, Nell and Erin hugged Johns extended family and wouldn't leave until every last one promised to come to the wedding. So waving to them as they crossed the bridge, they mounted up and rode back to Saltburn. As they pulled in at the Ship, they stabled and fed the horses and walked indoors. *Oh there you are, we was startin to think you'd gone an gotten lost, by god fellas rarther you than me getting wed to these two, they never stop talkin, ere ave a good look are me ears bleedin, the girls gave him a friendly punch on the arm, but nothing could take the smiles off their faces. C'mon then were've yer been all afternoon, can't tell you im afraid it would spoil the surprise, what surprise is that, oh no you don't you'll not catch us out like that either, anyway aint you gunna offer us weary travellers a drink to stave off the cold, ere'ya I'll get em, whats your poison ladies?* And after another hour of questions and no answers Nell started to yawn. *C'mon my luv lets ave you home it's been a long day,* so as the drinks were finished the two girls hugged John and said thank you one last time they climbed aboard the wagon and Nell fell immediately to sleep, closely followed by Erin. *Well Jeffrey I reckon it's your stimulating company mate,* and the men chuckled as they pulled onto the beach towards home. Somewhere in the undergrowth at the back of the Ship their leaving was logged.

On the eve of the wedding the whole of the Ship was buzzing with people arriving from far and wide the rooms upstairs were well gone and so folk had to sleep were they could. Near the fire was the best and favourite place to spend the night, apart from that funny smell emanating from that strange looking arrangement curled up by the hearth. Earlier that evening every woman within forty miles was in the kitchen preparing food for the wedding feast and once complete the door was shut and locked, unless of course you were the size of let's say maybe a cat and a small dog of dubious parentage that knew where the sea had weathered the lower bricks over the years and took no digging away at all, so with full bellies and a will to sleep it off, anyone that came close to moving them on got a vicious deep throated growl and a show of the teeth and if they were really persistent maybe a claw in the back of the hand.

The cock crowed at the dawn of a bright new day, full of expectation a day that non would forget for a very long time. As everyone started to wake and take their daily ablutions the two brides to be were fussing over each other, *I don't know how any bride could go through this on her own, its*

173

bleedin terrifying, wot if no one turns up, wot if too many turn up, oh I don't know if I can go through with it, my stomach is tied up in knots. Danniel! Samson! get out of bed an take the boys some tea over to the stables, an make sure they avent ran away, Danniel are you listening to me, can't do much else seein as your shoutin so bloody loud, Erin would you like two lazy brothers, their goin cheap, no I think their fine where they are. Danniel, I'm not gunna sa..oh there you are, right take the boys over some tea an meck sure they are gunna be alright. Over in the stables the two in question were just pulling round in the same hammocks that they used on the very first night that they came to the area *well son this is it the big day, aye, you still up for it. More than ever, you? Well the idea terrifies me but if I get my Nell at the end of it, I'll be a happy man. C'mon then we've got to skidaddle before the girls wake up, why is that then Jeffrey? I don't know it's just the way things ave teh be, get yourself dressed an we'll go see John an put the fryin pan on. Oye you two are yeh up an about, our Nell wants to know, aye were still ere an still alive, thank heavens for that I don't know whether I'd survive if you'd done one, ere'yah a cup of tea each, ah thanks Danneee… its ok you can call me Danny see'in as were almost brothers an all, thanks that means a lot Danniel, right c'mon you two ave ter bugger off drink yeh tea an piss off to Saltburn John will be expectin yeh, thanks mate we'll be off in a tick now go see your sister an tell her to stop worry'in, ok see yeh in a bit since boys.* and at that he left them alone to dress. The two grooms saddled up and left the stable, and if anyone had taken care to look behind them they would have seen two excited girls peeping from behind the curtains.

As the two pulled into Saltburn, they found an irate best man tapping his foot on the ground, *you ok John, I am now, I thought you'd had second thoughts, no mate just didn't sleep to well-being in the stables with the horses all night, ah well you're here now an that's what counts now come inside an we'll have some Dutch courage, count me in for that john, I'm bloody terrified,* as the three of them walked into the Inn the party had already started and the more sober of the crowd started to clap and pat them on the back, *good luck boys, all the best,* and before they knew it they had drinks in hand and all the best wishes than anyone could ever have. *Ok you two ave yeh got everything wot yeh need, aye I reckon so, how about the rings? Wot rings, well I don't know wot traditions they ave down in Hull but around these parts its customary teh put a ring on the brides finger, Bollocks never even crossed me mind John, wot'll we do? don't worry, the best man has come to the rescue once again, open your hands and close yeh eyes.* John fished around in his pocket and dropped a gold ring into both of their open hands, and both of them flashed open their eyes and stared. *We're still in the hammocks in the stables aint we David, not woke up yet. Bloody hell John were the hell did you get these from they must ave cost a small furtune. I made em, you wot? How? Well yeh know us masons we can turn our hands to just about anything, actually it's not difficult at all, the tricky bit is getting yeh hands on the gold coins, but I had a bit of a helping hand with that from Bonaparte look see there on the inside, that writing there is French that is. Oh John ow will we ever repay yeh, don't ave to them's is weddin presents to the four of yeh,* taking the moment Jeffrey rapped his knucklers on the table top, *ere everyone, a toast to the best, best man that ever there was.* The cheer was audible in the woods at the back of the ship. *I reckon it's going to be a busy day for me and you my friend, I hope you've got plenty of lead in your pencil.*

Over in Coatham the girls were starting to panic, so much so that everything that Nell touched either broke or went missing. Just then there was a shout from the front door, *anybody getting hitched in here today? Oh Sarah, girls come in, come in, we're at our wits end, nothings goin right, an were gunna be late an then the boys'll mad an they wont want to wed us anymore, an I'll die an lonely old maid, an…..that's enough Nelly Basham I don't want to hear another word I'm takin charge,* she then produced a large flask of gin and said *Ere drink some of this and then we'll make you the most beautiful brides that a groom as ever seen.*

Back in Saltburn time was a ticking. *Right, everyone who hasn't got a ride needs to set off now for the Church, it'll only take twenty minutes but we must get everyone there by twelve, now c'mon the lot of yeh, drink up an get gone.* As the soldiers watched the whole of Saltburn, Marske, most of Redcar and Middlesbrough, and a few stragglers from Staithes started for the Church. *This is no good I simply can't write fast enough. It doesn't matter we don't know anyone by name anyway just put male or female and then how many.* As john walked his horse from the stable and down to the beach, a thought occurred to him, he stopped and started to pat his pockets, then leaving the horse he ran back up to the Ship and dashed inside. Minutes went by until he reappeared from out the morgue. *Did you just see that, see what I'm still trying to catch up with this ledger. That fellow that picked the Major out of the stream, he just walked into the Inn, and out of the morgue, don't be daft you've been out here too long that's all, starting to see things.*

JOHN MOUNTED HIS HORSE, AND GALLOPED AT FULL SPEED TOWARDS MARSKE

Come on now's our chance, while everyone's at the wedding, hang on we were told to stay here and observe that's it, nothing about breaking into any buildings, but we won't get a better opportunity than this, there's no one left, just us. The two soldiers broke cover and started to work their way down to the Village, *let's try the morgue first it's the nearest, then we'll try the Inn.* The door opened with a groan and the soldiers slipped inside, *light a match, I can't see a damned thing.* As the morgue was illuminated they looked for another door, but try as they might there was nothing to be seen, just a big slab of stone on a stone plinth, in the middle of the floor and that's was it. *There you go I told you that you were seeing things, there's no way in or out but that front entrance, aye I guess you're right, c'mon let's try the Inn,* they left the Morgue and crept over to the Ship. *Bugger its locked well let's try the rear door, it's the same as the front locked solid, people only lock things if they've something to hide, there must be someway in a window maybe, have a look around that way and I'll go this I'll meet you on the other side.* Trying the windows as they went they were having no luck whatsoever until, *ah what have we here,* he knelt down and stared to pick at a few bricks, *what have you found? Holy cow don't go sneaking up on me like that, a few loose bricks not quite enough to crawl through but if I can loosen a few more…here we go, I've found us a way in. you go first your thinner than me, get lost, I'm not going in there, listen do you want to stay in this god awful place for another week or do you want to go home, well then get down on your belly and crawl through here.* Reluctantly he did as was asked, he was through to about his waist when he heard a low determined growl coming from inside. He briefly stopped to listen then all of a sudden wished he hadn't as out of the darkness came a fury of teeth and claws, as he started to scream his partner decided retreat was the best policy and ran back into the woods. With his arms down by his sides he had no way of protecting himself so he started to spit at this unseen enemy, the tirade stopped for a brief moment and then it spat back, and hissed like a rattle snake, he turned his head to get away from it and a sharp set of teeth clamped around his nose, by now he was so scared that he almost levitated back out through the hole, he got to his feet and overtook his comrade, who by this time was only half way to their hide out. If they had chanced a look back, they would have seen a mangy looking cat and a small dog of dubious parentage with their heads sticking out of the hole sniggering at them.

John had just brought his horse to halt outside the church when he spotted the bridal party immerge from behind the vicarage, he slapped his horse away from the doorway and ran inside, he slowed to a walk and appeared next to the terrified grooms. Up in the belfry the single bell started to sing, *where the hell have you been? I forgot something, like what, to pay the milkman? Don't start panicking boys, well what if they don't turn up, too late for that, there here,* and as the three turned to look, the two most beautiful visions were stood at the doorway looking back at them, with radiant smiles, and carrying a white lily. *Right boys you're on,* they took a couple of steps forward and stood side by side in front of the parson it was then that the choir started sing, and the brides were escorted up the aisle, by a beaming Dom and two very bruised brothers one with a definite limp, as they approached the alter the brothers handed Nell over to stand next to Jeffrey and Dom whispered to Erin, *your dad would have been very proud of you my dear* and handed her over to stand next to David. Sarah and the girls who had been putting the final touches to the brides dress's outside snuck in to sit at the back of the church and catching Johns eye he winked at them and smiled. The congregation started the prayers, and sang along with the choir. As the many voices faded the parson started his reverie, *we are gathered here* today to join this man and this woman, and this man and this woman, in holy matrimony… so if there are anyone here present who knows of any just cause or reaso…there was a commotion at the back of the church, and the brides stomachs turned over, everyone turned to look and John saw McCallister walking up the aisle, give me a moment, I'll be right back. As the two men met mid aisle, they started whispering to one another, *well I'll see what they say but it is rather unusual,* as he reached the alter he hunkered down to speak with the brides and grooms. There were astonished gasps and then a head would pop up and look to the rear of the church, finally John walked back to where McCallister still stood rather embarrassed, their two heads went down to whisper once more, and then the Sergeant walked to the back of the church and escorted Henri and Maureen to the alter, there was a few more whispers and then the parson voiced, *well ladies and gentlemen this is rather unusual however….and this man and this woman in holy matrimony, then hold your peace.* As the parson asked for the rings john reached into his pocket and pulled out three gold bands, *it's a good job I made a spare then aint it.* As the ceremony came to an end the parson said, *you may kiss the brides* the place irrupted into wolf whistles and clapping hands. As the six newlyweds walked to the rear of the church and out of the opened door the sun beamed down on them. *Oy you lot come ere,* the six of them walked over to where John held his horse. And stood in front of him. *Well did it go well or wot? Brilliant John thanks a million, oh you don't after thank me I wasn't doin much today anyway, right to business the girls dowries, wot dowries? These dowries,* he reached into his saddlebags and pulled out three heavy purses he tossed them one each to the brides surprise, he leapt onto his horse and galloped down to the beach. as each girl opened up the purses there was a shriek from each, seeing Jeffrey's puzzled looks Nell put her hand inside and pulled out a fistful of gold coins…*well bugger me!*

When John got back to the Ship Inn he noticed that the morgue door had been left open, which wasn't the way he'd left it he was sure. he strolled over to investigate and walked inside, nothing seemed untoward so he figured it must have been the wind playing tricks on him, as he went to leave and close the door something caught his eye, there on the floor was a spent match. His worst fears had come to haunt him. He ran over to the

Inn and noticed the bricks strewn across the pathway, quickly he reached for the key that was hanging from his neck and opened up, to hell with stealth, he ran from room to room, but could not find anything wrong, as he unlocked the pantry he slowly opened the door and could not fail to see the daylight that was streaming in through the hole in the wall, he also noticed something else, blood lots of it around the hole, something moved and he turned to look. There sat on the floor was a mangy cat and a small dog with blood all over its face, they both sat and looked up at him, and he could have sworn blind that the dog was smiling at him, he bent down patted it on the head and said *good dog,* the cat turned to look at the dog with venom in her eye and the dogs smile got bigger.

The wedding guests were starting to arrive and so the party began but not for John he went into the cellar and walked to the morgue he knew that the soldiers were onto him and he had to bury the evidence before they could find it. he was pretty sure that no one would discover the tunnel from the morgue, it was too well hidden but if someone really looked in the Ships cellar then they would discover it all so when everything had been moved to his satisfaction, he went back upstairs and walked over to the stables where he had hidden his gunpowder, one by one he rolled the barrels, over to the Inn and carried them through the back door down into the cellar, he carefully placed the explosives into weak spots and against the supporting timbers and used enough fuse to be lit from the Inn. Once complete he looked around and said *good bye old friend, we've had some laughs along the way aint'we an who knows when these idiots stop poking around we may yet again.*

As the soldiers were watching events they saw that there was someone toing and froing from the Inn to the stables and back, rolling barrels of what they thought was contraband liquor, it was at that moment that the penny dropped. *That's it, I knew I'd seen him before, that fellow that plucked the Major from the river, he was the same one as the fellow in the Dick Turpin that night of the party, he denied it of course when I asked him, said he'd been fishing or some such, but that was the key, d'you see, when the Major asked for a bottle of whiskey, and I went down stairs to fetch one, when I found no one about I took a bottle and left a note for the landlord saying to add the cost of it to our bill, well I never thought anything of it at the time, but when I brought it upstairs for the Major, he just uncorked it and took a slug to ease his pain and so that's what links it all together, the fellow that spent all night in the Ship Inn is the same fellow who was at the party, and the same fellow that saved the Major, he is.....John Andrew. When the Major took a slug of that whiskey there was no wax seal on it, it was contraband, right under our noses and not one of us noticed. We must inform the Major at once we need the troop here to apprehend the villain. Go and run to the main camp and bring them as quickly as possible, I'll keep watch while your away.*

John had finished his work in the tunnels, and so decided to return to the party. *Where the hell ave you been, oh just out back feedin the horses, well I hope your now going to enjoy yeh sell, here ave an ale,* he took the offered and started to circulate. *Well David ows it feel to be a married man then? No different than it did yesterday t'be honest with yeh mate, well, you can concentrate on startin your own family now, I know you'll mek a great dad, wots wrong John? Ello my dear hope your gunna look after this big lummox for me, why where are you goin oh no where just a turn of phrase ello Nell ow did you enjoy your day my luv? Oh John it would have bin nothing without you, give us a kiss yeh big softy, I reckon you've got yeh ands full ere Jeffrey, looks like you ave just now mate. Oh and here's the late comers you ad us a turn in that church Henri,* who gave him a blank look until Maureen translated he grabbed John by both shoulders and kissed him on both cheeks, *steady on lad no need for that, thank you John for everything, your very welcome dear cousin.*

SALTBURN PRESENT DAY

As Vicky opened the hatch they both looked down into its depths, *is there a light switch anywhere no this is where we leave the twenty first century behind and travel back in time grab a couple of those candles and we'll go see what we can find.* As they lowered themselves down the steps the room took on a musky smell which wasn't unpleasant but you couldn't wear it to say a night club, Ryan hit the floor first and was pleasantly surprised to find it relatively dry, he moved to one side to allow Vicky down. *God I haven't been down here since I was a kid, aye I bet you were the hide and seek champion at parties, get lost you wouldn't catch me down here by myself, no way.* As the couple searched Vicky asked *what exactly am I looking for, not sure, anything loose, eh! you know things that should be nailed down but aren't, something that would hide a hole, how about those old barrels over there, yeh that kind of thing, let's have a look, not likely there'll be spiders, you go look, ok mind out of the way and I'll go investigate.* As he started to move the top few he noted that some were relatively heavy *hey there's still something in these, yeh dad tried some when we moved here said it was bloody awful so they've been here ever since.* As he rolled the last few away all he saw was a stone wall he knocked on it a few times but to his disappointment nothing sounded hollow. *What's that over there, what that cabinet by hell it a beauty you should clean that up a bit and get flogged on the net, get lost have you seen how big it is you'd never get it through the hatch, I reckon that whoever wanted it must have built it down here from scratch, built it from scratch you say, yeh what of it? Well why would anyone go to the trouble of doing that, for storing bottles on, do you store bottles on anything like this, no they all come in crates and we just stack them on top of each other, exactly you can't move bottles about at a couple at a time because they'd roll all over the place and break so you put them into crates and stack them, so that being the case, what the hell is it for. Bring your candle over here a bit, and let's give it a good coating of looking at. Well there are no secret levers or pulleys but look at this, what? look what happens when I put the candle down the side of it see how it flickers.* Vicky started to knock on the wood as she saw Ryan do on the wall, *I don't think that will prove very much this oak must be an inch thick, who ever built this thing wanted it to last forever.*

SALTBURN 1812

As darkness fell the wedding guests started to drift away and John was there to see them off shaking hands and kissing the women all of whom congratulated him for such an enjoyable day, *what are you up to John? Oh hiya Sergeant, ave you ad a good time, aye but I've been watching you and something smells funny, oh that'll be the dog, you know that's not what I mean John, you're up to something walking about shaking hands and hugging folk like you'll never see them again, come outside and have a smoke with me Sergeant I need to check on the horses again… Ok out with it, their onto me mate, who is? them bloody soldiers that's who they've been poking around here when we was at the weddin, you sure? Sure as after every ones away tonight I'm gonna blow the tunnels and bugger off for a while. So you've thought it through then, aye, were will you go? Dunno, maybe the silk road, I've heard that there's little yella fellas wot can beat you up without movin, an you know me I'm always up for a challenge, Hah… is that so? Aye.*

SALTBURN PRESENT DAY

Would you have a brush close at hand, yup wait here. Vicky ran back upstairs and reappeared brush in hand, *here you go, well I never did, look at that, what is it? scratches in the floor this thing was made that heavy that its left us a clue, this thing moves, it was made to move, look see the curve in the dirt, it's got hinges on that side and if we get our finger nails between the wood and the wall it should….*

SALTBURN 1812

John look over towards the woods, see the lanterns through the trees there… aye, bet they didn't expect us to be out here waiting on them did they, reckon they was expecting us to be dead drunk enjoying the party, right saddle up my horse an keep an eye on them for me, it's a bit early but I've got to blow the tunnels right now. As he ran into the Ship he nearly knocked his sister to the floor. *Sarah I've got to go right now can you get the hangers on outside for me thankfully there's not many left now.* John ran to the cellar and finished off the rest of the fuse then with all his strength pushed the cabinet back against the wall and wedged it in place with a rock. *Shit… matches I've got no bloody matches, here you are catch, he heard his sister shout, thanks now get out,* he lit the fuse and ran up the stairs two at a time as he got to the front door he saw that McCallister was stood hold the reins of two horses. *What the hell are you doin? well you didn't think I was going to let you have all the fun by yourself did you? When will I see you again little brother, will I ever see you again? I don't know Sarah but if I don't go now the hangman will have me for sure,* she threw her arms around him and started to cry, *hey, hey no need for that I'll be back, d'yer promise? I promise, take care Sarah, and look after the old place while I'm gone.* The two men jumped into their saddles and with a shout they were off. *Ere John I didn't hear anything go…..bloody hell…..how much gunpowder did you use? No one's going to find that any day soon that's for sure.*

SALTBURN PRESENT DAY

It moved just a bit but it definitely moved, *would it help if I took that rock out of the way, yes that would be preferable sling it over there and give me a hand.* the two of them put all of their weight behind it as it moved further some loose rubble fell from behind and then it was open, but all they found was a collapsed passageway. *There must be tonnes of rock here we'll not get through there in a hurry, yes but we've achieved something that no one else has ever done, we've proved that the old stories were true after all, congratulations John Andrew you did a great job, hey look what's that?* Ryan crouched down and picked up a gold coin, dusted it down and passed it to Vicky, she looked at it, put her arms around his neck and kissed him.

SALTBURN 1812

As Sarah watched, she saw the two riders galloping across Hunt Cliff silhouetted by the full moon.

THE END

If ever you get the chance to visit St Germain's Church and grave yard on the cliff top at Marske you will find the graves of smugglers gone by, without inscriptions, just the skull and crossed bones to mark who and what they were.

I must mention Jack Anderson a local cobbler from Marske, who's font of knowledge of times gone by and the local area, was an inspiration, as kids we would sit, listening to his tales of smugglers and their adventures as he sat by his fire with his companion Winky the cat (Search Winkies Castle) and dream of someday finding the legendary tunnels full of John Andrews treasures that are said to exist to this day.

I dedicate this book to all the friends' I've ever known. If I could have my time again you would all still be in it.

Special thanks to Leigh my long suffering wife who is still mad at me for not mentioning her name in the pages of this book, but as I told her at the time she's my wife and I don't want to share her with anyone else.

Thanks also to my Father, who was not only my Dad, Hero, and Best friend he's also the guy that made me the man I am today, and whose only want in life was to be remembered.

'See yer in a bit since dad'......

CAST

Phillippé Oubre	Jeffrey, David, Wilf, Frank
Henri + Jean Verrel	Nell, Samson + Danniel Basham
Adrien + Claude Deveraux	Tom, Erin
McCallister	Mac and the mangy cat
Ryan + Vicky	John Andrew

The Teesside accent is unique to the area full of dropped H's, G's and slang words, I thought for a while that I should not try and write in the accent, however it is an intrinsic part of the area that I am proud to possess myself, nevertheless for anyone that might struggle with the phonetics here is a quick translation of some of the more common phrases:

Yer...........You
Yeh..........Yes
Aye...........Yes
Cause.......Because
Owt..........Anything
Mek..........Make
Nowt........Nothing
Aint...........Isn't
Gunna.......Going to
Dy'er.........Do you
Teh............To
Int're.........Into

About the Author

Mark Thompson is a retired contractor living in Marske by the sea in the northeast of England with his wife, Leigh, and two kids, Ryan and Erin. After starting Out of the Blue, he suffered a massive stroke, which left him on life support. He is still undergoing therapy to this day, though he's much improved. A keen local historian, he has aspirations to help reopen a smuggling heritage centre in Saltburn in honor of the smuggler John Andrew.

Printed in Great Britain
by Amazon

78280010R00116